The
MOMENTS
BETWEEN

Champion Books Publishing Company
NATALIEBANKS.NET

Printed in the United States of America

The Library of Congress has catalogued this edition as follows:
The Moments Between/Natalie Banks

ISBN-13: 978-0-578-60038-3

Other titles by Natalie Banks:

The Water Is Wide
The Canary's Song
The Dark Room

That Year by the Lake coming Spring 2020

CONNECT WITH NATALIE:

WWW.NATALIEBANKS.NET

INSTAGRAM: @officialnataliebanks

FACEBOOK: @nataliebanksnovels

NATALIEBANKSNOVELS@GMAIL.COM

The
MOMENTS
BETWEEN

NATALIE BANKS

A Champion Books Publication

praise for
THE MOMENTS BETWEEN

If you're looking for a heartfelt, authentic, and thrilling journey that walks the thin line between reality and dreams, this book is a must read. Natalie Bank's passionate writing and spot-on characterizations create a dynamic, realistic world where you feel like these characters are living people in your own life. The fast-moving plot is full of surprises and will have you enthralled until the very last word."

—Jennifer Moorman,
Bestselling author of *The Baker's Man.*

Beautiful tale with a terrifying premise. Your worst nightmare coming true. Watching events happen without being able to stop them, knowing the end is near. Natalie Banks writes of love, hope, and fears. Banks takes readers on a journey beyond worlds we can comprehend where anything and everything is possible. A world where the predictable is what you fear the most. It's the perfect book to get lost in, cozy up by a fire with a big cup of tea.

—Michelle Young, Author of *Your Move*

This is the second time I have had the privilege of reviewing one of Natalie Banks' novels. The Moments Between is a beautifully spun tale that will have your heart in your throat until the final page. Not surprising, if you have read any of her other work. Banks has a way of pulling you so deeply into the story that you are one hundred percent emotionally invested in her well-developed characters. You won't want to put it down until you know the answer to your burning question. Will Ben live? Don't miss this great story!

—Gail P., Carolina Portal Review

ACKNOWLEDGEMENTS

W ords can never be enough to express my gratitude to the people in my life that have helped me and supported me on my journey as an author.

I must start with my husband, Joe and my sweet children, Caroline, Ethan, and Elisabeth Grace who patiently wait for me when I sequester myself to write my novels and for supporting me and believing in me like no other! I am also grateful to my older children, Jesseca and Jake and my three beautiful grandchildren, Violet, Sawyer, and Hudson who also support and believe in me one hundred percent!

Without a few special people in my life, I wouldn't be where I am today:

Martijn and Bettina Atell with VOTEBASH.COM. Thank you for believing in me and my books, even when I was afraid to put myself out there.

Jane Ubell-Meyer with Bedside Reading who took a special interest in me and my books and has supported me like family! I would be lost without her!

Johnny and Diana Legg, Dee Dee Creech, and Kelley and David Morris who have been a HUGE support to me by keeping my books in their businesses and always believing in me!!

Last but definitely not least on this list, is my agent, Kelli Martin with Wendy Sherman and Associates, who has believed in me and my writing since the day we first met. With her encouragement and advice, I have grown so much as a writer and cannot wait to see what the future holds for us together as a team!!

I also have to give a big shout out to Jeanne McPherson who gave us refuge during Hurricane Florence! Because of her and her sweet family, I was able to have a safe place to go during the storm and was able to continue writing The Moments Between while there. Blood doesn't determine family, not in this case, anyway!

I am so grateful to my sweet friends Amy Hinshaw, Rose Hevrin and Heather Phillips, and Michelle Young, who have been a huge supporters to me and my writing. My beloved step-mother, Diana Hughes and my wonderful friend Michele Reber who always believed in me and my stories. A big thank you to Robert Charles Gompers, who is an extremely talented writer and friend. He has been there for me through the ups and downs of this writing process and I could never express how much I appreciate and love him! And most of all, my amazing father, Jim Banks, who has always encouraged me to follow my dreams. Thank you to all of you who have been there for me when I need feedback on my manuscripts. I am so grateful at how you all are always willing to jump in and read for me whenever I need it!

That beautiful cover that you see for The Moments Between is due to the beautiful soul and talented photographer, Bethany Schrock. She has been a huge supporter of me and my writing from the very beginning and I absolutely honored that she allowed me to use one of her beautiful photographs for this cover. There's more about her on the next page. Be sure to check it out!

A great big thank you to Colleen Sheehan with Ampersand Book Interiors for always making my interiors look amazing!

I also want to thank you, my readers, some of you are new, some of you have been with me for a long time, but I love and appreciate every single one of you! Thank you for reading my books, supporting me, following me on social media, and sending me letters! Everything I do wouldn't matter at all, if I didn't have you!

My heart overflows with gratitude to you all!!

cover photographer:
BETHANY SCHROCK

Photo by: Havner

Bethany Schrock has been creating things before she knew how to read. Growing up with learning disabilities like dyslexia made reading a book feel so daunting. When she was little, she'd draw you a picture book or paint you Landscape to describe something way before she would choose to use words to write it down. Years later and hurdles jumped, Bethany is still creating. Checking off one of her life bucket list items "To Photograph the Cover Of A Published Book" has brought us here, and gratitude is an understatement. She lives in the Midwest with her loving husband and fluffy pup. You can find her photo work and paintings at

BETHCATH.COM

The
MOMENTS
BETWEEN

CHAPTER 1

Despite every effort I had made, I failed to prevent what was to come. My body, poised in preemptive grief. Bare feet touching cold tile as I waited.

The lonely clock on the kitchen wall ticked louder and louder as the minutes passed.

It ticked, reminding me of the countdown that I had been living.

Three months to prepare…

To prepare for the death of my husband.

And now it was upon me.

THREE MONTHS EARLIER

The morning came earlier than I expected. I stirred without opening my eyes.

The boys were at my sister Mandi's house for their weekly Saturday night sleepover, aka my alone time to learn how to be me again. It was Mandi's idea. She wanted me to spend some time getting to know the new me. The widow me. The Ms. not Mrs. me. Who was this woman? I didn't know her, and I didn't know if I wanted to know her.

The last six months had been hard. No, actually they had been hell. The accident was to blame. It took the life of my husband. Tore our family apart. Changed life forever.

This version of me...my new life...just didn't have the same meaning without Ben.

I snuggled in deeper, not opening my eyes, blankets soft against my skin. Sleep beckoned me back into its arms as something foreign tiptoed across my mind. It called to me like whispers on the wind. A shadowy sound called to me again and again, rousing me too early from my slumber.

I pulled the covers up around my face, still not wanting to open my eyes.

Sleep was a luxury since Ben died, and I was looking forward to sleeping in this morning.

Sweet slumber, my escape. My single reprieve from reality.

But something wasn't right.

My brain struggled to decipher the intrusion that pulled me from blissful rest.

Clanging…banging? *What was that noise?*

Slowly it began to tune in, ever so slowly.

Downstairs?

Pulling the covers away from my face, I strained to listen.

Metal clanged on metal, followed by an occasional clatter.

The kitchen?

My groggy mind struggled, piecing thoughts together, and then all at once came into focus.

I sat up on unsteady elbows. The world around me, slightly off balance.

Someone was downstairs doing the dishes…and whistling.

No one should even be here this morning, much less doing dishes!

The strangeness of it not registering fully as I floundered, trying to reconcile the impossibility.

Was I caught in that elusive place between asleep and awake? Where dreams filtered into reality?

That certainly would explain it.

The intrusion silenced and the conclusion solidified.

I must've been dreaming.

I laid my head back down, sinking into softness, as sleep attempted to take me again.

But my reprieve was short lived, as footsteps sounded on the stairs.

Echoing in the stairwell, one by one, getting closer.

My eyes popped open as an icy wave of fear washed over me.

Who could be in the house!?

My thoughts disjointed and washed with fear as the steps got louder and closer still.

I was frozen in terror.

The bedroom door swung open and without thinking twice, I pulled the covers straight over my head and lay motionless.

Maybe they wouldn't notice me...

If they did, what could I do? I had no way to fight back...

My heart pounded in my ears as I steeled myself for what was coming.

I held my breath as the steps walked right past the bed and the bathroom door clicked shut, echoing in the room.

Stunned, I slowly peeked out from the edge of the blanket.

From behind the closed door, I could hear more whistling...and the water running. Followed by the distinct sound of someone shaving. The metal shaver clanking against the porcelain sink.

Before I could gather my thoughts, I heard more steps. The unmistakable sound of little feet, thundering in the hallway.

But it was impossible!

The boys weren't here...

I pulled the covers completely back from my face, straining to see into the hallway. Within moments they appeared in the doorway and bounded onto the bed. Their faces beaming with enthusiasm for life. And morning.

But as I looked at my boys, I noticed things weren't quite right...

Oliver was wearing the fuzzy, worn out dinosaur pajamas I had thrown out months ago. The ones where his big toe poked out of the right foot. They had gotten way too small, but they were his favorite. It was a battle to sneak them out of the house. Yet, somehow, he was wearing them now, and there was no hole in the foot.

My confusion grew as Grayson smiled at me, and I saw his two front baby teeth. He had lost those in July. The tooth fairy had left him two whole dollars in exchange for those teeth. Yet, there they were. Still there...

At five and seven, the boys were full of energy and gusto. This morning was no different.

Smelling faintly of baby shampoo and unbrushed teeth, they bounced, giggled, and climbed back and forth over my blanketed legs.

My head spun out of control, as I strained to put pieces together.

Everything was mixed up…

Surreal.

I had to be dreaming.

In an attempt to wake up I pinched myself hard… and it hurt. A red welp soon raised up.

But the so-called dream wasn't fazed by my attempt to pull myself back into reality.

Was I dreaming after all? What other explanation could be made?

My head continued to spin as the boys wrestled and argued over a Spider-Man action figure. Yanking it back and forth amidst whines and shrieks.

Without warning, the door handle of the bathroom jiggled and the door swung open.

Before I could scream, and seemingly as if by magic, out stepped Ben.

My husband stood in front of me, like he had never been gone.

The boys screamed, "Daddy!!" bouncing up and down on the bed, jarring me.

I gasped audibly.

The world underneath me began to twirl and spin, taking me with it on its journey around the sun. Turning my world at one thousand miles per hour, and I was powerless to stop it.

I closed my eyes and took a deep breath before opening them again. *He was still there.…*

A feeling came over me I had never experienced before. One that couldn't be put into words.

How could Ben be standing here in front of me, when he had been dead for six months?

Yet, there he was. His handsome face, cleanly shaven, and he was dressed for work.

He looked at me with a strange expression on his face.

"Claire? You okay?"

I watched him as he leaned over and began tickling the boys.

They squealed with fervent delight.

"Now boys, it looks like Mommy had a rough night, let's take it easy on her," he said as he tousled Oliver's hair.

He leaned over and kissed my cheek lightly.

"Take your time getting up, I'll get the boys dressed and fed breakfast. I have to go to the office for a few hours, but I promise I will be back in time to go to Mandi's birthday party."

My heart lurched forward as the words echoed in my head.

Mandi's birthday party?

My mind reeled, over and over, trying to process the implications of what he just said.

My lungs constricted, like a fish out of water, gasping for air.

It couldn't be...her birthday was back in March!! And that was months ago!

Before the accident...

I watched him as he walked out of the room carrying both of the boys. One over each shoulder.

An overwhelming feeling of nausea came over me.

I yanked my phone off he night table and looked at the date.

The hair stood up on the back of my neck as I stared at the screen in disbelief.

Unmistakably -it read March 3rd.

"Oh my God..." I said audibly. "What the hell is going on?" my voice cracked.

My mind faltered with confusion as I gritted my teeth, fighting back tears.

I looked over at the window as the morning sun peered in through the edges of closed blinds and a sliver of light streamed across the floor and onto the bed.

I looked back to the screen of my phone once again.

It still read March 3rd.

I numbly pulled the covers up to my chin, staring at the ceiling fan as it whirred and spun round and round, not fazed by the events of the morning.

A few moments later, Ben appeared back in the doorway.

He came and sat down on the edge of the bed.

I could smell his cologne and involuntarily inhaled the long-missed smell of Ben.

"Are you sure you're okay? You look pale," he said as he gently pushed the hair out of my face.

I still couldn't speak. My mind was lost somewhere in time.

Lost in confusion.

My Ben was back…

He stared at me intently, a look of concern on his face.

I needed to give him some kind of answer. To explain what was going on. But, how could I tell him when I had no idea myself?

His eyes were on mine. The same eyes I had looked into for the last ten years.

Then, the words came….

The only words that made sense.

"It was just a bad dream…" I stuttered. "A very, very bad dream."

By the time I got downstairs, the boys were in front of the TV watching Pat the Dog, and Ben was gone.

To work?

Isn't that what he said?

I scratched my head and staggered toward the kitchen, now beginning to wonder if I had actually imagined the whole thing.

Maybe it *was* a dream.

Could it be possible? Could Ben really be back??

I went to the pantry and pulled out a bag of coffee grounds. The earthy smell of the grounds laced with soft vanilla wafted up my nose, bringing me a strong sense of comfort.

Without a doubt, I needed caffeine this morning of all mornings. Something to set my mind straight. I stepped over to the coffee pot with the grounds in hand and stopped just short of it.

It was already made. Steaming hot and ready.

I stared at the red light on the machine as it glared back at me.

Ben had always done that for me before he died. Every single morning, he had the coffee ready and waiting when I came downstairs.

I had missed that since he'd been gone. The comfort of our morning routine.

It was one of many things that I missed...

I looked at the rich black coffee through the glass carafe as condensation ran down the inside of the pot.

My mind reeled again.

Ben...

His name caught on my breath.

I stepped forward with a trembling hand, tentatively grasping the pot's handle, and began pouring the coffee into a big ceramic mug. I stared off into space as I poured, filling the cup until coffee teetered on the rim, ready to spill over.

I stopped pouring just short of the flood.

Patterns danced on the kitchen floor around me, shadows from the leaves of the maple tree, just outside the window as the sun lifted higher in the sky.

Pat the Dog's voice echoed through the kitchen, followed by the boys' laughter.

I walked through the shadows on the floor to the refrigerator to get creamer for my coffee.

As I opened the door, I gasped and stared in disbelief.

A large white bakery box was on the shelf, staring back at me.

Mandi's birthday cake.

Red Velvet with cream cheese icing.

I had special ordered it from Magnolia Bakery on Tryon Street, in downtown Charlotte. One of the premier bakeries in North Carolina. Their reputation, known statewide, for their delicious cakes.

The fluorescent lights highlighted the carefully placed label on the box.

Magnolia, in beautiful scripted gold lettering, reflecting in the light.

It was the same bakery that had a huge kitchen fire, months ago, that destroyed all of their equipment.

The same bakery that closed down and never reopened.

I left the refrigerator door standing open, ran to the bathroom and threw up.

I sat on cold black and white tile resting my head on the edge of the toilet seat. Knowing that my hair would smell like urine after this. No spots were left sacred in the bathroom of a home where boys lived.

But I didn't care about that right now.

Everything felt wrong.

But how could it when everything was right?

I twirled the hem of my nightgown between my fingers as I stared blankly at the toilet paper caddy. It was empty and needed to be refilled. But my mind didn't register this necessity.

I was too lost in my thoughts for it to process.

"It was just a dream," I repeated out loud.

Suddenly, Teddy, our beloved tabby cat, came around the corner, meowing. The sight of him startled me so much that I had to stifle a scream.

Our sweet Teddy…

We had picked him up at a sidewalk adoption event, right after we were first married.

Our little Teddy bear, now eight years old, with sleek black and grey fur, came all the way into the bathroom and rubbed up against me, meowing and purring, making it clear he wanted his breakfast.

The sight of him would have normally brought me joy. I would've scratched under his soft chin and he would've purred louder.

But this time I lifted my head and puked again.

Teddy had been gone for months. He'd darted out of the back door and we never saw him again.

We had spent days trying to find him, but we never could.

Yet, there he was…right here in front of me.

Just like Ben had been earlier.

Was it all just a dream? Did none of it happen? It seemed so real…

My mind raced wildly, trying to understand, but I just couldn't.

I got up and numbly went into the kitchen, with Teddy on my heels, as trepidation twisted up my gut like a bad omen.

CHAPTER 2

M andi's birthday party was being held at Martini's Restaurant in the heart of downtown Charlotte. We arrived at the restaurant at 3:45 pm. We were fifteen minutes late. I rushed in the door ahead of Ben and a surge of air conditioning washed over me. Shivering in the cold air, I went straight to the bar and ordered a vodka martini. I needed something to steel my nerves. This morning had shaken to me to the core, and now I had to face Mandi too.

Ben came in quickly behind me, with the boys in tow, and whispered, "Don't you want to go in and wish your sister a happy birthday first?" His tone was firm, but I ignored him and waited impatiently for my drink. I glared at the bartender, who moved at a snail's pace, seemingly to intentionally irritate me. He hadn't started making my drink yet, and my intense stare had no effect on his speed.

The main dining room was empty, aside from an older couple sitting at a corner table. They stared down at their plates while they ate, not saying a word to each other. The whole place eerily quiet, aside from the occasional clatter coming from the kitchen. If this had been a Friday night instead of a Sunday afternoon, there would be standing room only, and a live jazz band would fill the whole place with music.

The building used to be an old warehouse and still had many of the original features with concrete floors, large exposed ductwork and piping overhead, and enormous wood columns. But the warehouse feel was broken up by mirror-polished stainless steel, laminated glass designs on the doors, and abstract art on every wall. After opening, it had quickly become one of the most premier restaurants in town. It was no wonder that Mandi had chosen this place for her party. For Mandi it was all about reputation, and Applebee's wasn't going to cut it.

Realizing I wouldn't be getting my drink any time soon, I sat Mandi's cake box on top of the bar. I stared at the golden lettering on the label, running my finger across it, feeling the raised letters of the word Magnolia under my fingertips. The stress and confusion of this morning weighed heavily on me.

The boys climbed up and down on black leather barstools, spinning them around, laughing and talking loudly. I didn't notice, nor care. The couple that had been eating in silence glared over at us, obviously not happy with the disruption.

Finally, after several minutes of waiting, Ben had had enough. He took the boys by their hands and led them away, leaving me alone at the bar. I watched as he walked over and opened the door to the private banquet room. The sound of music and conversation spilled out.

There had been about forty guests invited. Too big of a deal for a thirty-one-year old's birthday party, in my opinion. Of course, Mandi had to make everything a big deal when it had to do with her. She had always been that way. Even when we were kids, she was always showing off, one-upping and upstaging everything I did. I learned long ago not to care. Or at least I was really good at pretending not to care.

She was the older of the two of us by three years, but by her behavior, you would think she was the youngest. That was Mandi's personality, and nothing I did or didn't do was going to change that.

I looked up at the bartender who still wasn't making my drink. I knew that if it had been Mandi standing here, the drink would have already been made. My face reddened with frustration.

How could Mandi and I could be so different and still be related?
We were different in every way that sisters could be.

Looks and behavior.

I absentmindedly ripped a paper cocktail napkin up, piece by piece. Martini's name in red lettering torn into bits, scattered on the bar top, as memories of my sister floated through my mind.

The older couple in the corner paid their check and left, taking their silence with them. The sound of muffled talking and laughter from Mandi's party was getting louder and now could be heard through the closed door.

But I barely noticed, still caught up in the past.

I remembered one hot July afternoon when I was seven years old, one so sweltering that the air conditioner couldn't even manage to cool the house. Mom had opened all the windows and doors in the hopes of getting some air flow. Mandi and I were coloring on the back porch, and our older brother, Jonathan, was at work bagging groceries at the Food Mart down the road. It was his last summer home before leaving for college.

As Mandi and I colored in pictures of zoo animals, tires rumbled on the gravel driveway. A car door slammed, and we heard yelling. First coming from outside, then loud footsteps and more arguing coming from inside of the house.

"If she's so perfect, why don't you just go off with your bimbo secretary, already!?" I heard my mom yell. Her voice almost unrecognizable.

I sat up straight, looking at the back door.

My dad's response was low and angry, but his words weren't perceivable.

"Just go then!" Mom shouted. "Get out and don't come back!"

Mandi and I looked at each other. Our eyes filled with fear. We had heard many arguments lately over Dad's secretary, Linda. But never one this bad.

A few minutes later, the screen door creaked open and Dad came out with a suitcase.

He crouched down next to us. "I have to go away for a while, girls. But know that I love you, and don't forget I will always be your dad. Nothing can stop that."

Mandi stood up and started to wail. "No, Daddy, no! Please don't leave me here!" She grabbed him around his neck, nearly knocking him over.

He stood up. "Don't worry, darling, everything is fine. I'll see you soon."

I looked up at him, eyes wide open, blinking back tears. Confusion and grief swirled around my young heart.

He tousled my head, making eye contact with me for just a moment. Then picked up his suitcase and walked down the steps. Mandi followed quickly behind and latched onto his legs, making it impossible for him to walk. Her cries of despair disturbed a pair of robins nesting in the giant oak tree a few feet away. Leaves rustled and the branch shook as they took flight.

"Daddy…please Daddy don't leave me!" she cried out.

"I would take you with me if I could, sweetheart," he consoled her.

My eyes narrowed in jealousy. *He didn't want to take me.*

Mandi wasn't appeased. She continued to hold onto his legs so that he couldn't leave. He had to pry her off of him so that he could go.

Tears filled his eyes as he headed toward the driveway, stopping and looking back at us once more. He stood there for a long moment, and I thought he might actually turn around and come back.

He didn't.

I held back my own cries for him as they bubbled to the surface. I refused to be like Mandi.

I heard a creaking sound and looked behind me. Mom was there, looking from the screened door, her face red and swollen from crying. Her eyes on him as he turned and walked away.

I turned back and watched him too as he disappeared around the corner of the house.

Mandi's wails continued on as I sat on the porch, wiping away my tears, until long after the sun went down. Waiting. Hoping he would change his mind. That he would come back. And he never did.

I would never be able to forgive him for leaving us like that. For a woman, not much older than Jonathan, who soon grew tired of him and left him for a guy her own age.

And things were never the same after that.

Dad was gone.

Jonathan left for school and rarely came home to visit.

Our family was split into pieces. Never to be reassembled.

I stood alone leaning on the bar. Two girls came into the restaurant and were seated at the same table that the old couple had just left from. The server had quickly whisked away dishes and wiped down the table-top before they sat down. They were caught up in conversation and didn't seem to mind the short delay. I wondered if they were sisters. The rapport between them was intimate. If not sisters, then close friends.

I looked at them and then back at the party room where my own sister was and grimaced.

Mandi was Dad's favorite, there was no disputing that. He doted on her excessively. And I knew the way she fed his ego alleviated his guilt. She knew how to work everyone over to her advantage. It was a natural born skill.

Not to mention, she shined like a diamond.

Mandi was extraordinarily beautiful. Long strawberry blonde hair cut into layers that framed her face and seemed to flow like natural strands of silk. She had stardust freckles everywhere, even on her nose. She was tall and lean, with a perfect figure. Former cheerleader, with a million-dollar smile. There weren't many people that didn't turn and look when Mandi walked by. Men and women alike. There was just something about Mandi that stood out from the rest of the world, leaving me feeling insignificant.

She had been married to Lewis Maxwell for five years now. They met at the law firm where she worked as a receptionist for a short time. He was the managing partner there and twenty years her senior. He was already married when he met Mandi, but divorce soon followed. Mandi swore they were on the brink of divorce, anyway. Telling everyone that it was irreconcilable differences that had driven Lewis and his first wife apart. But I believed Mandi was the real reason behind it. Lewis was smitten by her, helpless against her womanly prowess. The way her voice purred when she spoke to him and the way her hand rested on his arm when they walked together captivated him. He couldn't have resisted even if he had wanted to.

I stared off in the distance out the front windows of Martini's as the bartender finally pulled out a martini glass. At last. But it went unnoticed by me; my mind was still on Mandi. On feelings that were still very much alive. Feelings that were deeply rooted in resentment.

I was the exact opposite of Mandi. I was a quiet child, one that liked to read books in the corner. Easy to ignore. Easy to forget. Especially when Mandi was around. I was used to it.

I didn't need the spotlight, and she did.

I wasn't tall, at five foot four inches, and I was fine boned. No freckles… and I was definitely not a cheerleader. I was sitting in the bleachers, while Mandi owned the football field. She walked across the field, swinging her hips side to side, flicking her long hair, with all of boys from the football team following.

My naturally blonde hair had been kept in a shoulder length angled bob ever since I graduated high school. I liked the ease of the style. With my tanned skin, turned up nose and brown eyes with distinct yellow flecks, I was pretty by anyone's standards, but compared to Mandi, I was insignificant.

Ben always told me that I was beautiful. If I really was, no one had ever sent me the memo, they were too busy looking at Mandi.

With that thought in mind, I looked through the six-pane glass door of the banquet room. As Ben made his way across the room, Mandi ran over to him and attempted to plant a kiss square on his lips.

I expected that. She always did it.

He stepped backwards right before her lips touched his so that they just grazed them.

Ben was expecting it too.

I laughed at his response.

He was the only boyfriend I ever had that didn't have his head turned by Mandi. Every boyfriend before him she had somehow stolen from me. When I brought a boy home, the ultimate test was his response to Mandi.

When I saw that Ben wasn't fazed by her beauty, her charm, her flirting… I knew he was the one for me.

However, his lack of interest in her spurred her interest in him even more. He became a challenge to her, and she was annoyingly relentless.

Even at our wedding, she was flirting with him. She dragged him onto the dance floor and pressed her hips against his, despite his apparent irritation. Later in the night, feigning being drunk, she fell into his lap and pressed her breasts against his face. To my relief, three eager groomsmen ran over to her aid and pulled her off of him. They were more than willing to provide assistance to the damsel in distress.

I didn't let it bother me too much. Ben was mine, and I knew I would never have to share him with anyone. I also knew I would never find another man like him. A man powerless to Mandi. A man who only had eyes for me.

Women were always admiring Ben. When I would see one of them flash their flirtatious smile his way, I would feel the burn of insecurity. But when I looked back at Ben, his eyes were on me. Looking at me, like I was the only woman in the world.

He was truly irreplaceable.

The thought immediately jolted me back to this morning.

Ben wasn't dead! He never was...

He was there, in Martini's banquet room, maneuvering his way away from Mandi and getting the boys seated at the long table decorated with flowers and balloons.

I jumped when the bartender brought my martini over, sitting it down in front of me. Along with the drink, he brought the check. This time he stared at me, impatiently waiting for my payment.

I almost laughed at the irony.

I rolled my eyes and handed him my credit card. After a few minutes he handed it back to me with the slip to sign, and I reluctantly tipped him two dollars on my eight-dollar martini.

I picked up the cake box and my drink, and headed to the party room.

My hands were so full that I had trouble opening the door. No one inside noticed my struggle.

As I attempted to get it open, two male servers walked past not even glancing my way. I was irritated that neither of them had offered to help. I knew if it had been Mandi struggling with the door, they would've both stopped.

After several tries, I finally got it open.

Once I stepped inside the door, something instantly felt wrong. I felt strangely out of place as an odd sense of déjà vu washed over me. And I thought for an instant, I might faint.

Reality was swirly and the space around me seemed almost pliable. Like the walls of the world weren't exactly intact.

As if I was existing a place where nothing was absolute.

But yet, everything was. I could feel the edges of the cardboard cake box cutting into my fingers and the cold weeping through the glass.

I walked over and sat the cake down at the end of the table, between two people I didn't recognize. The chatter in the room was overbearing, which irritated me even more.

And once I saw Dad sitting at the end of the table, my mood was sunk. He gave me a wave and I pretended not to see.

I didn't want to be here, but leaving wasn't an option at this point. Mandi spotted me from across the room.

"Claire! There you are! Where in the world have you been? You know you're 30 minutes late?!" She raised her voice just loud enough for the whole room to hear, then came over and kissed me on the cheek. I couldn't help but think of Judas' kiss in the Bible.

She looked down at the cake box and turned up her nose. Unable to hide the obvious disappointed look on her face. This was clearly not the appropriate location for her cake, I assumed.

She opened the box and lifted out the glistening white cake. The words *Happy Birthday Mandi* were precisely written in red on the top. She walked over and carefully sat it down in the direct center of the table for all to see. She took her finger and ran it purposefully along the edge of the icing, accumulating a generous amount. She paused, looked around the table, and smiled right before licking the icing off her finger, slowly and deliberately. I rolled my eyes as she giggled with all the men staring at her now bare finger.

Ben waved to me, and I went and sat down next to him. The boys were nibbling on cheese and crackers, shifting anxiously in their seats. They were already getting bored. I pulled two coloring books and a pack of crayons out of my bag and gave it to them. This seem to appease them for the time being.

Ben looked at my martini and shook his head. I shrugged in response.

He thought the drink was so I could get through the party. I'd let him keep thinking that.

And anyway, Mandi was part of the reason. She could drive anyone to drink.

The entire party was orchestrated to Mandi's exact specifications. We had a late lunch made up of four courses, which my boys struggled to make it through. It irritated me that she didn't even consider them in the equation when planning this, even though she was the one who was insistent that her nephews come.

Why was I surprised?

But what did surprise me is that Mom wasn't here. Where was she? She probably didn't want to see Dad any more than I did.

When it was time for cake, Lewis stood next to her, hand on her shoulder, seemingly to stake his claim.

Lewis wasn't a handsome man. He was completely bald and had the typical middle-aged male physique, but he was perfect for Mandi. Honestly, I think she liked the fact that she was out of his league because it gave her more power.

He beckoned to her every whim. What he lacked in the looks department he well made up for in the money one. He gave her whatever she wanted, and not to mention he turned his head when she flirted. Which she did often. This was part of her charm.

Everyone sang to Mandi as she blew out twenty-two candles. She refused to acknowledge any birthday after twenty-two. She had been twenty-two for nine years now and no one dared to correct her. We all just went along.

I looked over at Dad and he smiled at me. I gave him a quick wave. I had no intention of talking to him. I had nothing to say. He was here for his precious Mandi, anyway.

Ben got up and went to the bathroom, leaving me with the boys.

As soon as he disappeared out of my view, I began to panic.

Would he return?

With him out of sight, my grasp on reality was shaken. My thoughts disjointed.

I glanced from the door to my watch over and over again as time slowed to a crawl.

I braced myself, half expecting him to never come back.

My nerves, rattled. My world, unsteady.

As the party went on, I chewed on my lip. Watching. Waiting.

The door opened several times as servers bustled in and out. My heart sinking each time with the realization that it wasn't Ben.

Just when I couldn't take the waiting any longer, he finally reappeared, and a flood of relief washed over me. I looked down at my watch, he had only been gone for four minutes.

Why had it felt so much longer?

Just before the gifts were to be opened, Dad came over to speak to the boys. I gritted my teeth as he kneeled down next to them.

"How are my handsome grandsons doing?" he asked.

"Why would you care?" I hissed.

"Claire, that's uncalled for," Ben spouted.

Dad looked up at me, his face strained with emotion, but I was un-wavered by his crestfallen look.

"Why don't you go back and sit next to your beloved daughter?" I continued.

"Now, that's enough!" Ben almost shouted, his eyes fixed on me.

Dad stood up and put his hand on Ben's shoulder. "It's okay. She's got every right to be angry with me."

As he walked back to his seat, Ben gave me a disapproving look. I shrugged in return.

Soon after Dad took his seat again, Lewis brought the gifts over to Mandi. She opened them one by one, giggling like a five-year-old and dramatically proclaiming her love for every item.

As I watched her opening gifts, my stomach suddenly dropped as the realization hit me that I had left her gift at home.

Not having a gift for Mandi on her actual birthday was a punishable offense. It was just the kind of thing that she would be upset about, for a very long time.

I felt my cheeks redden in preemptive response.

I had so much on my mind when we were leaving, it had totally slipped my mind.

Honestly, I didn't even know if Mandi would have liked her gift anyway. It was a fabric journal and pen set that I had picked up for her at a boutique.

Who was I kidding?

She was not the kind of girl to journal. She was too busy living life to write about it. Suddenly, I felt that old familiar burn rise up in my chest, and pushed it down.

Mandi was the only person who made me feel this way.

Insignificant.

Next to her beauty, confidence, and glamor, I always felt washed up. The feelings were the strongest when we were teenagers, but now, years later, I was still filled with that same insecurity. I was powerless around her. Even if I tried to defend myself, she was always able to turn it around and make me look like the bad guy. It was a gift of hers.

When Mandi finished opening her presents, she looked around dramatically, searching the table around her and then leaning way over to check the floor like she had dropped something.

"Is that it?" she said as she turned and directed her entire focus on me.

I found my voice, but just barely. "I left your gift at home. I'm sorry…"

The expression on her face was instantly recognizable.

She was displeased.

"What did you say, dear? I can't hear you." Her eyes determinedly fixed on mine, wanting me to repeat it so that everyone would know about my offense.

The irritation that I had already been fighting multiplied rapidly.

Why was she always so intent on embarrassing me?

Why couldn't she just let something go for once?!

My heart pounded violently as my blood pressure went up. Anger coursed through me like a rocket. I wasn't going to be able to tolerate her behavior. Not this time. It was rare that she could get a rise out of me …but TODAY of all days…

Before I could complete that thought, Ben spoke up. "Mandi, I am so sorry. It's completely my fault. I left your gift sitting on the counter. Darned if Claire didn't remind me to get it too!" He chuckled.

With that, I felt his hand come and rest on my knee.

Mandi's shoulders relaxed as she leaned across the table. Just at the perfect angle for Ben to see down her blouse to her full bosom.

"Ah, no worries, handsome! You can deliver it to me personally, later." With that, she gave him a wink and flashed her quintessential million-dollar smile.

My eyes were on Mandi, anger still coursing through me. But once I looked back at Ben, my heart immediately filled with warmth. He always knew just what I needed, when I needed it.

He smiled at me, proud of his heroic deed.

A pang of guilt suddenly zapped me. I couldn't help but wonder if I had paid attention to these small kindnesses before?

Or now that I had experienced losing him, was I just only now noticing these acts of love?

It's funny how the things that you take for granted about the people you love are the very things that you miss the most when they're gone.

And oh, I had missed him so much. It had been so lonely without him. There were so many days that I just wanted to talk to him. To hear his voice. To tell him all the things that I wished I had said before he was gone.

Several times, I caught myself talking to the ghost of him, in the wee hours of the morning. Wearing his shirt, lying in the bed with a glass of wine, and I would imagine he was there, lying beside me.

My voice would echo in the empty room. Reminding me of the truth that he was gone.

That I was completely alone.

The reality of him being gone was unbearable. I didn't know how to do our family without Ben. He had made everything work for us...the boys and I...he made our lives wonderful.

I had taken it all for granted.

How I would've given anything for just one more chance to say thank you. To tell him how much he meant to me. The things that I never said enough before he was gone.

I had just assumed he would always be there.

Then he wasn't.

Like a vapor, he was gone. Leaving a gaping hole where he once stood.

Now, all of sudden, he was there, sitting right next me. His hand on my knee. I could feel the warmness of it through the fabric of my pant leg.

Not a wish. Not imagined.

Ben was really here. And I vowed I would never take him for granted again.

Finally, the party was over, and we walked the two blocks back to the parking garage where we had left the car.

I held Oliver's hand and Ben held Grayson's as we walked down the sidewalk side by side.

I sighed; my body filled with a flood of love.

Cars rushed by as we walked. Tires roaring on pavement.

People rushed past us on the sidewalk. Faceless. Nameless. Living their own lives.

And here I was with my own life. My own personal universe. Everything that mattered was right here with me.

The sounds of city suddenly faded away as I looked over at Ben.

"Who's up for some ice cream?" I asked.

Ben looked back at me. I could see the surprise on his face. Stopping for ice cream is something I would never do after one of Mandi's events. Usually, I just wanted to get home and crawl into a nice bubble bath with a glass of wine to recover.

The boys began bouncing immediately, chanting in unison. "Me, me, me, me!"

Ben smiled. "Ice cream sounds great, Mommy!"

Later that evening, after we got the boys tucked in, I stood in the living room, staring out the window into the night. The busyness of the day fading, leaving me to face my thoughts once again.

I stared out into the darkness as it mixed together with glimmery reflections of the streetlamp. My mind struggling to make sense of what had happened. I'd gone through the motions all day with precision, but inside, the memory of the dream was still with me.

As I stared out the window, Ben came up behind me with a bottle of wine and two glasses. I turned around to face him and he kissed me. Long and hard.

I felt my body instantly stirring in response, my pulse quickening at the thought of his touch.

He walked a few steps away, opened the bottle and poured us both a generous glass as my eyes followed his every move.

"I figured you needed this after the party." He laughed.

"I did." I smiled back.

I walked over with my glass and sat down on the couch. Ben followed, sitting down right next to me. He lifted his arm and put it around me in a synchronized motion. Moves we had memorized after years of replaying them over and over.

I sipped the wine, the taste tart and warm, and snuggled into the crook of Ben's arm.

Thoughts were still buzzing through my head as I fought to push them away.

I told myself over and over again...*it was just a dream.*

Just like I had told Ben this morning... *A very, very bad dream.*

Now, I just wanted to put it all behind me.

All that mattered now was that he was here. We were together.

I snuggled in closer to him.

It *was* just a dream.

And it didn't matter now.

What mattered at this moment was the feel of his arm around me and the taste of the wine on my tongue.

When the wine bottle was empty and our bodies were warmed, he led me up the stairs to our bedroom and closed the door.

He put his mouth on mine again and my body quivered with desire.

How long had it been since I had felt his lips on mine? It seemed like forever ago.

Was it?

How long since the last time he touched me? Since I had felt his caress? His hands on my body? I felt a tear slip out the side of my eye and quickly wiped it away.

He unzipped my dress and slipped it off my shoulders, one strap at a time. It fell to the floor in a crumpled pile. I began to tremble as he gently kissed my neck. His breath on me, like the flutter of wings. He unclasped my bra and reached down and slipped off my panties. Our eyes locked on each other.

He led me to the bed and I laid down. My body ached with an indescribable longing for him. The desire rose up inside of me like it was the very first time we had made love. An insatiable desire that I thought could never be extinguished.

He slid right up next to me. I could feel the hardness of him pressed against my leg as he ran his tongue down the side of my neck. Slowly, he moved his hands along my belly until he reached my breasts and caressed them gently.

I was filled with desperation. Months of longing engulfed me, and I couldn't bear it any longer. I turned and moved my hips against him, and he responded. When he entered me, a jolt of electricity spread through my entire body. The feeling so powerful, I had to bite down on my lip to keep from crying out and waking the boys.

We made love slowly and deliberately as my hands ran up and down his back.

I could feel the heat of his body on mine.

Ben...

He was here with me.

The memories of him being gone, drifted away. As if they never were.

CHAPTER 3

I awoke in the still darkness of the night. Moonlight filled the room with a muted glow.

And the dream called to me.

To remember.

It came back to me.

Images penetrated me against my will.

So vivid. So real.

The memory of it so close, that I could almost touch it with my fingertips. The pain so fresh, the echo of it rang violently through me.

Tears soaked my pillow as my mind succumbed to the memory of the dream.

The knock on the door startled me and I dropped the mug I was drying. It smashed to the floor, scattering hundreds of pieces all around me. Another knock, followed quickly by the ding of the doorbell. I tiptoed through shattered pieces of ceramic and looked up at the kitchen clock. It was 5:20 in the afternoon. I looked at the calendar on the wall.

June 3rd.

I wasn't expecting anyone.

Who could be at the door?

The boys had gone over to their friend's house and wouldn't be back for at least an hour. Ben was at work and wouldn't be home until after seven tonight. He had a meeting with a new client, and that would also require dinner out. Some guys considered it a perk of the job, wining and dining clients, but Ben hated it. He just wanted to get home to us.

The knock came again. It was louder this time. More insistent.

Soon after, the sound of the doorbell rang as I hurried toward the door.

My bare feet creaked on the hardwood floor as I walked through the open foyer. The foyer that Ben and I had just slow danced in last night to an old Marvin Gaye CD.

As I opened the door, the sunlight streamed in like a jet and nearly blinded me. Making it difficult to see who was standing in front of me. I put my hand up to my eyes to fight the glare.

"Mrs. DuPont?" a man's voice spoke.

"Yes?" I answered expectantly.

"May I step inside, ma'am?" he asked softly.

"Who are you?" I asked nervously.

Something about this situation felt off to me. My heart was pounding and I didn't know why. I stepped out onto the porch so I could see him better.

He looked to be in his fifties and was completely bald. He had soft but worn features and shockingly large ears. His striking blue eyes stood out from the rest of him. I guessed those eyes probably drove the girls wild in his younger days. He shifted uncomfortably in his grey suit. He was wearing a yellow tie that didn't quite match. Had he chosen it for himself?

"I'm sorry. I should've introduced myself. My name is Detective Nate Anderson, and I am with the Charlotte Police Department."

The Charlotte Police Department?

My mind reeled trying to think of a reason for him being here as he fished for something in his pocket.

How did he know my name?

He pulled out his wallet and opened it to an official ID to assure me of who he was.

"Can we step inside?" He asked again.

I stared at him blankly, not wanting to move. Not wanting to know what he had to say to me. Deep in my gut, something made me want time to go backwards. To be back in the kitchen putting away dishes and make it so that he never knocked on my door.

Everything around me felt as if it were moving in slow motion.

I closed my eyes and took a deep breath as we stepped inside.

We stopped just inside the foyer. A strange energy hung in the air.

I didn't want him to speak.

Was there a way to make him stop? To make him go away.

My breathing became shallow as he shifted nervously.

"Mrs. DuPont..." He cleared his throat, obviously having difficulty getting out what he wanted to say.

I took a step backward. I could sense in his voice that something wasn't right. Something wasn't right at all...

"Mrs. DuPont, I'm afraid that there's been an accident..."

I choked on a scream.

"My boys?!" My entire body began to quake.

"No ma'am...it was a train accident. Earlier today."

"A train accident?" I stammered, confused.

"Yes ma'am...and I am afraid your husband..."

Before he could finish his sentence, I let out a sigh of relief.

"No, no...my husband couldn't have been on that train. He's not coming home until much later."

He continued, despite my interruption.

"I am sorry to inform you that your husband was one of the seven victims that were killed today at 3:15. The three o'clock train collided with a transfer truck that had stalled on the tracks at the Central Avenue intersection, causing it to derail, and one of the cars detached and flipped, killing seven and injuring fourteen." He looked down as he spoke. I could tell he was uncomfortable with this assignment. I wondered if that was his job. Informing families of deaths. If it was, he didn't seem to be adjusted to it.

"Your husband was in the train car that derailed."

Once again, I corrected him. "No, my husband wasn't due to come home yet. I'm telling you, he was not on that train!"

"We were able to identify him by his driver's license." He paused. "Again, I am so sorry."

"NO!" I shouted. "You are mistaken!" I stumbled away from him and grabbed my cell phone off of the foyer table. With trembling hands, I steadied myself as I dialed Ben's phone number. My skin felt as if it was on fire. Burning me from the outside in.

"He's fine, I am telling you." I looked over at the detective defiantly.

He stared at me with a pained look on his face. I knew that I wasn't making his job any easier, but he was wrong and I knew it.

I waited for the ringing. I waited for Ben's voice to come on the line and tell me that everything was okay. That the detective was wrong. He had the wrong wife.

Instead, it went straight to voicemail. Ben's voice recording told me that he couldn't take my call right now and to leave a message.

I hung up and determinedly dialed it again with the exact same result.

Quickly, I dialed his office, assuming that his phone battery was dead.

The receptionist answered and put me through to his desk.

I looked over at Detective Anderson. "I'm calling him at work. We will get this all sorted out, right now."

I nodded my head assuredly. He just stared at me blankly in response.

The call was answered on the second ring. My heart soared.

"Ben! Oh, thank God! There's a man here..."

I was cut off by the voice of David Taylor, one of Ben's co-workers.

"Hey there, Claire! I am sorry but Ben isn't here. He left over two hours ago to go home. Said he had something he wanted to tell you. He didn't say what. Just left in a pretty big hurry. Is he not home yet?"

I dropped the phone, and it bounced off the foyer rug and onto the hardwood, sliding to stop at the man's feet. I could faintly hear David's voice calling my name to see if I was still on the line.

The detective picked up the phone and tried to hand it to me.

"No..." I choked out as I looked into the soft blue eyes in front of me.

He stepped toward me and I backed away.

"No!" I said again. "It's not true...it's not true!" My voice broke off.

I collapsed onto the floor sobbing. Electricity spread through my body like a zap of lightning. Every cell in my body fought against what was happening.

He came in close and lifted me from the floor. He took me by my elbow and gently led me into the kitchen. I sat down at the dining table and he sat down across from me.

Detective Anderson was speaking but I couldn't hear him. There was loud ringing in my ears, a screeching so loud that it was all consuming.

"Mrs. DuPont, is there anyone I can call for you?" he asked.

I couldn't process what he was saying.

Darkness was creeping in, slowly at first, but suddenly it encompassed me, and I fell off the chair and onto the floor.

When I came to, there was a woman in a police officer's uniform standing over me. For just a moment, I couldn't remember what had happened. I was baffled by her presence in my home. I looked across the room and made eye contact with a blue-eyed man whom I didn't recognize.

"Where's Ben? Where are my boys?" I demanded.

The blue-eyed man moved in closer and instantly the memory of who he was came flooding back. My body quaked violently and I began to sob.

The female officer patted my face with a cold washcloth. Blue terry-cloth with lime green gingham edging. It was from my own kitchen. She lifted me up, led me into the living room and sat me down on the sofa. She disappeared momentarily and returned with a box of tissues.

Where had she found them?

Maybe under the bathroom sink. Leftover from last year's flu stint that had made its way throughout the entire house.

The female officer then handed me a glass of water. I took it and stared at her. She seemed experienced at this kind of stuff. Her demeanor, calm and quiet.

She had blonde hair with streaks of brown pulled back into a ponytail. She was pretty but not graceful. She definitely had the cop look down, except for a tiny pair of pearl earrings that she wore. Almost seemed to be worn in a purposeful contrast to everything else about her.

I studied her face and wondered what her life was like. Was she married? Did she have kids?

Then, I remembered why she was here.

Sharp, jagged memories piled up in my mind. June 3rd. Train accident. Seven victims. Your husband...

I let out an audible cry of pain. A pain that threatened to completely crush me.

She got up and disappeared for a moment. When she came back, she handed me a white pill.

She whispered, "Here, take this. It will take the edge off."

She smiled sweetly despite her stern tone. I popped the pill in my mouth without even questioning her about what it was or where she had gotten it. Soon, the world drifted away and I fell asleep right there on the couch.

When I awoke, my mother was sitting on the couch next to me, and Mandi was sitting in a chair across the room. Her eyes were swollen and red. She blew her nose into some tissue.

"Where are the boys?" I asked in a hoarse voice.

I looked around and saw that the police officers were gone, and the sun was completely down. How long had I had slept?

"The boys are upstairs watching a movie," my mother answered. "The police officer called me from your phone and we came right away."

Mandi moved closer to me. She kneeled down in front of me as I tried to sit up. She put her head in my lap and started to cry. Almost as if she wanted me to comfort her. Of course, she would try to make this about her.

I had never hated Mandi more than I did at this moment.

I stood up, and in doing so her head flung off to the side. She looked up at me with a startled expression on her face. I wobbled as I tried to walk across the room. My mother got up and steadied me. I was surprised by her tenderness.

"Did anyone tell the boys...?" my voice broke in mid-sentence.

"No, we thought it was best for them to hear it from you."

I could hear Mandi's sobs coming from behind me in the living room as I climbed the stairs toward the boys' room.

I walked in the room and saw that they were already in their pajamas. And from their wet hair, I could see that they had been given a bath too.

I looked around their room and saw their dinosaur posters on the wall and the matching Spiderman comforters on their twin beds. A stuffed monkey from the zoo with Velcro hands hung from the curtain rod. There was a small lamp on the night table that stood between their beds. Lego men and Hot Wheels sat underneath the glow.

Just last night, I had stood in this very doorway while Ben had tucked them in and kissed them both good night. Now, Ben would never tuck them in again. A cry caught in my throat, but I pushed it down.

They were both laying in Grayson's bed. He was the oldest, and Oliver always looked up to him. Getting to lie in Grayson's bed was a real treat for him.

I went over and crawled into the bed with them. All three of us, tightly squeezed in. I wrapped my arms around both of them and pulled them closer to me.

Mom turned off the television and cleared her throat, as if to remind me of what needed to be said.

I knew what I had to do. I was just trying to let them have these last few minutes of innocence.

I slowly sat up and faced them.

"There's something Mommy has to tell you..." I kept my voice steady and clear. They needed me to be strong. Even though deep inside, I felt like I was one the one who died.

The days that followed were a blur. The visit to the coroner's office to iden-tify my husband's body, the meeting with funeral director, the paperwork. I moved through it all as if it were a dream.

At night, I would lie on his side of the bed, smelling his pillow. During the day I would wear his shirts. Wanting none of this to be real. Trying to keep him as close to me as possible.

The boys were noticeably sad, but seemed to take this more in stride. At least, better than I was able to. Though the last two nights in a row, Oliver had a nightmare and had called out for his daddy in his sleep. I had gone to him and held him tight until his sobs slowed and his breath-ing returned to a normal rhythmic pattern.

The funeral was small. I didn't want a big production. Ben wouldn't have wanted a big production either. Mandi tried to handle the planning and I refused to let her. I didn't want this to become one of her events.

There were about twenty-five people in attendance, and there were so many words of condolences, it all started to run together.

The faces and the words.

After the funeral, cars lined the street in front of our house. People poured in the front door with covered casserole dishes.

While everyone gathered downstairs to grieve and eat together, I slipped upstairs gripping the urn containing his ashes. I walked into our room and placed them on his side of the bed. I stepped back and looked at it. It sunk into the comforter and tilted awkwardly to the side.

A sensation of nausea came over me so powerfully that I had to swallow back vomit. My insides hemorrhaged with denial. I grabbed the urn off of the bed and shoved it into the closet. I couldn't bear looking at the reminder that Ben was dead. To be reminded that I would never look at his sweet face again. Or run my hands along his stubbled cheek from a weekend of not shaving. I would never kiss his soft lips or argue over the TV remote. We would never take another family vacation or go apple picking together. Never BBQ in the backyard again. We wouldn't grow old and wrinkly together. We wouldn't watch our boys grow up to be men and later see our grandchildren brought into this world. Everything that my entire life had been planned around was now gone. He took all my hopes and dreams into that urn with him.

As I closed the closet door, my bedroom door creaked open. Mandi quietly stepped inside. She was wearing a black low-cut V-neck dress that fit her curves perfectly and patent stiletto heels. She even looked spectacular at a funeral...

"Hey, you should come down here. Everyone is looking for you," she spoke softly.

I looked at her with contempt in my eyes.

"I don't owe them anything," I snarled.

"I know you don't, honey, but it would bring a sense of comfort to everyone if you would come down for just a little while. It would be good for the boys too."

I was shocked at her selfless words. That was a first for Mandi.

I made my way through that day and the days that followed, step by step. Minute by minute.

Hour by hour.

In some ways, it felt like he was still here, and in other ways, all traces of him had completely disappeared.

I barely slept at night. The moments I managed to sleep were filled with visions of his face. And my cries out for him would ring out into the darkness, startling me from my sleep and leaving me wide awake again.

Mandi began taking the boys on Saturday nights for what she called "their time with their auntie." She wanted me to start to practice some self-care. I was surprised at her willingness. It almost seemed like she was actually trying to care.

After the first few months, the days got a little easier. At least, I pretended it was easier. They say if you pretend something long enough, it starts to become truth to you. But even so, the nights were still long and lonely—and his side of the bed never lost its emptiness.

Before I knew it, six months had passed and the holidays were approaching. I was filled with dread. How could I get through them without Ben? Who would put up the Christmas tree? Who would put together Oliver's new bike? Who would help me fill the stockings on Christmas Eve?

I thought of last Christmas and how after we had put the kids to bed, we had made love on the rug in front of the fireplace. Afterwards, Ben had made us chocolate chip pancakes with whipped cream. We stayed up laughing and talking and didn't go to bed until nearly four in the morning. The boys were back up at six. We had just smiled at each other over our coffee cups as the boys tore into their gifts. Moments I didn't think much about...until now.

The memories...and regret...were never far from my mind. How I wished and even desperately prayed that somehow this wasn't my reality. That somehow, he had not died on the train that day and we would still be together.

That somehow everything was okay again.

Praying a futile prayer that never ceased.

I would see older couples holding hands in the park, and I would break down. It wasn't fair! He shouldn't have even been on that train! He shouldn't be dead right now. All the reasons why this shouldn't have happened flew through my head daily, on repeat.

I couldn't begin to understand how this could have happened to us. Not to us. Not when we loved each other so much…

All I knew is that I wanted my husband back, and if anyone had given me the opportunity to make it so, I would've taken it.

No questions asked.

Yet, he was gone and no power in heaven or on earth could bring him back to me now.

My body shivered with the grim images as I wiped away the tears from my face. I reached out frantically in the darkness for Ben. My hands found him there. I could feel the warmth of his body as his chest rose and fell with each breath. I scooted up to him and buried my face into his back. Soon after, the dream receded back into the depths of my mind and slipped away again.

CHAPTER 4

I awoke, the morning after Mandi's party, to the sound of the front door closing. And I found a note on Ben's pillow.

Went to work early. Didn't want to disturb you. Thought you could use the extra sleep.

You seemed restless last night.

I'll check on you later.

Yours Always,

Ben

I rolled over and looked at morning edging in through the window and sighed.

Everything was as it should be.

Nothing was amiss...

I thought about the dream. How real the events felt.

The pain so deep, and the grief so palpable.

It shook me up more than I wanted to admit.

But the fact was that Ben didn't even take the train. He had a perfectly good Honda Accord that he drove to work, every single day.

Reaffirming to me again...it was just a dream.

Despite my desire to put it all behind me, I found myself calling the Magnolia Bakery as soon I was out of the bed. And of course, they were open for business, as usual. When I asked about a kitchen fire, I was put on hold. The alarmed voice that returned on the line was stern and wanted to know my name. Embarrassed, I hung up, assuming they thought I was threatening them.

I drove the boys to school in a daze as they chit-chatted in the backseat. There was a distinct chill to the air, and I had dressed them in layers. This was the bi-polar time of year. The mornings ice cold, and the afternoons warm. The boys talked about Pat the Dog and Hoodie the Cat, laughing about an episode they had watched this weekend.

I couldn't quite focus on what they were saying.

I was thinking about the dream again.

June 3rd and the knock on the door....

With my thoughts not on the road, I nearly ran a stop sign. Screeching to a halt with the nose of my Yukon SUV poking out into the center of the intersection.

The red stop sign quivered in the wind.

Luckily, the street was empty. We were alone, with only the trees and squirrels to bear witness.

I sat there for a few moments to get my bearings before driving on.

I was thankful when I pulled up safely in front of Birchwood Elementary School. The tall brick building stood proud, as students filed in up the big steps and through tall double doors.

"Okay, guys, have a great day!" I said as I handed them their lunch boxes. "And Grayson, please be careful on the slide. I don't want you to fall again."

"What are you talking about, Mom?" Grayson replied.

"You're lucky you didn't get hurt more than you did, so please just promise me that you'll be more careful," I pleaded.

"Mom! I didn't fall off of the slide!" he said as he rolled his eyes.

I turned all the way around to face him in the back seat.

"What do you mean, you didn't fall? The school nurse called me…" My voice drifted off as I tried to place the memory.

I looked over at Oliver's wide eyes, blinking. I had scared him with my talk of falling.

I patted his knee. "It's okay, baby. Momma just worries sometimes…" *What else could I tell him?*

Tears of confusion stung my eyes as I looked at Grayson who was impatiently waiting to get out. The trickle of students had slowed.

"Mom, we are going to be late!" he whined.may

I watched them rush up the walk toward the building as my brain reeled trying to place the memory of his fall. I was sure that it happened. But clearly, it hadn't.

Standing in my kitchen later that morning, every cell in my body wanted to just let go of the dream and forget about it. But for some reason, I just couldn't shake the eeriness from my bones.

To distract myself, I began my normal Monday morning cleaning ritual. There was always a lot to do after the weekend. The familiarity of the cleaning routine helped soothe me. I moved in predictable patterns across the floor.

After all the dirty clothes were gathered, I carried the basket into the laundry room. The bright sun shone in through the small window over the washing machine. I balanced the basket on the washer lid and let the sun warm my face. I let out a sigh. I was starting to feel a little more like my normal self.

After I got the laundry going, I walked around and looked at our freshly cleaned home.

This was my dream come true house.

We had purchased this home when Grayson was eighteen months old, and I was pregnant with Oliver. Our apartment had been getting smaller and smaller by the day, but I never complained.

Ben came home early from work one day and surprised me with a pre-approval letter for a mortgage.

He smiled and said, "Want to go house shopping?"

I jumped into his arms, nearly bowling him over with my seven-month pregnant belly.

We only saw two homes before we made an offer.

As soon as I saw this house, I knew it was the one.

The relator had said that we were the easiest clients he'd ever had.

It was a historic two-story home on one of the most popular streets in the neighborhood of The Arts District. It was quite a stretch for our budget at the time, but once Ben saw the look in my eyes, he was helpless to say no.

It was a gray, traditional, two-story craftsman with black shutters, cobblestone columns, and a deep porch that was perfect for placing a couple of rockers and two large potted ferns.

In my mind's eye, I could see Ben and I in our old age sitting right here and rocking on this very front porch.

When I entered the open foyer, my heart instantly caught in my chest as I gazed upon the wide staircase and ornate trim work. As my eyes drifted up to the high ceiling, I felt as though I had stepped into a picture of the past. Every detail called to me, from the oil rubbed bronze hardware and crystal doorknobs, to the gleaming oak hardwood floors that ran through the main rooms of the home. But the home had an airy, open feel, despite its deeply traditional design.

The kitchen had been updated with stainless steel appliances, granite countertops, and brand-new tile. There was a large eat-in area with a huge picture window. The morning sunlight poured in, making it a perfect place for Sunday morning breakfast.

We climbed the stairs to see the three bedrooms of the house. The master on one side and two smaller bedrooms with a shared bath on the other.

Ben looked over and saw me smiling. In my mind, I was already setting up the furniture.

He took Grayson from me and we went outside to look around.

The backyard was a literal oasis with grass so green and lush that it felt like carpet underneath our feet, and the entire backyard was surrounded by a white picket fence that was lined with blooming flowers. It couldn't have been any more perfect.

We were determined to have it before we even put in our first offer.

We gave notice at the apartment and closed on the house forty-five days later. Just in time for Oliver to be born.

It was easy to turn this house into a home.

It was more than wood and sheetrock.

It was as if the house itself was a living breathing member of our family and had welcomed us under its wings.

But today, I felt out of place. Like somehow, I didn't belong.

I walked slowly into the kitchen, my footsteps echoing with each step.

I sat down at the table, staring off into space. The old house creaked and groaned in the silence around me. Outside, birds flitted and flew past the windows, preparing their nests as spring grasses rose up through the cold ground, bending with breeze.

Suddenly, I realized that I was sitting in the very seat where Detective Anderson had sat in my dream, on June 3rd.

I jumped up and involuntarily shook off the feeling of sitting there. I looked back at the empty chair and felt ill. My hair stood on end.

Dream or not, I didn't want anything to do with that day.

With that man.

I pushed the image of his face out of my mind.

Who knew if Detective Anderson was even a real person?

Most likely he was a complete figment of my imagination.

I was sure of that… yet the thought of sitting there… in that chair, where he sat in my dream…still felt wrong. Very wrong.

I made myself a cup of tea and sat down at the kitchen counter. Four barstools lined up in a row. One for each of us Ben had said the day he brought them home. The boys had spent many hours sitting here, coloring, snacking, living childhood to the fullest.

The thought of that brought me back to my own childhood.

To my own mother.

She was sitting at the kitchen table. Her expression washed with emotion. Pain and loss were deeply etched on her face as I struggled to try to understand. At ten years old, I didn't grasp the complexities of adulthood. I wanted to help her. Make everything okay again.

Her bitterness had become the central focus of our home. We had expertly learned how to tread cautiously around it. As to not to disturb it. She taught us well how to hide our emotions. To keep them in check. Our world was as fragile as blown glass, and we treated it as such.

"Mom," I said quietly. She didn't answer.

"Mom," I said again, a little louder.

The kitchen faucet dripped, making a loud splash in the sink below. I stood facing her, hands folded together in front of me. The innocence of childhood still coursing through my veins.

Her eyes met mine. Red rimmed and swollen. And I was filled with an instant knowing.

I should've left her alone.

"What do you want?" she screeched. Her voice, loud and stretched, made me shudder with fear.

"I thought you might be hungry…" I said, my voice barely above a whisper.

"You don't think I know how to take care of myself? I'm not some helpless victim here!" Her green eyes burned with anger as she looked back at me.

"It's just, you've been sitting here for hours and I thought…"my voice small and still childlike.

Before I could compete my sentence, the slap came. My cheek red and burning. My heart sinking. Tears stung my eyes, but I held them back.

"Don't you dare judge me! Why don't you mind your own business?" Her voice shook the room.

I turned and walked out, listening to her talking to herself. Complaining about being judged.

I went into my room and closed the door. Bitter tears broke through and ran down my cheeks as I touched the place where her hand had struck my face. The pain reaching deep into my spirit.

As I got older, I wanted to break away, to not be tied down to her.
To a broken family.
A broken mother.
But there was no escape for me. Not until much later.

It was funny how those memories didn't seem that far away, yet it had been many years. My mom eventually softened around the edges but never to the point where she was anything more than mother in name only.

Later in the day, I found myself at Greenbriar Lake Park, a place our family frequented often.

I walked down a shaded path and chose a seat on a park bench overlooking a small lake. It was situated in a strip of warm sunlight. Spring weather had set in early, but the wind was still cool. Cooler than I expected, and I shivered when the breeze blew, wishing I had brought a jacket. But before long the sunshine came in closer and warmed my whole body.

I sat back on the bench as people began to fill the park. I heard a dog bark in the distance. Playful and fun. Probably coming from the dog park across the lake. An older couple walked slowly, arm in arm, on the path in front of me. The man gave me a simple nod and I smiled in return. Not long after, a group of runners sprinted past like a flock of birds taking flight.

I looked out over the small lake as sunshine made diamond-like sparkles across the surface of the water. I watched tall grasses as they swayed along the edge of the lake, and butterflies flitted past me, searching for a flower to land on.

I looked up at a seemingly endless blue sky and I took in a long, deep, reminiscing breath.

Ben and I had been married in a place, tranquil and serene, like this one.

Our wedding day, so clear in my mind. We stood together in June, two starry-eyed lovers, saying their vows in a garden surrounded by Bradford Pear Trees shedding their blossoms. The blooms swirled around in the breeze, blanketing the ground with their snow-white petals. Our future wide open in front of us.

Truly, one of the best days of my life. A gust of wind kicked up and tousled my hair, almost if it was agreeing with me.

I reached for my bag and pulled out a worn blue leather-bound sketch pad. The edges of the pages were tattered and yellowed with age. I had owned this sketch pad for many years and had filled it with many different drawings. I tucked my hair behind my ears, and I began to draw on a fresh blank page. Empty and full of possibility. Waiting to be filled with anything I chose. I loved this about drawing and wished I did it more often. But running a household of boys didn't leave much time for artistic expression.

I sat there with pencil in hand and was lost in a world of my own.

And I found myself smiling.

Smiling for the first time in what felt like a very long time.

The sound of my phone ringing startled me. I didn't recognize the number, but I answered it anyway.

An older woman's voice was on the line. "Mrs. DuPont?"

"Yes?" I answered hesitantly, sensing an urgency in her call.

"My name is Carol Stewart, and I am the head nurse at Birchwood Elementary School. I was calling to let you know that Grayson had an accident today. He fell off the top of the slide and hit the ground pretty hard. Knocked the breath out of him. Don't worry, he's okay. But he's here with me now and asking to go home…"

I felt the blood drain from my face as she continued to speak.

Hadn't I just warned him about falling this morning?

After we hung up, I raced to the car. I didn't remember the drive at all. I just kept trying to comfort myself by repeating the nurse's words out loud: *He's okay, he's okay…*

As soon as I pulled up in front of the school, I threw it in park and practically ran up the front steps. I attempted to slow my pace and my breathing as I walked down the hallway toward the nurse's office.

I stopped in front of a slate grey door with a sign that read: Nurse's Office. The rippled glass window on the door casted sparkles of light onto the floor, reflections from the fluorescent lights above, as I slowly opened it and stepped inside.

Grayson was sitting on a chair in the small waiting area, holding an ice pack to his cheek. He looked up and smiled when he saw me.

I sat down and put my arm around him. He leaned against my chest and I took comfort in the feel of his small frame, safe and sound, next to me. Trying to ignore the sensation of dread as it worked its way through me.

How did I know this was going to happen? I had seen it so clearly in my mind this morning, as if it were a past event.

Maybe it happened in my dream? That certainly could explain it.

But I wasn't sure.

All I did know for sure was that something wasn't right.

Not right at all.

But I pushed the eeriness away. As far away from me as I could.

CHAPTER 5

I awoke to the sound of rain against the window. I snuggled deeper into billowy blankets, as slate grey skies stretched for miles; there would be no sunshine today.

Two weeks had come and gone with no more strange happenings. And with each passing day, the dream and the memory of June 3rd seemed to fade more and more. Becoming more of a passing thought, here and there, and life settled back into comfortable normalcy. The mystery of the slide incident had faded into the past, along with the dream, and I had begun to feel secure again.

And I found myself appreciating small things. Things I might have overlooked in the past.

I swung my legs over the side of the bed and stretched. From where I was, I could see Ben in the bathroom shaving. Oliver was standing next to him. Eye level with the sink. Fingertips pressed against the counter-top. Face filled with adoration.

I got up and tiptoed closer.

The smell of soap and sandalwood met my nose. I leaned against the doorframe and watched, neither of them aware of my presence.

The blade slid against Ben's cheek in a repeating pattern, revealing fresh skin in its wake.

"I wanna try, Daddy," Oliver begged.

"You're too young, son. Give it a few years and then you can."

Oliver's face was pursed in disappointment. Ben paused in his movement.

He picked up the shaving cream and smiled at Oliver, whose face had suddenly brightened up.

"Hold out your hands," Ben ordered.

Oliver cupped his hands together. Fingers still chubby with remnants of toddlerhood.

Ben pressed down on the trigger as a billowy white cloud of shaving cream piled up on Oliver's open hands. His giggles echoed on the bathroom tile.

I sighed and stepped away quietly. Not wanting to invade their intimacy.

The rain had stopped by the time I was dressed. I came downstairs in white shorts with a flowy navy three-quarter sleeve top, my hair pulled back into a low ponytail. I went into the kitchen and poured myself a cup of still steaming hot coffee.

Ben was in the living room doing a puzzle with the boys. Their voices trickled into the kitchen, light and melodious. Coffee cup in hand, I looked out the window as the sunlight glistened on wet blades of grass. Robins hopped from place to place, searching for worms displaced from the rain.

I took my cup of coffee out onto the front porch. The air was steamy as sun and moisture intertwined together in a slow-moving waltz.

I took a seat in a faded rocking chair, paint beginning to chip. The daily afternoon sun had left its mark.

With toes tapping the ground, I rocked back and forth, sipping on coffee, lost in my thoughts.

With the dream had come a sort of an awakening. A clearer vision of my life.

Casting my relationship with Ben into reflective contemplation.

We'd fallen in love in a rushed frenzy. Driven by an unspoken loneliness inside each of us. A yearning for completion. That completion we found in each other's eyes. When we were young and free, sharing our secrets, fears, and dreams.

I could still see us. Newly married. Walking together on busy sidewalks, hand in hand, to the Saturday Market to buy flowers and vegetables. Fresh baked bread, canned jams, handmade jewelry lined the aisles. Love and laughter surrounded us.

Memories rushed in. The image of Ben holding Grayson, only three weeks old, in the trickling light of dawn. Rocking, humming, soothing him back to sleep.

Our loft apartment, the center of the universe. Where we had spent many nights sitting on the patio, drinking wine, staring at the stars. Lost in conversation, as deep and vast as the ocean.

Now, business had left us careworn. Days slipping by without our noticing. Drawn into a synchronized dance of day to day child rearing. How I longed to take his hand and lead him back to where we started. Love, so fresh and new. Uncomplicated by life. A world all our own.

I'd never met a guy like Ben before. I never thought there would be another living soul who could understand the depths of me. Yet all of a sudden, he was there, standing in front of me, leaving me breathless.

I was working as a barista at a coffee shop in Pinehurst, a beautiful southern village located in the central part of the state, with miles upon miles of golf courses. The whispering pines told tales of historic golfing legends that walked the village streets in years gone by.

I grew up here. Accustomed to the influx of golfers, eager to play on courses traversed by the greats.

Ben had come to Pinehurst, with his company, to participate in one of the many tournaments that were held here every year. Ben worked for a company called Delta Services. A financial consulting firm, dealing mostly with wealth management. He had only been there a year but he was a favorite among his bosses. The only junior executive asked to come to the tournament.

Fall was descending upon North Carolina. Like a flower, slowly at first, then all at once. Leaves exploded all around us in a splendid display of color.

And this was a morning that was better suited as a poem.

The crisp smell of fresh cut grass and the earthiness of turning leaves mingled together and wafted up my nose as I got out my car.

I had arrived on the golf course just in time to deliver the specialty coffees that Ben's company had ordered. Requested to be delivered, thirty minutes before their tee time. I had four vanilla lattes, three mochas, and one double espresso with milk, all precariously double-stacked on two four-cup trays as I made way across the grounds. Just before I reached their tent, my foot caught on a tuft of grass and I fell forward. The coffees toppling down all around me. My white shirt stained brown and my pride irreparably damaged. I looked up, hoping no one had taken notice.

They had.

But Ben was the only person to come up and offer assistance. I stood up, wiping my shirt with my hands in a futile attempt to clean myself up, as he bent down to pick up the scattered cups.

My face flushed with embarrassment as he handed the cups back to me, sticky and covered with grass clippings. I looked down, avoiding eye contact.

"Hey, don't worry about all of this," he said softly.

"I'll go back and get you new coffees right away," I stammered as I attempted to put the cups back into the trays that were now saturated with coffee and dew.

The smell of vanilla bean and mocha was overpowering.

"No, no…it's not necessary, really. Those guys are too wired as it is." He chuckled as he looked in the direction of his team still standing under the tent. They were whooping and high-fiving each other over some unknown conquering.

He looked back at me and laughed again.

I looked at him fully for the first time and was taken aback at how attractive he was. He was tall, with an athletic build. Jet black hair, purposefully messy. Strong jawline. Vibrant green eyes that seemed to penetrate my soul. I broke away from his gaze, suddenly and acutely aware of my appearance. No makeup and drenched in coffee. When I looked back up, his eyes were still on me. Charming and flirtatious.

I was so taken aback by him; I couldn't formulate the words to say the *'Let's make it right for the customer'* spiel.

We stood together for a moment, surrounded by the sound of bird songs, the low murmur of conversation, and the occasional thwack of a well hit golf ball.

He was smiling at me.

What was he thinking about?

I wanted to leave, but I found myself frozen in place, unable to move away.

"How about I come by the shop after the game is over and we can settle this up?" he said, still smiling.

His eyes were soft but I could also see a playful spark in them.

A look that said there was more he wanted.

A look that said he wanted to see me again.

Did I imagine it? Surely, he just wanted to stop by and get the refund he was owed.

"Sure, sure…I mean, if that's okay?" I stammered.

He nodded happily and turned to walk away. Stopping after only taking a few steps, he turned back and looked at me. "By the way, my name is Ben…just in case you were wondering…"

He stood waiting for a customary response.

My name in return.

But I didn't speak. Time was standing still.

His name ringing in my ears.

Ben.

The sound of it made every cell in my body begin to tingle. It resonated inside of me somewhere deep. A place I had never been before.

He waited for just a moment for my response and when he didn't get it, a little dejected, he turned and walked back to his group.

Frozen. I watched him walking away, my chance to respond, getting further and further away. By the time I was able to speak, it was too late. He was back under the tent. And the opportunity had passed. My cheeks flushed again. I hadn't meant to be rude.

I pulled out of the parking lot with the determination to not be there when he came to the shop. How could I face him when I had embarrassed myself, twice over?

But despite my outward resolve, deep down inside, I was dying to see him again.

There was just something about him. Something I couldn't put my finger on, but it was there, drawing me to him. More than just his looks. I had dated attractive guys before. Ben was different. And something about him rocked me to my core.

I stretched in the faded rocker on our front porch. The mugginess of the morning had completely drifted away, while I was lost in memory. A breeze picked up, swirling around me, bringing with it the scent of freshly bloomed lilacs, signifying the end of cold weather, and I sighed.

I was ready for spring. In more ways than one.

A time to begin again. A rebirth for our marriage, perhaps.

A loud bang startled me, followed by the sound of laughter filtering out through closed windows.

I knew that sound well.

Playful wrestling. Boys being boys. And I was sure Ben was involved.

As the sounds of laughter faded, the memories called to me again.

As the dogwood branches adorned with fresh, new buds waiting to bloom swayed in the wind in front of me, my thoughts drifted back to the day we met.

After I left the golf course. I stopped at my apartment to change my coffee-soiled clothes. After putting on and discarding four different outfits, I stood in front of my closet staring. Finally, in desperation, I grabbed a long-sleeve black floral wrap dress and put it on, pairing it with a set of gold hoops and a pair of sandals. I threw some light curls in my hair, two strokes of mascara, and gloss on my lips.

I looked in the mirror and laughed. *So much for not being there when he came by!*

I got back to the coffee shop just as the morning rush was over. The clock ticked slowly as I busied myself with tedious tasks to pass the time.

After lunch, a man wearing a brown tweed jacket came in and ordered a cappuccino to go.

I inquired about the golf tournament. *Was it over?* He didn't know.

Hours passed and the afternoon drew to a close. And there had been no sign of him. In ten minutes, we would be closing, and I would never see him again.

After all the employees had left, I began the closing routine. Something I often did alone.

As soon as I stepped into the back room, the front bell chimed.

I had forgotten to lock the front door and someone had come into the shop.

An instant knowing came over me... he was here.

I stood where I was for just a moment, unable to move.

Compulsion pushed me forward.

And as soon as I stepped around the corner, I saw him.

His face strained with concern as he scanned the room. But once our eyes met, a broad smile came across his face.

I walked up to the counter and waited, my heart beating wildly as he approached.

He was wearing that same charming smile from earlier, all the way until he reached me.

There was no one here but the two of us in the soft light of the afternoon.

The fading sunlight filtering in through the front window, casting faint strips of light on the floor.

He leaned up on the counter, and his musky cologne filled the area around me. I could feel the heat of his skin even across the space between us.

I stepped in a half step closer.

"So, how can we make this right? I mean, you did jip us out of eight coffees." There was a mock seriousness to him, as he winked at me.

The Spanish Guitar CD that had been playing all afternoon ended, leaving quiet in its place.

A wave of nerves washed over me and my hands began to tremble. I quickly shoved them under the counter ledge, out of sight, as I attempted to speak.

To my horror, all that came out was gibberish. I tried once more, and got the same result.

I could feel my cheeks redden, in frustration. *What was happening to me?*

He laughed, seeming to enjoy my ineptness. "Oh, so what I think you're saying is that you're offering to take me on a date to make up for it, huh? Hmmm, I think that's a reasonable swap. Just tell me when and where...but it will have to be tonight, since I am leaving tomorrow morning." His eyebrows lifted as he emphasized the word *tonight*.

I could tell he was pleased with his own wittiness.

I let out a small laugh.

"Ah, I will take that as a yes!" His smile grew wider. "By the way, do you think you might tell me your name now?" he chuckled.

"It's Claire. Claire Everly," I offered quietly, still feeling the redness in my cheeks.

Did he notice?

"Nice to meet you, Claire," he said, his eyes fixed on mine.

I smiled softly in return, trying to not give way to the elation that was building inside of me.

It was agreed we would meet at seven, at the Mexican café across the street from the coffee shop.

I arrived a few minutes early and saw him before he saw me.

A shiver went down my spine in anticipation.

I looked at him as he stood waiting outside the entrance of the restaurant. Wearing jeans, a button up shirt and a sport jacket. Still as handsome as earlier.

I walked toward him, the joy of possibility all around me.

The sun was setting and cool breeze nipped at my arms. I was wearing fitted black jeans and a cream sleeveless top with a deep neckline. I had paired it with a set of black pumps. I now wished I had dressed warmer, as I shivered in the wind.

He turned around, and when he saw me, he smiled. A calmness enveloped me as he took my hand and led me into the restaurant. The feel of his hand in mine strangely familiar, though we had never touched.

We ate chimichangas and drank authentic Mexican beer while we talked.

"There's something different about you, Claire. Different from other girls I've gone out with," he said, his eyes fixed on mine.

"What do you mean?" I asked.

"I don't know, really. Just something about you feels familiar. Like I've always known you."

I nodded because I understood his sentiment. I could feel it too. There was a sense of home between us.

As we talked, we opened up to each other, sharing things about our pasts with ease.

He told me he was an only child and he had always felt alone. Feeling alone was something else I could relate to.

"My mother was an immigrant from Spain," he told me. "And my father, he came from a family of welders. Our family has been welding since the early 1900's and has built a very successful business that has been handed down generation after generation. Until now. I was the only son of four brothers and the one who was expected to take over the business when my father and uncles got too old to keep it going. But me, I decided to go in a different direction. I went to college for business. In doing so, I hurt my father. We were really close when I was a kid. I didn't mean to hurt him, but I had my own hopes and dreams to follow. It caused an unspoken rift between us. He never brought it up, but I saw it in his eyes every time he looked at me."

Ben paused and took a long sip of his beer as I sat patiently waiting for him to continue.

"When he got sick, my mom decided to take him to a faith healer's compound in Utah rather than getting him traditional cancer treatment. He died six months later. The guilt still eats at me sometimes. And my mom, I had a hard time forgiving her. I think if he had just gotten proper medical treatment, he'd still be alive. Now she's gone back to Spain and we rarely talk. So, I feel like I lost both of my parents." Ben's words were choked with emotion and trailed off as the waitress brought another round of beers.

When she walked away, he changed the subject.

I wondered if he had opened up to anyone like this before. My gut told me no. There was definitely something going on between us. Something I had never experienced before. A feeling of coming home, but like no home I had ever been to before. It was warm. Comforting.

By the time he walked me back to my car, the air was thick with dew and the entire city was asleep. The stop light's interchanging colors reflected down onto the empty street as we crossed over to where my car was parked. He put his arms around me, and I looked up at him with expectant eyes.

"I'm so happy that I met you, Claire Everly," he said as he put his lips on mine, soft and sweet.

And then he smiled.

It was the beginning, the beginning of us, and I knew it.

We were married in less than two years. Our relationship as deep and enchanting as an evergreen forest. Comforting even in silence. Made up of a million moments that said we were meant for each other.

The front door swung open and out came two little boys, followed by Ben. He was carrying a Nerf football. Ben tossed the football to Grayson and he caught it on the first try. Ben ran over and gave him a high-five. His eyes lit up with pride.

Ben loved being with his boys. They were a major priority in his life and it showed.

I knew his own upbringing influenced his way of parenting.

Ben often told me his whole world was wrapped up in me and the boys. His former life fading more and more into the background every day we were together.

As did mine.

Two halves make a whole, they say. And I certainly found that to be the case with Ben and I.

At dinner, later that evening, I was struck by how quiet it was except for the chatter of the boys.

Ben's eyes not meeting mine once.

Dishes washed in silence while the boys were put to bed.

Reading under lamplight.

A light kiss on the cheek goodnight.

A revelation of a vastness between us. How long had it been there?

I drifted off to sleep, deeply unsettled.

The next morning, I began to wonder. *Was he still in love with me?*
Like he was in days gone by…

That question shook me to the core.

He sat at the table reading the morning paper, sipping coffee.

I watched him as I wiped up spilled milk and Captain Crunch from the bar. Aftershocks from the boys' breakfast.

I laid the rag down, moisture still on my hand, and walked over to the table.

I took a seat across from him, my hands folded in my lap.

Bird songs drifted in from the partially open window next to the table. The thin curtain, moving with the breeze.

I studied his face as he intently stared at the paper open to the sports section.

As I looked, I noticed there were fine lines around his eyes. I hadn't seen them before.

How long had they been there?

Had he been completely invisible to me?

I had been going through the motions so proficiently that somehow, he had slipped off of my radar.

Not intentionally.

Life was just busy raising boys.

Dirty diapers led to potty training, that led to muddy-kneed jeans, school lunches, and PTA meetings.

A never-ending influx of activity.

Distraction.

A side effect of having two children in the house.

He continued to drink his coffee and read the paper without looking up.

Could he feel me looking at him?

Why wasn't he looking back? Was I invisible to him too?

He got up from the table and walked over to put his mug in the sink. I watched him as he moved through the kitchen and his shoes echoed on the floor.

I continued to watch as he rinsed his mug and turned it upside down on the counter.

Suddenly, I was filled with a wave of strong emotion.

I loved him so much. I wanted to tell him that he wasn't less important to me!

We'd just been busy. That's all...

I just didn't know how to say it.

Suddenly, the boys bounded into the room all dressed for school. They were wearing mismatched t-shirts and shorts. Grayson wearing plaid with stripes and Oliver's shirt on backwards.

I had been so lost in thought, I had forgotten about getting them ready for the day.

Their smiles, enormous. Proud of their independent accomplishment, and I didn't have the heart to make them change.

"Did you sillies brush your teeth?" I offered instead.

Their sheepish grins gave me all the information I needed.

Ben walked over and playfully swatted their behinds.

"Get upstairs and brush those teeth!" You could hear the laughter in his voice.

They giggled and disappeared upstairs.

I knew I needed to follow them and make sure the job was done properly, but I was frozen in place.

My husband was looking directly at me.

The world fell away, and it was just the two of us standing together in the kitchen.

"What?" I asked him, as the thunder of boy's feet could be heard on the ceiling above us.

Suddenly, his arms were around me.

"God, Claire…I love you so much. I hope you know that."

"Where did that come from?" I asked, astonished, wondering if he had been able to read my mind.

"You're everything to me. You and the boys. I am just so thankful for you. And I'm sorry if I don't show it like I should…" his voice trailed off.

"Hey, we are both guilty of that…." I said as I looked up into his eyes, sincere with love.

And then he kissed me. He kissed me in a way that I hadn't been kissed in a very long time. The kind of kiss that instantaneously makes you feel alive. The kind of kiss that makes you feel like a woman.

He turned, walked into the foyer, and picked up his briefcase. Before he walked out the door, he called out, "See you this afternoon, beautiful!"

The door clicked shut, and I stood there listening to the sounds of morning, basking in the wave of happiness that washed over me.

CHAPTER 6

Dreams.
   Tumultuous, captivating, and sometimes frightening, all unfolding in slumber's rapture.

Flying, soaring over tree tops, dancing with the wind. Laughter moving across the water. Pieces of life entangled with exotic places and unknown faces, reassembled into broken bits of reality. Creeping in the night to bewilder our minds while we sleep.

I had never paid much attention to my dreams before. They were side notes, fuzzy happenstances of the twilight realm. But lately my dreams had become something more. Frantic and intense. Filled with pieces from the dream of losing Ben, resurfacing and intertwining into hazy nightmares.

When the morning would come, moments of the images from the night before would come back in swirls, glimpses and strange disconnected details.

Then, slowly drifting away as the day unfolded.

The early morning sun poured in through the window, and I put my head on Ben's shoulder. Waking slowly, from another nightmare filled sleep.

It was still early and the boys were sound asleep. He ran his fingers along my shoulder softly, tickling me a little. I heard him sigh and I snuggled in closer.

"I was thinking about working in the yard today. The weather has been so nice and the flowerbeds have been begging for my attention," Ben's voice soft and throaty from sleep.

"How about the boys and I help?" I offered.

"I was hoping you would say that," Ben said as he pulled me in even closer.

I felt secure, wrapped up in blankets and his love, as the images of the night slipped completely away.

Before long the boys were there bounding onto the bed. Ready for the day to begin.

After a few minutes, I got in the shower as Ben took the boys down for breakfast.

The hot water invigorated my body, making the bathroom steamy, as I closed my eyes.

The water ran over my face, blinding me to the world.

There was a tap on the shower door and I jumped.

I opened my eyes and saw Ben standing there.

"Is there room for me in there?" he said, his eyes playfully looking me over.

"Wait. Where are the boys?" I asked, nervously.

"They're watching a new episode of Pat the Dog. A tornado couldn't pull them away." He laughed.

I hoped he was right.

He slipped off his boxers and stepped inside. He stood behind me and I closed my eyes, feeling his lips on the back of my neck.

My body electric. His touch precise.

The pulse of pleasure coursed through me. His breath warm in my ear. I turned around to face him as water rushed over both of us. I put my lips on his, enjoying the taste and feel of his tongue in my mouth.

Slipping himself inside of me, I instinctually bucked myself against him. He held onto my hips, meeting me with return thrusts. An explosion of fireworks erupted from my body. Leaving us both shaking in its wake. He kissed my cheek, my nose, my lips, as the water shifted from hot to turn lukewarm.

Reminding us we were on a time limit.

But neither of us were ready for this stolen moment to end.

Our eyes were locked. His surged with emotion.

"God, Claire, I love you so much…"

Before I could respond, the water turned ice cold and I screamed.

Laughing, Ben got out to get me a towel.

After breakfast, we loaded the boys up in the car and headed out to the plant nursery and garden center, only a few miles away. This was one of the highlights of the season for me. Wandering down the aisles of plants so deep and vast, it felt as if we were in the center of a dense forest, right here in the middle of the city.

When we entered the greenhouse, I was immediately swept away. Tall potted fruit trees and containers upon containers of pink, yellow, and purple blooms surrounded me.

A fine mist hung in the air, the smell of damp soil riding on it. The very whiff of it made me want to be elbows deep in the garden. I half wondered if they planned it that way so you couldn't leave this place without a cart full of plants.

Ben pushed the dolly cart around with the boys sitting proudly on top. I looked at all three of them, wearing baseball caps and black Nike tennis shoes. My guys, I thought happily.

My boys, little versions of Ben, with their good looks, dark hair and tanned skin. Their father made over. Except for their eyes. They both had my brown eyes with the familial yellow flecks. I was glad to know some part of me was put into their genetic makeup, but then again, I couldn't complain if they looked like their father. He was a beautiful man. Even after all this time, my heart fluttered when I looked at him. Especially after a morning like this one. The memory of our shower together made my cheeks instantly flush.

I had trouble choosing what plants to bring home. The choices seemed to be limitless. There were jasmine flowers, hibiscuses, roses, daisies, and lilies. There were climbing vines and flowering bushes. Not to mention the many varieties of trees and evergreens.

It was always hard for me to narrow down my choices, and I always left with more than I actually needed. This time was no different. Even the boys had picked out their own flowers to bring home and a set of windchimes to boot.

After we loaded our treasures into the car, we headed home. Only stopping at Frank's Pizzeria to pick up a pizza for our lunch. Saucy and delicious, authentic Italian goodness. A regular go-to for us.

After eating, we all headed outside to work.

With a symphony of bees humming, birds singing, and a warm breeze blowing all around us, Ben and I laid our plans in motion. While the boys sat happily in the middle of a clover patch trying to find a four-leaf treasure.

Ben began raking the fallen leaves, but once the boys saw him, they jumped into his piles over and over again, destroying them. For some reason, Ben didn't seem to mind their disruption. He just kept looking over at me, smiling.

I distracted the boys by getting them started on planting the flowers they had chosen. We had given them the flower bed that went around the large elm tree in our backyard for their plantings. Happily, they went straight to work.

While they were busy, Ben was able to finish raking the yard, and I cleaned out the bird bath and weeded the flowerbeds in the front yard.

When I walked back around where the boys were, they were covered in dirt from head to toe.

"Look, Momma! We did it!" Oliver called out.

Grayson rolled his eyes. "He crushed most them," he said, not hiding his disappointment.

I looked at the flowers partially in the dirt and partially out. Stems and petals crushed.

And I smiled.

"Looks like you fellas worked pretty hard here!"

Grayson shrugged as Oliver bounced up and down.

I looked at Grayson and whispered, "How about I help you neaten these up?" He shrugged again.

"Boys," I said, my face poised in mock seriousness. "I need someone to catch all those lady bugs that have been flying around the patio. Do you know anyone who could measure up to that job?" I looked around the yard, purposely avoiding looking at Oliver.

I made eye contact with Grayson and winked.

"Me, me, me! I can do it, Momma!" Oliver exclaimed.

"Ah, yes, I think you are just the man for the job," I told him as his face beamed with enthusiasm. I grabbed a bug catcher and sent him out to work while Ben refreshed the mulch in all the flower beds, and Grayson and I did right by his plantings. By the time we were finished, Grayson was smiling ear to ear, and Oliver was exhausted from his chase.

"I didn't catch any wady-bugs, Momma." he said as he handed me his net.

"Hey, it's okay! You tried and that's what really matters!" I said as I kissed the top of his head.

I took the boys inside and gave them a bath. Washing off layers upon layers of dirt.

Afterwards, Ben settled them in the living room to watch a movie.

I went into the kitchen, intent on whipping up some chocolate chip cookies.

As I mixed the dry & wet ingredients, I was filled with a deep satisfaction. My heart surged with love, filled with vast expansions of joy, just from the simplicity of life.

Teddy wound himself back and forth between my legs purring as I licked the mixing spoon, savoring the buttery sweetness.

Just as I added the chocolate chips to the batter, Ben came into the kitchen. "What can I help with?"

"I just need to figure out what to put them on when they come out since we don't have a platter anymore," I told him.

Ben looked at me strangely for a moment and then walked to the cabinet over the refrigerator. He slowly pulled out my white platter and held it up.

"You mean this platter?" he questioned.

I stopped in the middle of forming the cookie dough balls and just looked at him.

"That platter got broken...I thought..." I stammered.

My mind was muddled. *Didn't it get broken??*

I squinted, thinking harder.

"Looks fine to me." He laughed.

He sat it down on the counter next to where I was working.

"I swear that Oliver pulled that down off the counter and it smashed on the floor...." I continued.

"Crisis averted!" he joked.

I nodded, not convinced.

"You need anything else, beautiful?" he said as he walked up behind me and kissed the back of my neck.

I could feel a rush of warmness that spread all the way through me.

He wrapped his arms around my waist and looked over my shoulder as I tried to finish forming the cookies. It was a little more difficult to work this way. Usually, I would've sent him off to busy himself while I cooked, but it felt so good to have him here like this. I wouldn't dare send him away.

I finally got the cookies prepped and put them in the oven. Ben went into the living room and sat down with the boys to finish watching The Incredibles, a family favorite. The boys watched it at least once a week. They were obsessed with anything superhero.

Before long, the timer went off and I pulled cookies out of the oven, inundating the entire house with the soothing aroma of vanilla and chocolate.

I set them out one by one to cool on the platter. They were picture perfect. While they cooled, I went in to finish the movie with the boys and Ben. They were snuggled up, one on each side of him. I watched as Oliver's heavy eyelids opened and closed, fighting sleep. He didn't want to miss one moment of the story.

But as soon as the movie was over, he was wide awake again, and there was a stampede of little feet rushing into the kitchen. The cookies were calling to them.

I followed quickly behind so I could get the platter down from the counter. But before I could get there, and almost as if it were happening in slow motion, Oliver stood up on his tippy toes and reached up to grab a cookie, just out of his reach. And when he did, he pulled the whole platter down with it. It smashed all over the kitchen floor, the sound ricocheting off the walls.

Oliver's wails soon filled the kitchen.

I had seen it in my mind's eye, and I knew he was going to pull the platter down, but it all happened so fast. Before I could call out.

For an instant, the whole scene had a nightmare quality about it.

Ben ran into the room and looked at me, his faced washed with shock and bewilderment. After a few seconds, he quickly ran to Oliver's aid. Ben picked him up, dusted him off, and held him close. The shock of the smashing sound and the loss of the cookies was more than Oliver's five-year-old heart could bear. He sobbed in his father's arms.

I numbly got out the broom and swept up the broken platter and ruined cookies as the scene replayed in my mind.

Both the boys were moping over the lost treats, so Ben loaded them back up in the car and took them to the grocery store bakery for some fresh chocolate chip cookies.

After they left, I walked outside and sat on the back patio, feeling numb. I watched absentmindedly as butterflies flew around the garden, landing on our freshly planted flowers.

I replayed the event over and over again in my mind as the newly hung windchimes dinged softly over my head.

How had I known the platter would be broken? Something else from the dream? It had to be!

And as quickly as the questions entered my mind, an uneasiness settled deep into my bones and cold distinct fear began to take ahold of me.

Ben never mentioned the platter to me. He acted as if nothing unusual had happened. I tried to ignore it too, but I couldn't get it off of my mind. As I slept that night, I kept dreaming of the moment the platter smashed on the floor, over and over again. It roused me from my sleep each time it hit the floor.

Finally, I gave up on sleeping and quietly got out of the bed around four in the morning. I tiptoed downstairs and made myself a cup of tea. I took the tea into the playroom and turned on the computer.

The quiet of the night surrounded me. Every sound amplified. The wind rushed through the trees outside, making a roaring sound, and I could hear the echo of a hoot owl in the distance.

I sipped on my tea and searched in Google for premonition type dreams. In my mind, this was the only explanation of my knowing about the platter and the slide accident before they actually happened.

The search results confused and frustrated me even more.

I turned the computer off and sat in the darkness. I was at a complete loss.

Maybe I'm making too big a deal of this?

I sat numbly lost in thought, turning the lamp on the desk off and on, again and again. The soft yellow hue filling the room, only to be quickly pushed away by the darkness again.

When the sun finally came up, I heard Ben's footsteps coming down the stairs.

"Claire?" he called to me.

I went to him and wrapped my arms around him. He hugged me back.

"Are you okay, honey?" he asked tenderly.

"Yes, I'm fine. I just couldn't sleep…"

I didn't want to tell him the truth. How could I tell him what I was going through? He wouldn't understand.

Ben was too practical. He would never believe that it was anything more than a coincidence. After what happened to his dad, Ben did not believe in anything outside of the normal, predictable world.

And I had already spent too much time worrying about my dream.

…and Ben was fine.

Everything *was* really fine.

At least, that's what I kept telling myself, trying to ignore the darkness in the pit of my stomach.

CHAPTER 7

E aster weekend slipped up on me before I even realized it. Mom had invited us to come over to her house to celebrate. She was cooking a big meal and wanted all of us kids there. We didn't usually celebrate Easter together, so I was surprised by her invitation.

But lately Mom had been on this kick, saying we didn't see each other enough. So, when she invited us, I wasn't going to be the one to disagree. Especially when Mandi and her husband Lewis had already agreed to come. Not to mention my brother, Jonathan, was actually coming too.

I knew Mom was lonely. I was always encouraging her to get out and make some friends. She had made a few at her bridge club, and she also attended a book club once a month. But, honestly, it wasn't enough. What I really wanted her to do was find a man to spend some time with. But she was completely against it. She had not dated anyone since the divorce.

Time's gone by. Mom's heart long cold, made bitter by disappointment.

I could remember when my parents were still in love. Standing outside my room after tucking me in for the night, kissing under the orange glow of the hallway lights. Whispers of their love rushing in and surrounding me. We were all happy then. Our lives, filled with joy and laughter. Abundant and running over.

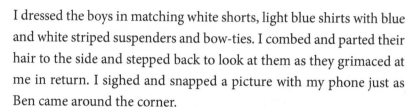

I dressed the boys in matching white shorts, light blue shirts with blue and white striped suspenders and bow-ties. I combed and parted their hair to the side and stepped back to look at them as they grimaced at me in return. I sighed and snapped a picture with my phone just as Ben came around the corner.

"Whoa, those are two handsome young men right there!" he exclaimed.

He walked up and high-fived both of them as wide grins spread across their faces.

I looked at Ben, wearing a t-shirt and gym shorts.

"Ben?" I tried to hide the irritation in my voice.

He looked back at me expectantly, feigning ignorance and holding back a smile.

"Are you going to change?" I continued.

"What?! You don't like my outfit?" He laughed.

I stood with pursed lips and folded arms. We were already running late.

"Okay, okay. I'll go change!" he scoffed.

He stopped before he walked away and looked at me, his eyes amused. "But only if you give me a kiss, and I mean a real kiss."

The boys immediately began to moan and scream in protest about the kissing and disappeared down the hallway.

"Don't mess up your outfits!" I called after them.

When I looked back, Ben was still waiting for my response.

I laughed. "You're ridiculous!"

"Ridiculously in love!" he proclaimed as he swooped me up and laid his lips on mine.

Mom lived on Evergreen Street in Gastonia, which was only a forty-minute drive from us. She had moved there after Grayson was born so she could be closer to help me with the baby.

One of her many attempts to try to repair our relationship.

She lived in a historic cobblestone cottage she had been renting for years. It was located just a few miles off of the interstate, making it easy to get to. It was a small two-bedroom house with all original windows and floors and a large fenced in backyard with beautiful mature trees. The house was also within walking distance of the local library. Making it even more appealing for her.

When we arrived, everyone else was already there. Cars filled her small driveway. When we got out, the boys ran up the walk and straight inside without looking back.

Ben took my hand and we went up the walkway together.

I took a big, deep breath just before we stepped inside.

Jonathan and Lewis were sitting in front of the television watching basketball when we came in. The playoffs were on. Ben walked over and shook both of their hands as I went into the kitchen, where Mandi was talking to the boys.

Mom was pulling the ham out of the oven when I walked in. I was struck by how beautiful she looked. Radiant.

Her short blonde hair was now tinseled with streaks of white and her silver hoop earrings sparkled as she turned, smiling when she saw me.

She's smiling? That's a new one.

"Claire, could you grab the hot plates and set them down on the counter for me?" her voice light and melodic.

I grabbed them just in time for her to set down the hot roasting pan.

The kitchen was strangely comforting, filled with the aroma of cinnamon and warmth.

Mandi came up and lightly hugged me. She smelled of Chanel perfume and hairspray.

Her hug was brief, and afterwards she brushed herself off.

I couldn't help but roll my eyes. She saw me and glared back.

"What's your problem?" she asked.

"Nothing," I responded.

She nodded her head. "Yeah, whatever!"

She turned and walked into the living room.

I watched her walk away in her mini skirt and stiletto heels, and I grimaced.

"Why does she always have to be like that? It's pathetic." I looked over at Mom who was serving out steamed broccoli onto a platter.

"Like what?" Mom answered without looking up.

"I don't know. Dressing like a prostitute for starters…"

"Claire! That's enough!" Mom retorted. Her face red with anger.

I dropped it, but I was still annoyed. Lately, my patience for Mandi was razor thin.

Years of not standing up to her had taken its toll. For some unknown reason, I could never stand up to her. Every time I had ever tried, I ended up getting tongue tied and flustered.

I remembered just after Oliver was born, Mandi had stopped by to see the baby. I was excited to see her, but as usual, that excitement was short lived.

She stepped inside the front door, looking as if she had stepped off the runway. Wearing a deep v white blouse with skin-tight leopard pants and black thigh high boots. Her hair perfectly wind-blown. Lips so red, they looked like blood. I stood in front of her in a baggy t-shirt and sweat pants, hair unbrushed for days and felt suddenly self-conscious. I ran my fingers through my hair, nervously.

"Where's my new nephew!?" she exclaimed as the foyer filled with the scent of her perfume. I led her into the living room, where she bent over the cradle and cooed. She stood looking at him for several moments, her back to me.

"Do you want to hold him?" I offered.

She whipped around. "No, no! That's quite okay!"

She stepped back from the cradle shaking her head.

Mandi and Lewis didn't have any children. She proclaimed she would never have kids. Too much work, she would say.

"So, I see you haven't lost any of the baby weight…" Her eyes on my post-baby widened hips. I tugged on my shirt, pulling it down over my waist trying to cover any bulge that was spilling over.

"God, I would never want to ruin my body in that way." Her face was crinkled up with distaste. "I just don't know how you do it, Claire." Her eyes now on my unbrushed hair.

All that was going through my head was: *Bitch, Bitch, Bitch.*

I had just had a baby for god sake. What did she expect?

But I didn't say a word. Everything I wanted to say sitting on the tip of my tongue, right until she walked out the door.

I knew deep down her put downs weren't intentional, but most of what came out of her mouth was taken that way. It was just a natural side effect of being around her.

I walked over and started picking at and eating pieces of the ham, the drippings burning my fingers, while Mom looked on disapprovingly.

"Take this dish outside for me," Mom said as she handed me a bowl of stewed apples, trying to deter me from nibbling before the meal. I walked out the back door to where the table was set up. A paper table-cloth flapped in the wind. She had set a table up out here because her house was too small to have one big enough to accommodate us all. Luckily the weather was perfect for outdoor eating. We had just had a small cold snap, with days in the fifties. Luckily today was warm. I walked around the table and looked at tiny floral place holders, each one holding a card with our individual names. I placed the apples near a large flower arrangement of daffodils and white lilies that sat in the center of the table. I narrowed my eyes suspiciously. She hadn't done anything like this since I was very young. She had even planned an Easter Egg hunt for the boys. The colorful eggs were already strewn all over the yard. Purple, orange, lime, and pink peeked out from the blades of green grass.

Jonathan came out with the ham on a large platter. He sat it down next to the apples, and I looked just past him and saw streamers hanging from the tree limbs.

"What's up with Mom?" he asked, as if he could read my mind.

"How am I supposed to know?" I retorted, instantly regretting my tone.

"Well damn. You live by her and I don't. I would think you'd know." His voice was edgy. I wondered if this was going to turn into an argument. Jonathan and I had never argued before. But we didn't talk either. Our conversations normally were limited to small pleasantries.

He actually had a closer relationship to Ben than he did me. When we got together for the holidays, they would immediately get together and start laughing and joking about everything. Feeding off each other to the point where sometimes it would get out of hand. Especially if they started poking fun at Mandi.

I wanted to talk to him, really talk, but I didn't know how. To find a way to bridge the distance that had formed over the years.

I adored Jonathan when I was little. When he still lived at home, he was my hero. Especially right after Dad left.

Before he left for school.

He had been an anchor in an unstable world.

One particular night stood out from the rest. It was the week after Dad left. Mom had locked herself in her bedroom again and wouldn't come out. Jonathan came home from work with McDonald's for Mandi and I for dinner. He knew we would be hungry. Later after eating, Mandi and I were watching a video when Jonathan called out to us from the backyard.

Mandi and I stood out on the porch, looking out at him.

"I thought you were going to your friend's house to watch the meteor shower?" Mandi spouted.

"I was. But then I thought who better to watch the meteor shower with than my best two girls?" He smiled. His body still gangly with youth.

Mandi huffed and walked away, going back to the video. The truth being, she had no interest in what Jonathan was talking about.

I looked up at him with expectant eyes.

"What's a meteor shower?" I asked.

"Let me show you," he said as he took my hand and led me off the porch to where he had a laid a blanket out on the grass.

We laid down on our backs and looked up at the darkened sky.

"It's a perfect night for this!" he exclaimed enthusiastically. I nodded, still not quite understanding.

I put my hands behind my head like Jonathan did as the wind moved through the trees and the crickets hummed their nightly tune.

The sky was a deep ebony etched in sparkling stars, blanketing the sky as far as the eye could see. I was entranced by the night sky. Enveloped. Consumed. As if I were becoming one with its vastness and majesty.

Time seemed to stop as we lay motionless.

Then, the first meteor blazed across the sky with trail of dazzling light behind it. And I gasped.

"Woah! Did you see that?" Jonathan asked, his face as bright as the meteor itself.

I nodded in awe.

"*That* was a meteor," he said with pride.

As we laid next to each other and watched for more meteors, Jonathan taught me about the constellations. He pointed out Orion's Belt, The Big and Little Dippers, and Cassiopeia.

This became a nightly ritual for us. Star gazing. It lasted right until he left for school, and we never stargazed again. In fact, we barely talked either. He became a distant relative, one you barely saw and one you barely knew.

My brother had practically disappeared from my life. My young heart experiencing its first real taste of heartbreak.

I looked at Jonathan, now a grown man, a physicist at UNC-Chapel Hill with his own life going on. I felt a surge of sadness as I watched him walk back into the house to get more food for the table. The streamers that Mom had hung rustled in the wind behind me.

I wanted to say something to him. Start a real conversation. Maybe find a way to reconnect. I rehearsed in my mind what I would say, but when he came back out with the mashed potatoes, Mandi was on his heels, and any conversation I had hoped to have was over.

After we ate, Mom let the boys hunt for the Easter Eggs. Oliver was lagging behind, wanting to open each egg as soon as he found it, giving Grayson the advantage. And he was quickly clearing the yard of eggs. Jonathan went out and helped Oliver pile his basket high. Oliver's eyes filled with admiration, as his and Jonathan's laughter rang out across the swaying grass.

Jonathan left right after the egg hunt, before I got another chance to talk to him.

After the boys finished devouring pieces of melted chocolate, I took them inside to wash their hands. When I stepped inside, I overheard Mom on the phone with someone. She spoke in a hushed tone, but I heard her say, "I miss you" to whoever was on the other end of the line.

When she saw me, she immediately hung up the phone.

"Mom, who were you talking to?" My eyes steady on her as she stood motionless in front of me.

"Oh, that was just Betty, my neighbor. She was seeing if we needed anything for the meal, but I told her we had just finished up."

She moved to the counter and began cleaning up.

"Why did you tell her that you missed her?" I pressed.

Mom's face instantly reddened. "I did not say that!"

I ran it back over again in my mind and was certain that she did.

We stood looking at each other for just a moment, and then she turned and walked out the back door, without another word.

I walked the boys on to the bathroom, passing by family pictures hung on the wall. There was one of all five us. Taken before the divorce.

Taken when we were still a real family.

It seemed so long ago, it could have been another lifetime.

As I stepped away, a strange longing overtook me, so I went back to look at them again. The afternoon light poured in through the front windows, giving the hall a soft glow.

The boys washed their hands and darted past me, back outside.

I stood motionless. My eyes fixed on the family photo again. Nostalgia flowed as I looked at my dad's face.

Young and handsome. Strong. Broad shoulders.

Nowadays he seemed smaller to me. Weathered.

A part of me missed him, but we rarely talked. I had never been close to my father. There was a wall between us that neither seemed to be able to penetrate. I just couldn't forgive him for leaving Mom the way he did, for leaving us alone to deal with the after effect of her bitterness. But more so, for always favoring Mandi. He always had eyes for Mandi and Mandi only, and I would never be enough.

Not to mention the last time I saw him, we had a big fight.

It was Oliver's first birthday party. Dad had come to the party and spent the entire time talking to Mandi. Giving her advice about her latest loser boyfriend. He didn't even see Oliver eating his smash cake. I stormed over and told him he needed to leave. I ended up yelling at him, saying he wasn't wanted.

He left soon after, with Mandi chasing behind him. I felt bad for yelling at him, but it was infuriating to me that he couldn't take his eyes off of Mandi long enough to see his grandson celebrating his first birthday.

I knew I should try to make more of an effort to talk to him...to see him... but for some reason I couldn't. I knew deep down inside, I would never compare to his precious Mandi, and my heart was locked up tight. All my life I loved him, but I would never let him love me. He didn't deserve that privilege. I walked away, ignoring the empty space stirring inside of me.

When I came back outside, the sun was getting lower in the sky and I didn't see Ben anywhere. When I finally spotted him, I saw that Mandi had him cornered. As I approached, I could see her leaning in close. She was running her finger along his jawline, proclaiming her love for his weekend stubble, as he tried to politely edge away from her. His face twisted in frustration.

I walked up behind them and cleared my throat. She whipped around and laughed, trying to deflect anything I might have been thinking about her actions.

Before I could say another word, Oliver came running up. I crouched down to hug him and he ran right past me and into Mandi's arms.

"Aunt Mandi, will you play hide and seek with me. Pweease!"

She looked at me and smiled a smile I knew was reflecting a deep satisfaction. It didn't go unnoticed by her that he ran right past me and into her arms.

"Sure, I will, baby boy! You know your auntie would do anything in the world for both of you boys!" With that, she took his hand and they walked off together.

I stood there glaring at the back of her head.

"Why do you let her get to you that way, Claire?" Ben spoke up.

"I don't know. She just…ugh…I don't know!" I was still looking in her direction as I spoke.

"I think you're being silly. After all, Mandi is just being who Mandi is. The star of the show."

I whipped around and looked at him. "The star of the show?"

He laughed and pulled me to him. "You're the only star of my show and that's all that matters."

I shrugged and pulled away so I could continue to glare at Mandi.

"It's actually a little pathetic, if you think about it, Claire. She is so desperate for somebody to validate her. She is always seeking approval from everyone around her. Can you imagine living that way, day after day? That's why she comes after me. She could never even begin to compete with you, and she knows that deep down inside. You have got to stop letting her behavior get under your skin." I looked at Ben as he spoke, and I could see he was serious. This wasn't the first time he had lectured me about her. But he didn't know Mandi the way I did.

I turned and looked back at her, stumbling in her heels trying to chase the boys, and she looked absolutely ridiculous.

For just a moment, I actually kind of felt a pang of sympathy for her. But only for just a moment.

CHAPTER 8

I t was the beginning of April, and spring had arrived in all its splendor. Bringing with it weather so warm, I was sure that summertime would come early this year.

Here in the Carolinas, spring was a time of celebration and renewal.

As the Dogwood trees bloom their signature white blooms, the grass grows greener, the nests fill with baby birds, and the azalea bushes explode in color, the whole state comes to life.

It was almost as if we were all going through some sort of baptism of hope and rebirth. Everyone seemed to smile a little more and breathe a little easier, despite the thick yellow pollen that dusted everything in its path.

On a whim, I'd decided to sign up for an art class. It was a beginner's course in acrylic painting. I wanted to expand my artistic expression beyond doodling.

The class was being held at the Midtown Center for the Arts, right down the road from our house. They offered many different classes like art, dance, pottery, photography, and acting. During the day it was filled with moms like me and retired men and women who wanted to learn new artistic skills. In the afternoon and evenings, children's voices filled the halls.

The Center had been converted from an old brick building that used to be a large daycare facility. And now was filled with well-appointed studios and a small theater for the performing arts.

My class was held at ten in the morning, which afforded me the time to grab a fresh latte on the way in. A little luxury just for me.

I walked into class with my coffee in hand and took my usual seat in the back. The teacher had placed fresh canvases on our stand-up easels. I ran my fingers along the blank canvas, relishing in the unlimited possibilities.

Out of the corner of my eye, I saw Sarina come in. A self-proclaimed psychic and she dressed the part. She had shoulder-length, curly, black hair with scattered wisps of grey and steel blue eyes that were lined with dramatic black, winged eyeliner. She wore a flowing floral kimono over a long grey maxi dress. Around her neck she wore silver chains with several natural stones dangling from them, their edges raw and uncut. Sometimes when she would speak, I would see her grasp one of the stones and move it around delicately with her fingers. I didn't know if it were a nervous habit or if there was something more to them that I wasn't aware of.

As she walked in, I avoided eye contact. I had never been around anyone like her before and she made me uncomfortable.

She passed by me and smiled. "Good morning, Claire," her voice soft and friendly.

I nodded in response as the smell of essential oils wafted up my nose.

She took her place at the easel to the left of me.

I pretended to sort my paints and brushes to avoid conversation.

Not long after, Mr. Thompson came in, smelling of coffee and Old Spice aftershave, and claimed his spot on the other side of me. He was, what I guessed to be, in his late seventies. A retired police officer and a widower.

He was tall, had a square jaw, and a head full of thick gray hair. Something he always bragged about. He would always ask us if we knew of another old man with as much hair as he had. Even if anyone did, no one would object to his claim.

He nodded to me and cleared his throat as he sat down on the stool by his easel.

"Hope you're well this mornin'," he said as he gave me a denture filled smile.

I smiled back.

I looked at him, noticing that his shirt was slightly wrinkled. I felt a pang of sadness, with the thought of how his wife was no longer there to make sure he had nicely pressed shirts. She died of breast cancer four years ago.

He didn't say much about her.

We only knew her name was Lola.

The two paintings he had done so far in class, he had said they were for his Lola.

He was a nice man but his presence here…his loss of Lola… it shook me to the core.

I came here to escape. To not think about the dream.

And his grief, his pain brought the memories to the surface.

Not long after he sat down, the music started.

Our teacher, Amanda Quick, always said creativity flowed better when it had a soundtrack. She had us listen to the likes of Yoyo Ma and Kevin Kern while we painted. The notes floated through the air, enrapturing us into another realm, where we freely connected with our creativity.

Our class had a total of six students. I hadn't gotten to know the other three ladies in the class yet. I figured them to be my mom's age. They sat in the first row right by Amanda's easel. They were eager to be the teacher's pets and seemed to have their own clique going on, leaving Sarina, Mr. Thompson, and I with our own awkward little gang.

Amanda looked to be in her twenties and always wore her medium-length, brown hair in two braids that she tied up with pieces of colorful yarn. Every time I saw her, she was wearing a white tank top with paint splatters and varying wide legged patterned pants that somehow seemed to match the paint splattered shirt perfectly. She also wore fifties style cat eye glasses that were lime green. She was a bit eccentric, but her smile was genuine and her laugh was contagious.

When class was over, I walked to my car with a painting of a beach dune under my arm, breathing in the warm spring air. I passed by bushes full of bright pink azalea blooms as tiny birds poked around underneath them, looking for food.

I had just settled into my driver's seat when my cell phone rang.

It was Jamie calling. I was happy to hear from her. It had been a while since we last spoke.

Jamie and I had been friends since we both moved to Charlotte. We met in the parking lot of Harris Teeter. She was loading groceries into the back of her Volkswagen Bug, when she dropped a bag of red apples. They rolled in every direction possible. I quickly ran over to help her wrangle all the apples back into the bag. We both laughed as one of the runaway apples was smashed by the tire of unsuspecting car.

We stood in the parking lot making small talk, that suddenly flowed into a rush of conversation that has never ended.

She was older than me by ten years, but we appeared to be same age. She was newly married too, but for the second time around.

She told me her first husband never grew up. "That was grounds for divorce, right?" she said, as she laughed heartily.

Her second husband's name was Mike, and he was my age. She was always bragging about being a cradle robber, though, he was prematurely bald. Jamie always laughed and said that was God's way of evening things out.

Mike was one of the top salesmen at the Mercedes dealership, giving them a comfortable life. They had three children in the span of time I had my two. Two girls and a boy, all under the age of seven. She laughed and said she was trying to get all her baby making days in before she was too old.

With her naturally red hair and vibrant green eyes, she was stunning and, in some ways, reminded me of Mandi. But Jamie had a heart of gold. If you ever needed to feel better about yourself, you could spend some time around Jamie. She had a way of making everyone she was around feel like a million bucks.

Before I could even say hello, I heard Jamie on the line. "Took you long enough, lady!"

I laughed. "You know I had art class today..."

"Oh, I forgot." She snorted a little. "Did you paint a masterpiece?"

I just laughed again in response.

"So, you have your deposit for the trip?"

"What trip?" I asked.

The phone was silent for a moment.

"What do you mean, what trip? This was your idea!"

"I thought it was cancelled," I answered bluntly.

"Claire, are you okay??" she responded.

I sat quietly trying to figure out what was going on.

"God, Claire, you know, the trip to Asheville!?" she spouted.

"Yes! Of course, I know... but we cancelled that trip... because Annie broke her ankle...remember? We decided to reschedule it... for next year, right?" I stuttered a little, trying to remember the exact details myself.

There was silence on the phone for just a moment, a rarity for Jamie.

"Annie's fine, Claire... Are you sure *you're* okay?" Her voice was clearly strained with concern.

I watched the teacher's pet trio pass by the front of my car, lost in their own conversation.

Dizziness overtook me as I tried to put the pieces together.

I definitely remembered Annie getting hurt and us rescheduling the trip. But why didn't Jamie know about it?

Wasn't she the one that called and told me?

We had planned a girl's only trip to The Grove Park Inn, a luxurious historic hotel in Asheville nestled next to the mountains. We needed a getaway. An escape. And The Grove Park Inn was ideal. Just by walking in the door, you would immediately be swept away by the lavishness of the inn, gigantic stone fireplaces, expansive views, and the uniformed concierges as they stood by, waiting on your requests. We planned on getting the works, with two deluxe rooms and a view of the mountains, wine every night, and spa services galore. The cure for mom-burnout.

Annie and Jessica were Jamie's neighbors and had become my friends by default, and the many summer days we had spent together, with all of our kids playing in Jamie's backyard, had bonded us for life.

Jessica was the prettiest and youngest of our group at only 23 years old. She had long dark hair that she usually kept in a messy bun, yet still always looked fabulous. She only had one child but she fit in with us perfectly. Her bubbly personality and bright outlook were good for all of us, but her perfect figure was the envy of all. Her body didn't seem to have betrayed her after having a baby the way ours had. She would always say how she needed to lose five more pounds, and we wondered to ourselves and often out loud where she thought she was going to pull five pounds from?

Annie was the same age as Jamie and had her two children later in life. She had been an executive with JP Morgan and Associates for fifteen years before deciding to give it all up to be a stay at home mom. She was a smart, bold woman with strong opinions about the world, and she wasn't afraid to speak her mind. She wore a pixie cut and always dressed like she was going to a casual business meeting. Her stony demeanor was undercut by her soft voice and kind blue eyes.

I enjoyed the camaraderie and friendship given to me by these women. We got together as much as we could, including the occasional bar-beque on the weekend, when we brought along our husbands. There would always be plenty of hot dogs, hamburgers, cold beers, and great conversation to be had.

This trip was the first for our group, and we were really looking forward to getting away from it all. That was until Annie fell down her front porch steps. She had tripped on a Lego and broke her ankle in two places.

But that didn't happen…did it?

Her ankle was perfectly fine and we were going on the trip….

I re-steadied myself before I spoke, not wanting to flag Jamie that something could potentially be wrong.

"Oh, sorry Jamie…I don't know where that came from…I guess I'm just a little out of it today…" I said it as lightheartedly as I could, surprised at my own acting ability.

She didn't respond.

I gave a loud fake laugh, intent on changing the subject. "Anyway, I will send you the deposit through Venmo or something today. Cross my heart!"

"That's fine… as long as you're sure you are okay?" I could hear the worry still in her voice.

"Yes! I am fine!" I said emphatically.

That seemed to appease her and we talked for several more minutes, exchanging the latest on our kids.

After we hung up, I sat in the parking lot staring out the window, thinking again about Annie. The more I thought about the memory, the more difficult it was to place.

Could it be another thing from the dream?

I put the car in drive, and as I pulled forward, I nearly ran over a little old lady that had stepped in front of me, carrying red dancing shoes. I jammed on the brakes, causing my bag of paints to fall and spill out all over the floor board.

The old lady gave me a disapproving look before continuing on toward the building.

Every year around this time, we always went to Bentley's Farm in Huntersville to pick strawberries. It had become a family tradition of sorts, something we all looked forward to each year, and I always got enough strawberries to freeze and use throughout the entire year.

Today was the day. Ben had gone to work for a half day, and I was expecting him to be back around lunchtime. The boys waited on the front porch for him to arrive. They sat together on the top step, side by side. One just a little smaller than the other.

I got out my phone and snapped a picture.

Brothers. Captured in time.

I was busy packing our picnic lunch when they came running in the door yelling, "Daddy's home!"

Ben appeared in the doorway moments behind them, coming straight into the kitchen to give me a warm kiss, promising to be ready in a few short minutes. The boys followed him all the way up to our room, to ensure his speediness.

On the drive there, we opened the windows and welcomed the fresh spring air in as it swirled around the car. Filling it with the fragrances of honeysuckles and wisteria as we drove down the road. As we passed by houses, the smell of freshly cut grass joined the medley and I sighed.

That scent brought back many childhood memories.

Good memories. Before my dad left.

When Mom used smile all the time.

I could still see her, with permed hair, in her crop top, high waisted shorts, and oversized sunglasses, working in the flower beds, while Dad cut the grass with a push mower. Mandi and I would play with our dolls on the front porch. The smell of the cut grass thick in the air. Mom would come out and bring us lemonade in tall glass cups.

I could still taste the tartness on my tongue.

Those were happy days for us. When everything was right in the world of two little girls.

I looked over at Ben and then back at my boys and smiled, thankful for my own happy family.

Ben turned on the radio to our favorite Motown station. He turned it up louder as we all sang along. The boys sang too, getting most of the words wrong, making me laugh.

"We are raising our boys right. On good classic music," Ben said, with a tone of deep satisfaction.

I nodded my head in agreement.

We drove on, passing by landscape, lush and deep. The highway stretched through the countryside, comforting and familiar, passing by fields boasting of cows and horses grazing happily on spring grasses. Driving by white farmhouses with wide welcoming porches and red barns, buzzing with activity. Springtime planting well underway. Soon, the fields gave way to patches of pine forests, stretching for miles.

Finally, we arrived at the farm's entrance, tires crunching on gravel. We found a parking spot next to a fifteen-foot-tall strawberry statue. Faded from years of sun exposure, but it still held impression. There was no mistaking what you were here for.

After we parked the car, the boys got out and ran to the back of the car to get their baskets for picking. Ben was right behind them.

When I came around to where they were, I saw Ben crouched down, eye level with the boys, lecturing them on what good behavior was and wasn't.

They both squirmed, adamantly repeating back to him, "I know...I know..."

Ben looked up at me and smiled. "They know..." We both laughed, our eyes meeting for a just a moment.

I grabbed the cooler with our lunch from the trunk and headed toward the picnic tables just outside of the main entrance to the farm.

I spread a soft, blue and white, gingham tablecloth over a worn, wooden table that sat next to a large hand-painted sign, listing of all the ways you could use the strawberries you picked. Strawberry Jam, Strawberry pie, Strawberry Chutney, Strawberry salad and the list went on.

We ate lazily, while the sunshine warmed our faces and the bees buzzed by in search of sweetness. The boys chattered on about who was stronger, Batman or Spiderman? Ben kept chiming in on both sides of the argument, just to see them get worked up. Each time he did it, he would look back at me and wink.

After eating, we meandered the strawberry fields, picking sun-warmed, ripened fruit. The boys' fingers turning red with juice as they taste tested every other one that they picked. Scissor-tailed Swallows swooped over us repeatedly in a seemingly synchronized dance, in a bright cloudless sky.

Ben walked beside me in a comforting silence as the boys endlessly searched for the most delectable juicy berries, bright and ready for the picking.

Before long, the boys grew tired, their faces flushed with the warmth of the afternoon.

They lagged behind, as we headed back to the car, and fell asleep before we even hit the highway. Ben and I looked at each other and smiled as a deep satisfaction flowed through me.

On the drive back, Ben and I talked in hushed tone, as to not wake them.

"Oh, I forgot to ask you!" he said in a rush. "Did you hear about the Magnolia Bakery?"

"No, I didn't…." I responded, curiously.

"Apparently, they had a huge kitchen fire and it destroyed all of their expensive equipment. No insurance either. Somehow their policy had lapsed and no one knew. From what I am hearing, this may put them out of business for good."

My heart lurched forward.

Did he really just say that Magnolia Bakery was closing down? From a kitchen fire?

My breath grew shallow as I tried to process the reality of what he said.

I stared out the window as we passed the familiar landscape.

Ben was still going on about what a shame it was for such a great bakery to be going out of business and didn't notice that I wasn't responding to him.

He finally noticed my silence and asked, "Claire, is everything okay?"

I didn't answer. I couldn't.

"What are you thinking about?" he pressed.

"Nothing…" I finally answered, knowing it was a lie.

"Sure was a nice day, wasn't it?" he offered with a smile.

I wished I could share in his sentiment, but my day had turned on a dime.

My mind on the news that the bakery was closing.

It was a coincidence, right? It couldn't possibly mean anything at all. In the dream they had closed, yes. From a kitchen fire, yes. But didn't that mean anything else, did it? I decided to go with no. It didn't mean anything at all. Nothing at all.

I looked over at Ben, and a cold chill went down my spine.

CHAPTER 9

Oliver crawled up to the front seat to give me a kiss before jumping out the car, with Grayson right behind him.

The carpool line for school had been longer today.

Or maybe it just felt longer.

After I got home, I found myself standing at the counter eating strawberries, firm and juicy, feeling troubled in the wake of the news about the bakery fire.

The thought of it was beginning to consume me. Pushing aside all rationality.

It couldn't just be a coincidence.

If that came true, what else was going to come true?

Ben dying?!

That thought rattled me to my core, like an earthquake, jostling and shaking everything inside. The comforting pattern of my life, suddenly derailed.

I held onto the counter, trying to steady my mind.

What if my dream actually meant something?

But it couldn't! Could it have?

A gust of wind rattled the window, startling me.

I jumped backwards, almost stepping on Teddy, right underneath me.

Anxiety pulsed through me. I needed someone to talk to.

An outlet for my fears.

I picked up the phone, and against my better judgement, dialed Mandi's number.

I needed my sister right now.

She answered on the third ring, her voiced muffled.

"Mandi?" I asked.

"What is it, Claire?" she huffed in return.

"Can you talk?" I offered reluctantly, the regret of calling already filling my mind.

"God, Claire, can't this wait? I am in with Swami Advani right now, getting the most divine massage, which you have so rudely interrupted."

"I'm sorry...I just wanted..." I stuttered, unable to formulate what I wanted to say.

Bitterness coursed through me.

If she didn't want to be interrupted, why did she have her phone on in the first place?

So, she continued. "Look, doll, I would say that I would call you after-wards, but I'm having a pedicure right after this, and then I'm headed to the country club for lunch and a tennis lesson this afternoon. How about I call you tomorrow?" The counterfeit kindness in her tone was more insulting than her words.

I couldn't speak, anger was prickling under my skin.

It didn't go unnoticed; she hadn't asked me if everything was okay.

"Okay, then! I must go! Ta-ta for now," she said, making a kissing sound as she hung up.

With the phone still to my ear, bitter tears stung my eyes.

Honestly, I was angrier at myself than her.

Mandi was just being Mandi. Just like Ben said.

How could I have expected anything different from her?

I hated myself for putting my faith in her. Again.

Why did I always go back to the hope that she could just act like she was my sister? To be my friend, my cheerleader.

Why were we always at odds?

Of course, we had never acted like sisters. We've never had that sisterly bond, that beautiful camaraderie that I had seen with my friends and their sisters. The shopping trips, the long phone calls. The undying loyalty. All of that was foreign to me.

We had none of it—and I had accepted that fact a long time ago.

Yet, it still hurt. No matter how hard I tried to pretend like it didn't. It did.

In some ways I felt it would almost have been better to not have a sister than to have a sister, *that wasn't a sister at all.*

I longed for one. A real sister.

Especially on a day like today. When I just needed someone to talk to. To comfort me and tell me that everything was going to be okay.

Was it going to be okay? Every day, June 3rd got closer and closer.

I poured some hot coffee into my cup and took a sip. Warm richness flowed over my tongue.

I walked the floor, with my coffee cup in hand, pacing back and forth from the kitchen to the living room and back again, afraid I needed to see a psychiatrist.

I passed through glistening, wooden door frames, sock covered feet treading lightly across the floor, thinking, wondering.

I looked up suddenly, blinking. Remembering pieces of a conversation that I overheard Jonathan and Ben having had last Thanksgiving.

Jonathan had been telling Ben about his latest research on how thoughts in people's minds were linked to physical outcomes.

Thoughts. Outcomes.

It wasn't dreams and outcomes… but it was as close as I was going to get at this point.

And at least talking to my brother was better than going to a doctor.

Even though he was my brother, I was hesitant to call him. I couldn't remember the last time we had spoken on the phone. Not to mention, honestly, I barely knew him. Time and distance had made him a virtual stranger to me.

But the same blood coursed through our veins, and I hoped that would be enough to connect us.

I decided it was best to go unannounced. I didn't want him to have the opportunity to blow me off, like Mandi did.

At least, that was my excuse to not call first.

I got my purse and left the house before I chickened out.

Luckily, the boys were going over to their friends' houses this afternoon and wouldn't need me to pick them up at 3:00 pm when school let out, giving me plenty of time to make it to Chapel Hill and back.

Around three o'clock, I arrived at the seven-hundred-acre campus. Traffic grew dense and slowed to a crawl as I drove through the university's tree lined streets. I passed sprawling green lawns in front of historic buildings and streams of students walking, wearing backpacks and smiles, lost in deep thoughts or friendly conversations.

Finally, I spotted the sign that read Phillips Hall and turned in. The parking outside of the brick-sided physics building was limited, but I finally found a space on the backside.

I got out of the car and stretched my legs as a gust of warm air rushed against me.

I took a deep breath, my stomach in knots, now regretting not calling first. The mid-day sun shone down through the scattered trees in the parking lot, casting freckled shadows everywhere. Song birds were in chorus all around the building, giving the place a welcoming feeling, opposing to how I felt.

As I walked across sweltering pavement, beads of sweat began to form on my forehead and chest. It was incredible how spring had given way to summer like temperatures already.

Sweat permeated my blouse before I even reached the doors to the building.

As I pulled open the heavy glass door, three students caught in heavy conversation were coming out. I stepped past them into the air-conditioned building, and ice-cold air quickly cooled my skin, making me shiver from the dampness on my blouse.

I walked under tall ceilings, my steps echoing loudly on tiled floor, as I found my way to the elevators and the building directory.

It didn't take me long to find Dr. J. Everly's name. His office was on the third floor.

I pushed the elevator call button and before long heard the groaning and straining of its approach. The doors opened and I stepped inside. As the doors I closed again, I had to fight the urge to run back out and go home. The feeling only fleeting, and after a moment, I was able to push the button for the third floor.

As the elevator made its short journey, I wondered what would I say to Jonathan?

How would I explain just showing up like this?

When the doors opened again, I stood frozen in place for just a moment, uncertainty paralyzing me. I could hear the sound of distant talking and knew I had to make quick decision.

Stay or go home?

After a few seconds of indecision, I finally committed myself to moving forward.

The directory had said he was in room 336. There was a deep hallway to my left and right. I stepped forward and looked as a group of guys came out of a room down the hall to left. There were about fifteen of them, all carrying books. I assumed that their class had just been dismissed. A couple of them eyeballed me as they passed. I nodded in their direction, out of nervousness and the desire to blend in. After they got on the elevator, I walked down the hallway to my left, underneath piping that ran along the ceiling, watching the numbers on the doors climb.

Within a few minutes I was standing in front of a wooden door with a pane of frosted glass with the number 336B etched on it.

I knocked and a young woman answered.

Startled by her presence, it took me a moment to speak.

"I'm looking for Jonathan Ever...I mean, Dr. Everly," I stuttered.

She narrowed her eyes and looked at me warily.

The young woman looked to be about my age, with shoulder length chestnut-brown hair that was neatly pulled back on the top by a barrette. She was wearing an A-line skirt with a white button up blouse, sleeves cuffed at the elbows. Around her neck, she wore a small scarf with dainty flowers tied to the side. Her style reminiscent of the fifties. She had a slender nose and wide-set hazel eyes, giving her a natural girl next door kind of beauty.

"My name is Sheila Donovan and I'm his personal assistant. What can I help you with?" she said, as she straightened her shoulders and faced me squarely. Giving me the clear message that I had to get through her to get to him.

I sensed this demeanor was in contrast to her normal personality, and I had to wonder about her response to me. But once Jonathan came around the corner, I understood at once.

As soon as she saw him, her eyes lit up and her cheeks became a rosy pink color.

"Dr. Everly, this woman is here to..."

Jonathan held his hand up to her and smiled. "I know her. Sheila, this is my sister, Claire."

Jonathan came right up and hugged me tightly.

Sheila's shoulders relaxed and she smiled. Undoubtingly grateful to realize I wasn't a threat.

"What are you doing here?" He asked, clearly happy to see me.

I was surprised by his warm response, but extremely grateful.

I was happy to see him too.

As I looked at my brother, I saw the same brown eyes with yellow flecks I saw when I looked in my own mirror. I looked at the scar on his chin that he got from a skateboarding accident when he was fifteen and the dimple in his right cheek you could only see when he smiled. He was wearing a plaid button up shirt tucked into khaki dress pants with a brown leather belt, definitely befitting of a scientist.

I cleared my throat. "I need to talk to you about something. If you have the time. I'm sorry I didn't call. It was rude of me but…"

Jonathan spoke before I could finish my sentence.

"Gosh, don't apologize, Claire! You're my sister. You don't have to have an appointment to see me. Let's go into my office."

He put his hand on my back and guided me to the room adjacent to the one Sheila was in.

Sheila followed behind us. "Can I get you anything? A coffee? A tea?" she offered, her voice slightly quivering.

Jonathan looked at me for a response, and I shook my head.

"We're good, but thank you, Shelia," Jonathan responded.

We stepped inside of his office and he closed the door. He pointed in the direction of two large cushioned chairs with padded arms just in front of his desk. I took a seat in the one to the right and felt myself sink deeply into the back of it. I tried to adjust myself so I could sit up straighter.

He sat down in front of me at a large mahogany desk. Books and papers were scattered all over it. Nothing seemed to be in any recognizable order. It reminded me of his room when he was a teenager. I remembered Mom always complaining about it.

I looked around his office. A non-descript gray carpet covered the floors. There was a blackboard covered in mathematical formulas I couldn't even begin to understand. To the right of the blackboard, there hung numerous framed awards and certificates in Jonathan's name.

Along the other three walls, there were bookshelves filled to the brim with books.

Just behind his desk was a large window. I looked out of it, and from my seat I could see large white clouds floating in the sky outside.

Jonathan leaned forward across his desk and looked at me. I couldn't help but notice how much he looked like our dad now, with his strong jawline and broad nose. His medium-brown hair was now speckled with grey and neatly parted to the side.

And when he smiled, I could see my own smile reflecting back.

"So, what's going on with you, Sis?" his voice, warm and friendly.

"What's going on with you?" I countered, eager to delay this conversation.

"You can't tell me that you came all this way just to find out how I was doing?" he said with a half laugh.

I couldn't tell if he was being funny or sarcastic.

I shrugged, not breaking eye contact.

He leaned back. "Ah, I'm doing fine. Busy. As usual. Working on a big research project right now. Always feeling like I'm on the brink of a big discovery..." He chuckled to himself.

"Are you seeing anyone?" I asked, thinking of Sheila.

He laughed out loud and shook his head.

"Nope!" He said, emphatically.

"Why not?" I persisted.

"I don't know.... Girls just don't get me. I'm not, in any way, a lady's man. Not to mention, I spend every waking moment in the office or in the lab. Where do you suppose I am going to meet a girl?"

"How about Sheila? She's pretty and she likes you...I can tell." I smiled, remembering how she lit up when she saw him.

His eyes immediately took a glimmer that wasn't there before, and I knew I was right about my initial gut feeling.

"We just work together…" he protested, but I could see his mind was starting to calculate what I had said. "Why, did she say something to you?" His eyes narrowed.

"No…but girls can tell about other girls. The way she looked at you… You should ask her to lunch sometime." I smiled.

He shrugged, but by the expression on his face, I knew he was suddenly looking at Sheila through new eyes.

"How are the boys?" he asked, quick to change the subject. "They sure are growing up fast. Too fast!" he said, shaking his head.

"Yeah…they are…" I answered.

Just then, the phone on his desk began to ring. He picked it up, holding up one finger to me, letting me know he wouldn't be long.

After five minutes of him talking to the caller, I got up and walked to the window to get a better look out.

It overlooked the back-parking lot, where I had come in.

Now much emptier, with only a few cars left.

I went over to the wall where Jonathan's certificates were hanging. I was astonished to see all the degrees he had and all the awards he had won. I had no idea about all of his accomplishments. I felt a lump of shame rise up.

I looked over at him, still talking on the phone. He was arguing with someone about a formula. When he saw me look at him, he smiled and held up his finger again. Obviously, the debate with the caller was professional in nature.

"So, you want a tour?" he offered after he hung up. Clearly sensing and respecting the fact I wasn't quite ready to talk about what had spurred my visit.

I nodded, relieved to not have to talk about it.

Not yet, anyway.

He took me through his auditorium style classroom and then to his personal lab. He unlocked the door and waited for me to step through. The lab was small and nondescript, with no windows. I was surprised by the starkness of it. The room was odd, with a small empty desk and an adjacent table with several desktop computers. In the corner were several other machines I didn't recognize. There were also two closet sized rooms attached to the main one with one-way privacy windows to each, but he didn't take me into them.

I didn't know how he could spend so much time in those rooms.

After the tour was over, we headed back to his office. When we passed by Sheila's office, the door was open. She stood up and smiled when she saw us, her face taking on that same rosy glow from earlier.

Jonathan stopped in front of her door, stuttered a little and then walked off in a huff.

I thought of when I first met Ben and couldn't speak properly myself. Apparently, not being able to talk to people we were attracted to was an inherited disorder.

As I walked away, I saw her face was strained with confusion.

I smiled as I passed by her, knowing by the way he acted he would ask her out soon.

We went back into his office and took our respective seats.

"So, now will you tell me why you came?" He looked at me inquisitively. "I mean, if you're more interested in just sitting here and looking at me awkwardly, I'm fine with that. I'll sit here with you. But I have a feeling there's something going on…"

I wrung my hands in my lap, trying to figure out how to start.

He sat patiently waiting for me to speak.

When I finally found my voice, it sounded like someone else was talking.

He listened to me intently without saying a word, aside from the occasional question to get clarification. When I finished speaking, he leaned back in his chair and put his hands on the back of his head, lost in thought.

I patiently waited for his response.

Maybe he would have some answers.

It was several seconds before he began to speak, but when he did, I knew he had taken me seriously.

"First of all, I want to tell you that you're not the first person to ever experience something such as this. There are many recorded stories of this very thing happening, all over the globe. Don't feel like there's something wrong with you because of it. Studies have shown that at least twenty percent of people claim to have had a premonition type dream that came true.

The Ancient Greeks and Egyptians believed some dreams contained pertinent information for the dreamer. They took dreams very seriously back then. The dreams of rulers and royalty were often interpreted and studied for any symbolism that might give insight into their future."

"How did they know which dreams were to be taken seriously, and which ones weren't?" I asked, leaning in closer to his desk. The smell of dust and polished wood wafted up my nose.

"Well, honestly, they didn't. The only clue is that the usual precognition dream is negative in nature and usually involved disaster or death. From what I have learned with these type of dreams, the events usually follow within hours or days, but sometimes not for several months. There are no clear standards."

I readjusted myself in the seat and listened to the sound of a hidden clock ticking somewhere in the room as he continued.

"And the length of your dream seeming to span six months is unusual, but not completely unheard of. Numerous studies have shown that dreams usually last for only a few seconds, even though they may have been experienced as taking place over hours or days. This is a function of accelerated dream consciousness. It's a whole different universe in the dream world." His voice had a serious tone to it.

"How do I know if my dream means anything or not?" I pressed, still confused.

He nodded his head and leaned forward slightly before he answered.

"When you analyze the event of a precognition type dream, one that someone remembers in their waking consciousness, it brings up the element of entanglement. Leading us to question, is it the dream that predicts the future, or does the dream influence it? Meaning, that having a dream that one was going to die, it is entirely possible that in focusing on that dream, it can actually cause that person to draw death to themselves, via entanglement or laws of attraction. According to one physics' theory, every behavior, every choice, every action, every thought, can create a new reality, paving the way for innumerable possibilities."

I sat still, trying to digest what he had said. I stared out the window as the branches of a large oak tree danced and swayed in and out of my view.

He continued with his explanation.

"Let me put it like this. Instead of a linear timeline that goes forward along a single line, the universe would be more like a tree within a forest with countless branches and twigs, each of them being a different possibility of events that could happen. When you make a choice, one of those paths or branches are chosen and this becomes your reality. And each time you make a new choice, you are set on a different path. You may ask, does this mean that by dreaming about the events that you did, that you are in some way bringing that path into existence?

Maybe. I do personally have a tendency to believe that the things that we focus on are drawn into our realties. In truth, we just don't know. The most important piece of Quantum mechanics is uncertainty. We can't experience more than one choice at a time. Our observation changes the nature of reality, so we have no idea what would be happening if you hadn't had the dream in the first place. You are where you are because you did have the dream, and the way you process the events that are happening are being affected by it."

He rubbed his temples and laughed a little.

"So, in other words, I have no idea how to help you figure this out. If I could, I would be a sure thing for the Nobel Prize. Maybe one day we will understand more about dreams, but what we know right now is still so much in the beginning learning phase."

"That's it?" I looked at him questionably. My heart sinking. I was no closer to an answer than I was before.

He got up and came around the desk to face me. He kneeled down next to the chair and put his hand on my arm.

"I'm so sorry, Claire. I really am. I wish I could've helped you somehow…I just don't know what your dream meant, but I can tell you that the best thing you can do right now is not dwell on it," he said with his eyes, genuine.

"I know you're right. But, it's just so scary. I feel like my life is off balance right now. It just doesn't feel right," I responded.

Jonathan stood up and walked over to the window and looked out. He rubbed his forehead, lost in thought. The shadows from the trees outside danced on the window sill.

After a few minutes, he turned around and looked at me. "Maybe it wasn't even a premonition, Claire. Maybe it was nothing. Sometimes an apple is just an apple. I just really think you need to let it go and stop worrying so much."

I nodded and smiled weakly.

What else was there to say?

And he was probably right. At least, I hoped he was.

Though my gut told me a different story.

He looked up at the clock. It was six o'clock already. "You hungry? I haven't eaten all day."

I thought about Ben and the boys being at home without me, trying to find something to eat for dinner and the urge to say no overpowered me. "I really should go back now…" I responded, reluctantly.

"Aww come on, grab a bite to eat with your brother! It's been way too long since we hung out!" he insisted. His face pursed with hope.

How could I say no?

I texted Ben and told him to pick up the boys and grab a pizza for dinner just before we walked out of Jonathan's office.

I stepped past him into the hallway as he turned to turn off the lights and lock the door.

As we passed by Sheila's office, he paused for half a step.

She was already gone. The door closed and locked.

I wondered if he had been considering inviting her to go with us and I smiled, pleased with myself.

As we walked down the corridor toward the elevator, I noticed all of the hallways were now empty and most of the offices were dark.

We stood together waiting at the elevator, and when the doors opened, we stepped in.

An old man stood inside, leaning against the elevator wall wearing a wrinkled blue jumpsuit, clearly the building janitor. His embroidered name tag, in red letters, said Larry. He stood quietly next to his mop bucket, with disheveled grey hair that fell down long past the nape of his neck. Barely looking up, his expression forlorn.

"Howdy!" Jonathan said to the man.

Larry nodded back in response.

Jonathan studied him for just a moment before speaking again.

"I really appreciate the work you do around here. I know it takes a lot of effort and you do a great job."

The man looked up with a new expression. Eyes, sparkling. Clearly, the compliment had gone a long way.

When the doors opened again and we stepped out, Jonathan turned back around, smiling at the old janitor.

"Take care, buddy!" he called back to him.

As the doors closed, I caught a glimpse of the man and he was smiling.

The kindness Jonathan had shown him spoke volumes to me about the kind of man he had grown into.

We walked out of the building into lingering sunlight. I shielded my eyes as they adjusted to the change in lighting. The day had gotten soft around the edges, the heat no longer oppressive.

We headed to my car, since Jonathan normally took the bus to work, and we walked together in a comfortable silence across the parking lot into fading light. Brother and sister together. Our footsteps echoed across the virtually empty lot.

Even the birds had quieted their music for the day.

When we got in the car, Jonathan looked at me. "What are you in the mood for?"

I shrugged. "You pick! I can eat anything, and plus, I don't know enough about the area to decide."

His face brightened immediately. "Actually, I know just the place."

CHAPTER 10

⸻ ⟡ ⸻

"This is it!" Jonathan told me as we pulled into a small parking lot next to a brick apartment building. It was five stories tall and looked like it had been standing there since the seventies.

Jonathan pointed up to a window on the third floor. "That's my place!" He beamed with pride.

We got out of the car and stretched in the early evening air. His apartment was only five miles from the campus, but because of traffic, it had taken us every bit of thirty minutes to get here.

"The place is only two blocks away, so we can walk from here," he said as he closed the car door.

The sky had turned to a shade of lavender and orange as we walked side by side over uneven sidewalk. People were everywhere, filling the area with conversation and laughter. The smell of fried foods wafted out from several places that we passed, making my stomach grumble. I hadn't even realized that I was that hungry until now.

Just like Jonathan promised, the walk took only a few minutes, and we arrived at a pub restaurant called The York. When we got inside, we found it was packed wall to wall with hungry students. The smell of beer, sandwiches, and pizza wafted up my nose, making feel a little dizzy with hunger. I didn't know how long I could make it without eating. But after only a fifteen-minute wait, we were able to get a high back booth near the back.

While Jonathan ran to the bathroom, I looked around. The bar was dark, with wood paneling covering the walls. The floors were concrete and unfinished, reminding me of the inside of an old garage. There were pool tables and dart boards not far from where we were sitting. Framed vintage beer advertisements hung over every table. Old couches were scattered around intermixed with the tables and filled past their seating capacity.

Voices and laughter blended in with the music playing from overhead speakers. I looked over and saw several girls dancing, cocktails in hand. Suddenly I felt very old. Though in reality I was only a few years ahead of them, it felt like a century.

When Jonathan came back, the waitress came over. She stood at the table with a notepad in hand. Short and stocky, with drugstore dyed red hair. She had a tattoo with the word *Blackbird* on her wrist. I wondered what it meant.

"What can I get ya?" she said, as she smacked on her chewing gum.

We decided on two Philly Cheesesteak sandwiches and a giant basket of cheese fries. While we were waiting for our food, Jonathan insisted we get a couple of beers. Because, according to him, how often do a sister and brother get to go out together? What I realized immediately is that he meant how often does he get to go out at all? But I knew now that Sheila was in the picture, that would soon change.

While we were sitting at the table, I saw numerous girls look over at Jonathan and smile. And he was oblivious. *Why didn't he see the affect he had over women?*

The overhead speaker played "Have You Seen Her?" by The Chi-Lites. I was instantly overcome by nostalgia and looked over at Jonathan.

"Do you remember when our parents used to dance to this song?" I asked him.

He listened to the song for a moment before it clicked. "Wow, I haven't heard this song in years! Didn't they have this on an old LP?"

"Yes, they did. I remember watching them dancing in the kitchen to it. With me staring at them like they were magical creatures." The image in my mind, hazy and surreal.

"Yeah, that was before they hated each other." Jonathan laughed.

"What happened to them? How could their marriage fall apart like that when they were so in love?" I hoped since he was older and saw more of their relationship, he would know.

"I don't know, really. I mean, they used to be really happy, I think. One day, things kinda changed. And suddenly they were distant. Dad had his own thing going on and Mom was raising us kids. I mean, don't get me wrong, Dad was still around all the time, but him and Mom, they weren't really a couple anymore."

"What happened? Why would Dad go off with Linda like that?" I pressed.

"What ever happens to any couple? Things go wrong and distance grows between them. Who knows? I was a teenager and caught up in my own life." He looked down as he spoke.

"Yeah, there's no telling what Dad was thinking when he left," I offered.

"Well, I can tell you what he was thinking!" Jonathan's voice, sarcastic and sharp.

We both knew what was on Dad's mind.

Linda. His attraction to her, purely physical.

The waitress came back and brought us two more beers, and we were happy for the distraction. After she walked away, we changed the subject.

When we were finished with our sandwiches, we nibbled on leftover fries and sipped our beers, making small talk and laughing.

Suddenly, Jonathan's expression changed. "This has been a lot of fun having you here. I'm so glad you came. I hope you'll come back again sometime…" His voice trailed off.

"Why don't you come home to visit more often?" I asked. "I mean, it's only a couple of hours away."

He paused, looking down at the withered French fry in his hand as he twirled it round and round, deciding whether to eat it or not.

He looked back up at me and shrugged. "I don't know. I guess I just feel out of place. After I left for school, Dad hooked up with Linda and things were really weird at home. I was mad at him. I was mad at Mom for being in a bad mood all the time. So, I just stayed away. Hung out with my friends, you know. And soon, that was the habit. Staying away. When I come home, I feel like I'm the third wheel. I'm just so out of the loop these days. You guys have your lives and I have mine."

"A third wheel? Are you kidding me? Do you not know how much I missed you?" I exclaimed.

"You did?" Jonathan said. His face perplexed. "It just seemed like you and Mandi had your own thing going on, and I just didn't fit in anymore."

"Oh, Jonathan. You always fit in! You were the light of the world to me. I always looked up to you. Had you on a pedestal, really. I grieved our relationship. I just wish you would've known how I felt about." I stopped mid-sentence, interrupted by the tightness in my throat.

"I needed you, Jonathan. I felt so alone. And I needed you to be a buffer for me against Mom…"

A wash of strong emotion came over me and I had to wipe back my tears. I hadn't realized how much my brother's absence had affected me.

"Man, I am sorry, Claire. I really didn't know. I was young and stupid, I guess. It just never occurred to me," his voice strained.

I could tell my words had stung. That wasn't my intention.

I reached across the table and touched his arm. "Listen, I should've made more of an effort too. It's on both of us. And we can make up for it now. Honestly, I would love it if you came around more often. The boys would love it too. It would make me happy. I've really missed you."

Jonathan looked up at me, a smile now in his eyes. "You know, I think I will take you up on that offer!"

I smiled back. Jonathan wasn't a stranger after all. He was the same brother I had always known and loved.

The waitress cleared the table of our plates, and as she leaned past me, I could smell cigarettes on her clothes.

"So, how's Mandi doing?" Jonathan asked after she walked away.

Irritation crawled up the back of my neck.

Why did everyone care so much about Mandi and her life?

"She's fine. I guess," I answered without making eye contact.

"Boy, she really gets to you, doesn't she?" His tone was light, not realizing he had stepped into a bee's nest.

"What's that supposed to mean?" My voice had an edge to it I instantly regretted.

"Ouch, I touched a nerve." He half laughed. "I'm sorry. I was just asking."

I let out a loud sigh. "No, I'm the one who should be sorry. You're just asking about your sister. Mandi and I don't get along that well, in case you haven't noticed." I half laughed, trying to lighten the mood.

He laughed too and leaned back against his bench seat. "Yeah, I think it's pretty obvious that there's some tension. But my question is why? I have never understood the rivalry between you two. Even as little girls, you were always competing for our parent's attention. I mean, in all honesty, it was really Mandi that was pushing you to the side and stealing all of the attention. But it just doesn't make sense. You both are wonderful girls, in your own way."

"I've just never felt good enough, compared to her..." I couldn't believe I had said it out loud. The words I had been fighting against my entire life.

Jonathan listened patiently as I continued.

"And I have a lot of bitterness built up. After Dad left, it became my responsibility to look after her, even though she's older. I did it because it had to be done. Things had to be taken care of when Mom was too depressed to get out of bed. And Mandi wasn't going to help me. I was the one who made sure we got up in time for school and that we had lunches to eat. But eventually I got bitter. Mandi thought she was so much better than me. But even so, I still tried to be a good sister to her. Always covering for her when she was sneaking out with boys. Lying to Mom over and over again to protect her. She didn't appreciate anything I did for her, and she still doesn't." I looked down, ashamed of my outburst.

"Claire, you're just so tender, and I mean that in the best way possible. You've always worn your heart on the outside of your chest. And Mandi...well, Mandi marches to the beat of her own drum. You should never compare yourself to her. You're a real gem and Mandi, she's like one of those chameleon lizards. You know the ones who change their outside to match their environment? Bless her, but in all honesty, she's the one who should feel less than. Not you. Don't get me wrong, I love my sister, but I also know her. She's always been this way and she always will be."

He reached his hand across the table and patted my hand. "You need to believe in yourself a little more. Anyway, what do you think you can do to change any of it? Things move on, you have to move on too or be bowled over by it."

Could the past just be the past? I didn't know.

I smiled. "Thank you, Jonathan. I'll try." Deep down inside knowing the dynamic between Mandi and I was never going to change.

After we finished our beers, he wanted to play a few rounds of darts, and much to his happiness, he won every single round. I wasn't that great of a player to begin with, and I had trouble getting into the game.

My thoughts were elsewhere. Memories flitted in and out of my mind, like wisps of wind.

I couldn't stop thinking about Ben and O'Malley's Pub. It was a place we frequented after we were first married, playing darts every time we went.

I could still feel Ben's arms around me, as he taught me the proper form to throw a dart while the jukebox played oldies in the background.

Sudden tears threatened to flow. I involuntarily fondled the wedding rings around my finger.

Not wanting Jonathan to see my emotions, I rushed to the back of the bar to where the bathroom was. I twisted the doorknob and it was locked. A metal sign on the door in front of me read: Chicks. I looked over at the men's bathroom door sign and saw one that read: Chick Magnets. I wanted to laugh but there was no humor inside me. Shortly after, two girls came out together, laughing. I could overhear them talking about a group of guys that had been hitting on them all night. After they passed me, I opened the heavy wooden door and walked into the bathroom, locking it behind me. The overpowering odor of urine and perfume nearly knocked me over. I stepped carefully over the wet toilet paper, strewn all over the floor. I looked at the toilet and I decided to avoid it. It had seen better days.

I walked over to the sink, looked at myself in the discolored mirror and sighed. There were dark circles under both of my eyes, and my skin was pale from lack of solid sleep. I turned on the water, took two handfuls of it and splashed my face.

When I came back out, Jonathan was standing by the door with two tequila shots, two lemon wedges and giant grin.

I shook my head no and he nodded his yes. In the end, he won. I sprinkled salt on my hand and turned up the shot glass. The warm sensation of liquor went down my throat. I quickly bit the lemon to combat the bitter taste, as a couple of onlookers cheered.

Four Jose Cuervo shots later, we were both feeling the effects of the alcohol ...and Jonathan was ready to go home. He had to work tomorrow.

We stepped out of the bar into a beautiful night. The stars were out and the air was warm.

Jonathan stopped and looked up at the night sky.

"Remember when we used to stargaze?" he asked.

"Yeah, I do. Some of my best childhood memories," I answered softly.

We looked at each other for a moment, wanting to say more. We were interrupted by a group of drunk guys, laughing as they pushed their way past us.

The moment over, we walked arm in arm, back to his apartment building.

CHAPTER 11

The alcohol made its way through me, spreading slowly, limb to limb, disconnecting my thoughts. The longer we walked, the more it seemed to be affecting me.

By the time we reached Jonathan's apartment building, I was barely able to climb the stairs, my gait unsteady. We walked into Jonathan's place just after midnight, and he showed me where the bathroom was; nature was calling.

Coming out, I ran straight into the door jam, the world spinning around me. My thoughts, clustered and confused.

Jonathan walked out of the kitchen with a glass of water.

"Drink this," he said as he handed it to me.

"I'm really drunk," I said, slurring my words.

"I noticed." He laughed. "Looks like you'll be staying here tonight."

He went to the closet and came back with some blankets and a pillow, and settled me on the couch as my head began to spin even more.

"Ben. He doesn't know I'm not coming home," I whispered, trying to clear my head.

"I'll call him for you. Don't worry." Jonathan's tone, gentle. "Let me know if you need anything."

He kissed me on the top of my head and disappeared out of sight

I could hear him from another room. He was on the phone with Ben, talking in a hushed tone, assuring him that I was alright. I listened for just a moment before sleep overtook me.

A beeping sound woke me from a deep slumber. I stirred, not wanting to wake up. My body, stiff and uncomfortable. My eyes flitted, not wanting to open. When I finally did, bright sunlight burned them and I coughed, my tongue feeling like dry cotton. I looked through hazy eyes, images blurry, for several minutes.

The inside of the apartment was quiet, but I could hear some rowdy students outside the window.

I needed to get up.

I sat up too quickly and my head began to throb in response.

I stumbled to the bathroom to rinse my mouth and face. When I came out, I realized Jonathan wasn't home. I glanced at the clock. It was nearly eleven o'clock already. Jonathan had probably left for work hours ago.

I looked around at his apartment for the first time. The couch where I had slept sat facing two large windows that looked out over the parking lot where I had left my car last night. Adjacent to the couch sat a small dining table with two chairs. The kitchen was a galley style and had been updated with modern stainless-steel appliances and cabinets. Along the far wall, there was a television, flanked by bookshelves filled with almost as many books as I had seen his office yesterday.

I went over to the window and looked out. There was no sign of the rowdy students I had heard earlier. The window ledge caught my eye and I saw the culprit of the beeping sound that had awoken me. It was coming from a Bluetooth speaker, still beeping. I pushed the button on the front of it and the sound stopped.

My head still throbbing, I walked back over to the couch to fold the blankets that I had slept on. I glanced at the side table and saw a note with my name on it.

It was a handwritten note from Jonathan. I sat down on the couch and opened it right away.

Dear Claire,

    After you fell asleep last night, I stayed awake all night and thought about what you confided in me about the unusual dream that you've had about Ben. I wish that I could've helped you more, but when dealing with these types of phenomena, it's almost impossible to predict what is going to happen. Even with all the research that has been done, psychic phenomena are poorly understood.

    If it is just a dream, then no big deal, but if it's not, there's something you need to know.

    There is a phenomenon called The Butterfly Effect. It's the conceptual belief that everything affects everything.

    I will say it again. Everything affects everything.

    I am telling you this because I want you to be careful. I know that sounds crazy, but you have to trust me. There've been studies to prove that something as small as the flap of a butterfly's wing could change the course of history, hence the name.

    My concern is if you try to change something from the dream, like Ben's death, it could have disastrous effects.

    Claire, you're in reactive mode. You are basing your feelings and reactions to life right now on the dream. It's affecting how you look at the world, and I just don't want you to do something that could lead to something even worse. I know that's hard to imagine but it's true. There are worse things. Just stay out of it and let things happen the way they are going to. I know that's hard advice to hear because it's hard for me to give it.

    There are all kinds of ways to win, and sometimes when you think you've lost, you've actually won. So, don't give up on yourself. No matter what happens with Ben. You've still got a lot of life to live and a future in front of you. Nobody makes you, you. They just add or they take away. You are still the best part of your life, sis, and I'm proud of the woman that you've become.

I love you and I am really glad you came to see me.
Call me if you need me!

Love,
Jonathan

Four hours later I was sitting in front of the boys' school waiting for them to dismissed for the day. The late afternoon sun seemed dimmer than usual. Maybe affected, by my still throbbing head.

Five school buses were parked and idling in front of me in line, waiting for their passengers. Diesel fuel exhaust seeped into the vents of my car, making feel nauseated.

I turned the car off and got out to wait, taking in a huge breath of clean air.

As I headed up the walkway toward the school building, my phone dinged. I pulled it out and saw it was text message from Jonathan.

"Guess who I took to lunch today?"

"Oh my gosh, Sheila?! How did it go?" I pushed send and smiled.

His response came in a few seconds later. "It was great. I only spilled a drink in her lap. LOL! But I think you're right. She likes me. Thanks, Sis."

I texted back a heart as a wave of happiness washed over me.

Soon groups of students began to trickle out the front door. It wasn't long before Oliver came down the steps. Running in his direction, I met him on the last step, picked him up, wrapped my arms around him and squeezed.

"Hi, Momma." His voice meek, like a mouse.

I kissed his cheeks repeatedly, relishing in the little bit of babiness still left in him. Grayson would have been mortified if I had kissed his cheek, even once, on the front steps of the school.

"Hi, baby. How was your day?" I asked.

Before he could answer, Grayson appeared.

"Mom! What are you doing out of the car? Parents are supposed to wait in line!" he whined.

Even without kissing his cheeks in front of the school, I had still managed to embarrass him, and I laughed.

We walked together to the car, with Oliver still in my arms. He laid his head down on my shoulder as I strained under his weight. He definitely didn't feel like a baby any more.

On the drive home, I called Mom to invite her to dinner. We had barely seen her lately, and the boys had asked about her several times.

The phone rang twice before she answered.

"Hi, Mom. You have plans for dinner?" I offered immediately.

She cleared her throat before answering. "Oh, thanks for the offer, but I've got plans tonight."

"Plans?" I questioned.

"With friends. Why are you being so nosy?" she retorted.

I wondered, *what friends*? But didn't dare to ask.

"Have you talked to your sister lately?" Mom asked. "She's been acting a little strange, and frankly I'm worried about her."

"No, she's too busy to talk me," I answered bitterly, remembering our phone call yesterday.

"Well, you should call her," Mom pushed. "She is your sister, after all."

I could feel myself getting irritated.

Mandi hadn't even bothered to call me back after she was so rude yesterday.

But I ended the phone call with a promise to Mom that I would call and check on Mandi.

A promise I knew I wouldn't keep.

I stood at the sink, coring apples for a pie, when the door opened. I heard Ben's footsteps behind me. I turned and saw him, his face showing slight stubble from the day.

"How was your time with Jonathan?" he asked.

I wondered if he was mad that I didn't come home, but he didn't seem to be.

"Good. We made up for a lot of lost time," I said, wiping my hands on a towel.

Ben came up and kissed my cheek, sending warmth down my spine.

"Want to grill out?" Ben asked, smiling. "I could make my famous burgers!"

Ben's "famous" burgers were made with shredded cheese and chopped onions mixed into the meat before grilling. And they were so huge, I could never finish a whole burger in one sitting. He always swore it was a prize-winning recipe, but what contest he entered, I had no clue.

While I finished making the pie, he rushed upstairs to change. When he came back down, he whipped up the burgers and then went outside to light the grill. I followed with warm baked beans and sweet tea, placing them on the outdoor table. Grayson came out behind me, with paper napkins, plates, and cups.

The grill gave off the aroma of seared meat and smoke. Ben stood shirtless over the grill, flipping the burgers over as they hissed in response. He didn't see me watching him, my eyes filled with love.

Thunder rumbled in the distance. A rising breeze tossed the napkins and they sailed across the yard, with the boys chasing them in laughter.

Ben pulled the burgers off and we sat down together to eat.

I watched as Oliver bit into a burger nearly the size of his head. Ketchup and mustard squirted out the sides and ran down his shirt. He looked at me and laughed. I couldn't help but laugh too. I noticed he was getting freckles on his nose. I always heard that freckles were angel's kisses, and as I looked at Oliver's sweet face, I believed it.

Grayson sat close to Ben, complaining to his dad.

"I'm the only kid in my class that hasn't lost any teeth! Even Christopher lost a tooth last week. And he's the shortest kid in school!" Grayson's face crinkled up in genuine frustration.

Ben tousled his head. "Don't worry about it! Don't you know that the late bloomers always produced the best buds?"

I could see by Grayson's face he had no idea what that meant, but he nodded his head in agreement.

Ben gave me a knowing smile, and I smiled back as the afternoon sun slowly slipped away and gave way to evening. There was more thunder in the distance, but Ben assured me it would pass.

After we finished eating, Ben gave the boys each a glow stick, cracking them gently to reveal their fluorescent glow. As the boys ran, chasing each other with their mini light sabers over darkening grass, Ben built a fire in the fire pit. I watched as the flames ignited, dancing together slowly at first, and then all at once engulfing the wood. Crackling and spattering, in song.

I sipped on red wine, entranced by the firelight and the sound of the boys' laughter. Ben took a seat next to me and I sighed. I closed my eyes, willing this moment to last forever. Everything was right in the world right at this very moment.

Then without warning a raindrop hit my cheek, followed by another. Raindrops fell, landing on my face and arms in dollops, as the sky opened up.

CHAPTER 12

I woke up just before dawn, quietly got out of bed and slipped on my robe. Ben still had a few minutes to sleep before his alarm went off, and I didn't want to wake him.

I tiptoed downstairs and made a pot of coffee. The aroma rich and comforting as I poured myself a cup and took it out with me onto the patio. The rain had pushed out, leaving a damp chill in the air. I tugged on my robe and pulled it closed a little more tightly.

Night was still silencing the world, and I had my own private showing of the sunrise about to commence. I sat down on the chair with my coffee in hand and took a deep breath, as orange streaks spread through the ebony sky and the early morning song birds began their chorus. I quietly took it in the new day as it emerged.

As the light pushed away the darkness, I thought about what Jonathan said in his letter.

I didn't want to live in a reactive state. If he was right about the things we focus on being drawn to us, I needed to put this dream as far behind me as I possibly could. I didn't want to think it about it anymore.

I mean, after all, it was only a dream. I was the only one giving it power over my life. I was putting it behind me, once and for all.

After Ben got home from work later that day, he went upstairs to shower and change. I put the oldies station on the kitchen radio and started making dinner. Meatloaf, mashed potatoes, and a garden salad.

As Otis Redding's voice filled the kitchen, the boys came running in with offers to help cook. I pulled up two chairs to the counter and let them prep the salads.

Oliver beamed, "I'm a big boy!" as he tossed lettuce into the salad bowls.

I nodded. "Yes, yes you are."

Just as I turned back to the stove, Ben came around the corner playing an air guitar. Both of the boys started laughing. Oliver's hand came down on the counter and turned over the bowl of cherry tomatoes, spilling them out. They rolled across the counter and onto the floor. As Grayson got down to help clean them up, his elbow caught the plastic bowl of chopped lettuce and it flew off the counter and bounced on the floor, throwing lettuce everywhere.

The boys looked over at me wide-eyed.

I laughed and shrugged. They both let out a deep breath of relief.

Ben stopped playing his air guitar and looked at the floor. "Well, that certainly gives new meaning to a tossed salad, now doesn't it?" A roar of laughter filled the room.

Once the salad disaster was remedied, we sat down to eat dinner. The boys were chatting on about their day, when Ben chimed into the conversation.

"So, guess who came to see me at work today?"

The boys bounced up and down in their seats with anticipation, saying, "Who!? Who!?"

"Auntie Mandi!" Ben snickered.

I looked up from my plate, feeling the blood rushing to my face.

"What did *she* want?" I hissed.

"Oh, she wanted to take me to lunch. Which of course, I said no. But boy did she cause a stir!" He laughed.

"What happened, Ben?" I said, my voice sharp and jagged.

"Well, she came in wearing a slinky dress and heels, you know the kind of stuff she always wears. I wasn't in the office. I had gone down to the third floor to pick up some documents. When I got back up, every single guy in the office was waiting for me at the elevators. I was like, what is it my birthday or something? They all started commenting on the chick that was waiting for me in my office. They were elbowing me, calling me an ol' sly dog. I was super confused until I walked into my office and saw her. I turned around and all the guys had followed me to the door, hoping to catch a glimpse of her again. I shut the door in their faces."

"You closed the door with Mandi in there with you?" I tried to keep my voice from shrieking.

"Come on, Claire, let me finish the story. God, you don't have to get jealous over this. It was funny."

I narrowed my eyes. *It wasn't funny to me. Not at all.*

He continued, "Once I closed the door, she came up and hugged me. She said she was just in the area and thought she'd stop by and take her favorite brother-in-law to lunch. Which of course, I informed her I was her only brother in law. She just laughed and laughed, like I was a paid comedian."

I could feel my heart pounding in my ears. "What did you say about going to lunch?" I insisted.

"Of course, I told her I wasn't going to lunch with her. And she protested profusely. Once I finally had her convinced to leave, she kissed my cheek, leaving a giant set of red lip prints on my cheek. Which of course, I didn't notice until after she was gone. The guys followed her all the way to the elevators, trying to talk to her. Once the elevator doors closed, they came running back to me to get all the dibs on her. I had to field questions for a half of an hour!

And don't worry, I told them there was nothing going on between us, and that Mandi just wanted what she couldn't have. But boy did they ever give me a hard time, especially over the lip marks on my cheek. I don't think I will ever live that one down." Ben's face was red with laughter.

My brain was swirling as I pushed my chair back with a loud screech. I quickly stormed out of the room with Ben following behind me.

"Claire! What are you doing?"

"I am calling her!" I shrieked.

All the stress of the last few weeks had worn me down, and I was ready to fight.

I picked up my phone and searched for her name.

"God, Claire! She didn't cause any harm. Seriously, if there was any concern about something going on between me and her, I would understand! But there's nothing there. She's just a broken person, can't you see that? You need to cut her some slack."

"Ben, honestly, I don't care what she is! I am sick and tired of her playing games. I'm tired of her trying to tempt you."

I finally found her name in my phone and clicked it.

"But she can't tempt me. I don't want her. I never have and never will! Like I said at Easter, it's actually kind of sad. You should just try to be there for your sister and not attack her. You're a better person than this…"

He was still talking when she answered my call.

"Mandi?" I shouted into the phone.

Ben turned and walked away from me, shaking his head.

"Claire? Is that you?" Her words were slightly slurred.

"Are you drunk?!" I shrieked.

"I've had a few glasses of wine, that's all." She laughed.

"Why did you go to Ben's work today?" I demanded.

"What's wrong with wanting to take my brother out for lunch?" she protested.

"He's not your brother."

She laughed. "Oh yeah, brother-in-law…"

"You have no business going to his office, Mandi! You need to stay away from my husband! I have been fed up with you hanging all over him and making a scene every time you are around him for a long time now, but going to his work, that is just beyond unacceptable. What the hell is your problem? Don't you have enough already? You want to take what's mine too?" I could hear my voice was shaking no matter how hard I tried to steady it.

"Gah, Claire! Get over it already. If I wanted your husband, I could've had him a long time ago." She laughed again.

"Well, that's where you are wrong. He would never have you! Do you not get that? He doesn't want you! He thinks you are pathetic, Mandi! I don't know what your damn problem is, but you had better back off because I am not going to put up with your crap any longer!"

"Has anyone ever told you that you're a bitch?" she exclaimed.

"No, how about you!?"

"Touché!" she replied.

We sat in silence for just a minute, neither knowing what else to say. I stood in the foyer, listening to the sound of Ben getting the boys in the bed.

Finally, Mandi spoke up.

"I didn't mean anything by it, Claire."

"Sure, you didn't," I replied bluntly.

"Why can't you just be nice?" she asked.

"Be nice? Be nice? Are you kidding me, right now?" My voice decibel rising again.

Mandi mumbled something to someone in the background. I assumed it was Lewis.

"I've gotta go," she said, quietly.

"Stay away from Ben, Mandi. I'm not kidding around." My voice stern, proud.

After we hung up, I found Ben reading in the living room.

I went in and quietly sat down on the couch next to him.

"I'm sorry I got so mad. She just brings out the worst in me."

"You don't say!" he half laughed.

"Are you mad at me?" I asked, quietly.

"No, I'm not. I just wish you wouldn't get so worked up over her antics. And all over jealousy? I don't get it. You just don't realize how much I love you. Do you? I love everything about you, Claire. The way you tuck your hair behind your left ear. The way your cheeks redden when I tell a dirty joke. How you look at me like I could save the world."

He shook his head in disbelief. "I am in love with a girl who can't see her own worth. A girl who fell into the shadow of a sister who was never competition to begin with. I just wish you could see that and stop letting her get under your skin."

Ben's eyes were steady on mine. Deep down inside, I knew he was right in some ways, but after all these years of dealing with Mandi, I didn't think things could ever change. She would never change, so how could I?

Ben began reading again and I snuggled up next to him, still thinking about what he said.

Mandi had always known how to push my buttons. Something that came naturally to her.

She wanted everything that was hers and everything that was mine. She wanted it all.

We were in high school and I had just started dating Jeremy Whittle. We'd been going out for just over a month when I invited him to come over after school. We were going to do homework together. Mom was gone to a doctor's appointment and Mandi had cheerleading practice. I had used this opportunity to get to hang out with Jeremy, just the two of us.

We sat together, laughing and talking, having difficulty focusing on schoolwork. I'd had a crush on Jeremy since middle school and was over the moon for him.

Jeremy was just about to kiss me, when we heard the loud roar of a V8 engine. My heart dropped when I realized it was the sound of Mandi's boyfriend dropping her off. She busted in the house, dropping her books by the door with a loud thud.

I hadn't told her about Jeremy, and she stopped in her tracks when she saw him sitting there with me. I narrowed my eyes at her, giving her a warning message, which she ignored and gave me a broad smile in return.

"I thought you had cheerleading practice?" I asked.

"Cancelled!" she answered.

She skillfully turned around and bent over, taking off her shoes in deliberate slow motion. Giving Jeremy and me a full view of her pink lace panties underneath her short skirt. Jeremy's mouth was hanging open. I elbowed him in the ribs as Mandi disappeared into her room.

Not long after, I went into the kitchen to make some microwave popcorn for Jeremy and me. I stood waiting with the hum of the microwave as the popcorn exploded like fireworks.

When I came back around the corner, bowls of popcorn in hand, I caught sight of them.

Jeremy and Mandi, making out on the couch.

"Mandi!" I screamed, dropping both the popcorn bowls on the floor. Kernels flew everywhere as Jeremy got up and ran out the door. He never spoke to me again.

One of many painful things I had experienced, at the hand of Mandi. But not this time.

She wasn't ever going to have Ben. No matter how hard she tried, she would never win him over.

I knew that.

Honestly, the thing that bothered me the most was that she didn't even really want Ben. She only wanted him because he's mine. She would be willing to destroy my entire marriage just so she could satisfy this whim.

I wanted to talk to Ben about it more. To explain my actions, but he wouldn't understand. He would just tell me to let it go, as he always did. No one understood what Mandi did to me. How she made me feel… and no one ever would.

CHAPTER 13

S everal weeks had passed and May was upon us. Everything outside exploded in green splendor, and the morning rushed in with a luscious breeze. I opened all of the windows to allow freshness to expel stagnant winter air from the house. The breeze billowed through the halls, lifting papers on the countertop as I hummed to myself.

I walked out onto the front porch with a broom in hand and swept away leftover yellow pollen and watered the two ferns, flanking the door. When I finished, I took a deep breath as the wind swirled around me, making me feel like I could take flight.

I sat down on the top step and listened to the birds singing happily. I watched a squirrel as it ran up the trunk of the old oak tree in our front yard. Its large branches spread over the driveway, making a beautiful canopy. I looked up as the sunlight sparkled down through the leaves like golden raindrops.

I loved this old tree. Ben kept saying we needed to have the branches cut back. He said they were dangerous and could easily fall in a storm. But I protested. I couldn't stand the thought of it being pruned. The tree was a signature part of our front yard and provided wonderful shade in the summertime. I refused to let him hire the tree trimmers. He wasn't happy about my rebellion, but he reluctantly agreed to my veto.

I looked over and saw Grayson's baseball bat lying next to the hedge wall that separated us from the neighboring house. It was a tall green wall of hedges that we had one on each side of our property. It gave a sense of seclusion and privacy. Not that we really needed it.

We had never really gotten to know any of the neighbors. We had an occasional wave from the older lady, Mrs. Parks, who lived across the street. But mostly, she completely kept to herself. This neighborhood was full of people who kept to themselves. I tried to start a neighborhood Christmas cookie swap, and the people who actually answered the door weren't interested in participating. I pretty much gave up on connecting with anyone after that.

I walked over to the hedge, with my eyes on the bat but stopped just short of it, startled by a rustling sound. I peered through the hedges and could make out some movement on the other side.

"Hello?" I called out.

I had never met the neighbors on this side of the hedge.

I heard someone answer but couldn't quite make it out.

"I'm sorry, I can't understand you..." I called to the unseen person.

I followed along, as someone paced back and forth along the greenery, mumbling.

I strained to see and could make out that it was an elderly man with white hair.

He was talking, his voice muffled.

What was he saying?

I strained to listen.

Suddenly, I caught a few words.

"...watch out..." His voice, irritable. His words, hard understand.

I could only make out bits and pieces.

"What do you mean?" I called back to him.

More words came into focus. "You know it's coming...stop fighting...it can't be stopped."

I could feel tears beginning to sting my eyes.

"I'm sorry, I can't hear you. What did you say?" The hair on the back of my neck was standing up.

He didn't answer.

Was he talking about my dream? How could he possibly know?

"Sir, what do you mean? Please tell me..." I called out.

He responded, "You can't stop fate..."

His voice got even louder as he came closer, but I still couldn't quite make out what he was saying.

His face was next to the hedge. I could see splotches of him through the leaves. Crystal blue eyes reflecting in the sunlight.

He shouted, "Death is coming!"

He was mumbling again when the shock of what he said overtook me. I stepped back away from the hedge and screamed, falling over the bat that I never picked up.

I jumped up and ran back into the house, slamming the door behind me as terror ran through my veins.

I sat down on the floor in foyer trying to calm myself, my breath ragged and coming in rapid succession.

Who was that man and why did he say those things to me!?

A million thoughts ran through my head.

And the question burned in my mind, *why did every time I resolve to forget about the dream, something else happens to trigger me?* I couldn't get away from it, no matter how hard I tried.

It felt as if the dream was pursuing me, targeting me, and I began to cry in protest.

Teddy came in and rubbed up against me, trying to comfort me. I reached down and stroked his soft fur. He purred loudly in response.

Time passed without my recognition as I replayed the man's words in my head over and over again.

I didn't get up until I heard the phone ringing, standing on wobbly legs to answer it.

It was Jamie calling.

"Hey girl! So, I just have one question for you! Are you psychic now or something? I mean, seriously, did you ever call it! It's just so crazy that you knew!" her voice was high-pitched.

"What are you talking about?" I asked, perplexed, beat down.

Jamie laughed out loud. "What am I talking about? I am talking about Annie breaking her ankle! She fell down her front step yesterday because she tripped on a Lego! Poor thing broke it in two places. Man, you called it, sure enough. You said the trip was cancelled and well, now it is!"

I dropped the phone, ran to the toilet, and threw up.

I steadied my shaking hands as I made spaghetti and meatballs for dinner. I strained the pasta and served it on our nicest dinnerware. I topped each plate with a generous amount of sauce and meatballs, sprinkling fresh grated parmesan over the top. Keeping my mind fixed on making the best spaghetti and meatball dinner that was ever made.

Keeping me focused. Keeping me sane.

There had to be an explanation for all of it. Nothing like this had ever happened to me before. My life had been simple. Predictable. Now, nothing was steadfast.

I ate my dinner in silence as the boys rattled off their day's events. Oliver had learned how to add single digits and kept asking us to guess the answer to two plus two or three plus one. Ben kept saying the wrong answer to tease him.

Grayson got up and brought back over a paper mâché alligator that he had made in art class. Green with brown spots. I saw Ben's eyes light up when he saw it. He immediately began to tell them the story of the alligator that was seen in Charlotte, years ago. I knew it was a tall tale, but I let him go ahead and tell his story.

Ben told them the alligator was spotted right in the courtyard by his office, in the middle of downtown. The courtyard was shared by several buildings and was just across the street from the train station. In the center of the courtyard was a fountain where people loved to gather to talk or eat a quiet lunch. On nice days, you would often find musicians or performers in the courtyard with their donation buckets. Hot dog stands and gyro carts littered the courtyard at lunchtime.

This is where Ben's fictional alligator was spotted, right by the food carts.

Ben made roaring sounds as he told how the alligator snarled and snapped at all the people who passed by. The boys wide-eyed as he told how the dog catcher brought a net and captured the alligator in it. The boys cheered as Ben described how the man wrestled the alligator into the back of his van. He ended the story with the alligator being released to his family in the Florida Everglades. A happy ending for everyone.

After the boys were in bed, I went downstairs to finish cleaning up the dishes.

The lights were low as I washed our dishes. Warm water on my hands, my thoughts pulsing.

Ben came in and leaned on the doorway.

"You sure look good in this lighting," he said. "Well, actually, you look pretty good in any lighting."

I turned to look at him as I dried my hands on the kitchen towel.

"Ben, do you know the man that lives next door, to the left of us? You know, the white house with green shutters?"

"No one lives next door that I know of," he answered, approaching me. He had that look in his eyes. The look that said he was ready to go upstairs so we could make love. A look that I knew well.

"There was a man there today. He said some strange things," I persisted.

I wasn't interested in going upstairs. I wanted to talk about the neighbor.

"No one lives there, Claire." His voice has a low lusty sound to it.

He put his arms around my waist and pulled me in, kissing my neck.

I forcefully yanked away from him. "There was a man there today, I am telling you!"

"Claire, dammit, I said no one lives there! That house has been vacant since we moved in! The realtor said the man that owned it died right before we bought our house. His family refuses to sell it. What's with you tonight!?"

The only thing that I heard him say was that the house had been vacant since we moved in. I didn't hear the rest of what he said. I knew he had spoken to me sharply, but I didn't care. I was already out the door, on my way to the front steps of the old man's house.

The night air was cool and the moon lit up the sky. Full and round, sitting just above the horizon.

I ran, fast legs underneath me, toward his house.

He was there today and nobody can tell me that he wasn't! And I needed to talk him now! He needed to explain to me why he said those things!

I stopped running when I stepped into his yard. My breath sharp as I walked toward the house. Only darkness could be seen through the windows. I stepped tentatively up onto the porch. An old set of wind-chimes dinged as I approached the door, weathered boards creaking underneath my feet.

I knocked and no one answered.

I waited and then knocked on the door again. Louder this time.

Still no one answered.

Panic rose up like a storm inside of me, and I repeatedly hit the door with both fists.

He had to be in there! I didn't imagine him!

"Answer the door!!" I screamed.

I heard a sound behind me and jumped.

When I looked up, I saw Ben.

"Honey, stop…no one's there," he said softly as he came up the porch and put his arms around me. I jerked away from his grasp and beat on the door some more.

"Claire! That's enough now. This house is vacant!" he yelled.

I looked at him and then looked back at the darkened house. I was defeated.

We walked back together in silence toward our own house, lit up like a lantern in the night, leading us home.

When we climbed into bed a little later, Ben rolled over and looked at me.

"Is there anything you want to talk about?" he said as he gently brushed a stray hair from my face.

I answered with a sharp, "No."

Ben rubbed his cheek, clearly frustrated.

I flipped over, turned my back on him, staring at the wall, regretting my tone.

I had no reason to be angry with him. None of this was his fault.

But still I stayed with my back to him.

He lay there for several minutes, not saying a word, and then rolled over himself. And soon, I could hear his soft snores.

I tried to sleep, but kept tossing and turning. My night filled with nightmares of trying to save Ben from some sort of death. Different scenarios playing out in my dreams. It was always up to me to save him, and I never could.

I never made it to him in time.

When the sun finally rose, I got up, emotionally drained and physically exhausted.

I pulled into the parking lot at the Arts Center and parked near the entrance. Part of me wanted to leave and part of me wanted to stay. I sat in the car, looking at the window as people drifted in for their 10:00 am classes while the morning's golden light filled the day.

Finally, I opened the car door and got out.

As I passed through the covered walkway leading to the building, I could see a tiny sparrow nesting in the rafters. She flitted and flew back and forth over my head, gathering materials for her home. As she worked, a flash of blue caught my eye. A Blue Jay perched nearby, watching her. A predator. A danger to her home. Seemingly to notice it at the same time that I did, she squawked voraciously and charged this bird, much larger than herself. Fortunately for her, the large jay flew off. I marveled at how she had no concern for own well-being. Her main objective, to protect her nest.

I could relate.

Once inside, I stood in front of my canvas with brush in hand, staring off into space. I must've stood that way for a while because Amanda came by and asked me if I was okay.

I nodded to reassure her, knowing the real truth. I looked up from my still blank canvas and saw Sarina. She looked up too and smiled in my direction.

A strong impulse came over me. One that I had never explored before. I watched Sarina as she began working on her painting again and wondered.

Should I talk to her? Should I ask her about the dream? About Ben? I mean, after all, she is a psychic.

She looked up again, sensing my eyes on her, and I looked away quickly, my cheeks instantly reddening.

I deliberately took paint to the canvas in front of me, laying out a blue and green washed background in an attempt to keep busy until class ended.

When it was over, I stopped Sarina as she passed by me.

"Would you want to get a cup of coffee with me?" I asked, trying to hide the truth in my eyes.

She looked at me warily for a moment and then smiled.

"Sure, that would be nice," she responded. "When were you thinking?"

"Now..." I looked at her hopefully.

She looked down at her watch and shifted.

"I have an appointment in thirty minutes..." she paused as she studied my face. The anxiety I was hiding betraying me.

"But I think I can reschedule it..."

I let out a sigh of relief and had overcome to the urge to hug her.

We agreed to meet at The Coffee Beanery, just two blocks away. The coffee shop was small and run by locals. I liked it because it wasn't one of those big chains. There was a quality to their coffee that you couldn't find at the mainstream places. This was the place where I always picked up my pre-class lattes. They knew me well. My order would already be being prepared before I even reached the counter on most days.

I walked inside ahead of Sarina and sat down at a table for two. I twisted my keys in my hands over and over again as I stared up at a piece of folk art hanging over the table. A tree with a large trunk and spidery limbs, exquisitely carved from dark maple wood, laid over slats of whitewashed planks. Reminding me of the tree in our yard.

I kept glancing out the window. There was no sign of Sarina.

I didn't know what I was going say to her.

What do you say to a psychic?

Soon she appeared, and I saw her as she came in. As the door closed behind her, a gust of wind slipped in and tossed her curly hair up. Her flowy skirt twirling as she stepped inside. Her movements nimble and graceful.

After she ordered a coffee, she came and sat down at the table with me.

"Thank you for agreeing to meet me." I looked down, feeling my cheeks burning again.

"Of course, you seemed like you needed a friend." Her voice kind and soothing.

I noticed how her skin was pale in stark contrast to her brown eyes and dark hair. She put her hand to her face to push back a stray hair, and her rings flashed in the fluorescent lighting.

I wanted to speak, but I couldn't find my voice. Apprehension was silencing me.

"What did you want to talk to me about?" she asked gingerly, almost seeming to sense my dilemma.

She wasn't at all like I expected. Not that I knew what to expect from a psychic.

Suddenly the words came. Bursting forth like a broken dam. I told her about everything that had happened since Mandi's birthday, in great detail. I hadn't expected to say so much.

She sat quietly for a moment taking it all in, sipping her coffee, before she spoke.

"What I really think is that you are beginning to develop intuitive abilities. These can be very scary at first, but you can't let fear get in the way. You have to trust yourself and follow your inner wisdom. This is truly a gift, but only if you use it wisely." Her eyes fixed on mine.

"I don't want this so-called gift. I didn't ask for this. Honestly, I just want it to go away. My life has been so confusing and stressful ever since this started." I meant every word but was embarrassed by my impulsive response, especially considering her line of work.

She hadn't seemed to take offense. She reached across the table and patted my hand.

"There's a reason why this is happening to you, Claire. I can't tell you why it's happening. I just can tell you there's a reason for everything."

Ben's face immediately came to my mind.

This all started when I thought he was dead. Was that the reason?!

"Sarina, please tell me…is my husband going to die?" The desperation in my voice was impossible to disguise.

She closed her eyes for a moment, and when she opened them again, she smiled gently.

"Claire, I don't see anything to indicate that your husband is going to die, but I cannot give you any guarantees. I am not God, my dear."

I took in a deep breath and sighed. That was enough for me.

I looked at her, tears filling my eyes. "Thank you so much, Sarina."

Her face suddenly took on a serious look, and she began to speak again.

"I will give you one word of caution. If events continue to match the pattern of the dream you had, I would pay very close attention. Don't ignore the signs when they are there."

Before I could say another word, she stood up.

"See you next week in class!" she said as she turned and left the coffee shop.

The bell on the door dinged as she closed it behind her.

I sat at the table alone, reeling.

Don't ignore the signs? I had no idea what she meant by that. What was I supposed to do?

The events *were* matching the pattern… and I was helpless to stop any of it.

CHAPTER 14

The days after my talk with Sarina were filled with dread and apprehension. I was looking for a monster around every corner. Everything made me jump.

And Ben was always giving me the side-eye. He knew something was up, but he couldn't put his finger on it. I wasn't doing anything in particular that he could say was wrong, but I definitely wasn't myself and he knew it.

I couldn't tell him what was going on with me, and I especially wouldn't dare tell him about my talk with Sarina. Ben was a skeptic, at best. He grew tense around the subject of spirituality. He didn't believe in any power outside of himself. The experience with his dad and the faith healer had soured him permanently.

When Oliver's toe burst through the right foot on his dinosaur pajamas, Ben and Grayson laughed at Oliver wiggling his toe out the hole...and I cried. Ben thought it was because I was sad Oliver was growing up.

If he only knew the real reason...

I refused to let it be another foretelling, so I took the pajamas and sewed the hole back up, only for his toe to pop right back out the next day. And I cried again.

Could I not even change something this small? Was I completely powerless?

I filled my days with busyness to avoid thinking about my dream, filled with a desperate sense of responsibility that I had to keep watch over everything happening around me, so nothing could go wrong.

And strangely enough, the nightmares stopped.

But my compulsion did not.

I struggled to recall the events that happened in the dream, but most of the details were fuzzy, with only a few sharp images remaining.

Terrible images. Painful images…of Teddy going missing…and Ben dying.

Thank God, neither of those things had come to pass… but the terror…the nagging fear of it looming over the horizon…was just about more than I could stand.

Thinking about the man next door became an obsession. Watching, waiting for him to reappear. His crystal blue eyes searing my mind. While the words he spoke swirled around in my thoughts. "…You can't stop fate…Death is coming…"

Every time I was in the front yard, I would look for him, but he never appeared again.

Where did he go?

It seemed impossible that he didn't exist. I remembered his voice… and his crystal blue eyes so distinctly. Unique and intense.

I found myself trespassing on his property, repeatedly. Hoping to catch a glimpse of him again. To solidify to myself that he was real. My quest went unanswered.

In a desperate attempt for answers, I accosted Mrs. Parks. She was checking her mail when I spotted her. I moved quickly across the yard, bare feet on grass, to talk to her.

As soon as she saw me, she moved quickly to get back inside, not interested in conversation. I called out to her as she shuffled away in fuzzy pink slippers.

I caught up with her just as she reached her porch. A rounded portico.

"Mrs. Parks, I am so sorry to disturb you." My words choppy, out of breath.

Her face, cold and taut. There was no hiding her displeasure in my company. Her hair was snow white, cut into a chin length bob that curled perfectly under her chin. The lines on her face, deep and trenched. Her eyes a deep brown, and from her facial structure, I could tell she was a beauty in her day. On her face she wore thick-lensed glasses with an oversized frame. She pushed them up on her nose as she studied me warily. My eyes went to her floral housedress, slightly askew. She straightened it right away as if she had read my mind.

"What do you want?" she asked curtly.

"I wanted to ask you about the man across the street." I glanced over at the old man's house as I spoke.

"I don't know any men around here," she said, as she turned to walk away.

"The man...the man who lives next door to me," I said as I followed her onto her small portico. There was barely enough room for the two of us.

She turned and eyed me narrowly. "What man?" she said coarsely.

"The man who lives to my left, in the white house with green shutters." I pointed back across the street.

She looked at me with uncertainty and then eyes drifted over to the old man's house.

Her face immediately softened.

"Are you talking about Ed?" There was a tone in her voice that hadn't been there before.

"Actually, I don't know his name..." I answered.

"Ed has been dead for ten years, young lady. He was my…my friend…
and now he's gone." Her voice crackled as she spoke.

Her eyes glistened with a far-off look. Lost in time. And then they
filled up with tears.

"He had the most beautiful crystal blue eyes…" she trailed off, still
lost in memory.

Every hair on my body stood on end.

She continued to mumble to herself as she went inside and closed
the door behind her. I stood on her porch looking at her closed door,
red and faded from years of sunshine.

The rush of shock gave way to a deep sense of uneasiness.

Crystal blue eyes?

That was definitely him….and he had been dead for ten years.

The days were long and the nights were longer. I still wasn't sleeping
well. Images of the old man's crystal blue eyes filled my mind every
time I tried to fall asleep.

Fatigue and paranoia didn't make the best combination.

And then the day arrived, where I came completely unraveled.

"Oliver! Come play outside with me!" Grayson called out. His voice
echoing through the house. I walked around the corner and saw him,
with the back door standing open.

"Grayson, shut that door, we don't want Teddy to get out," I told him,
remembering my dream.

But it was too late.

Just as Grayson stepped forward to close the door, Teddy darted right
past his legs and out into the yard. Disappearing out of sight immediately.

I pushed past Grayson and ran out after him.

"Teddy!" I called out desperately. My heart in my throat. Not wanting
this to be real.

It was almost as if he had vanished into thin air. We searched the neighborhood, under every bush, car, and porch. Ben got in the car and drove around for hours looking for him as I walked the sidewalk with his food, calling out his name.

We never found him.

Now, the fear of losing Ben was all consuming. I was barely functioning. When Ben said he needed to talk to me, I knew he was concerned for my stability. I could hear it in his voice.

We sat down on the patio together. Ben opened a bottle of wine and poured us both a glass as I sat in the chair, knees drawn up to my chest, not looking at him.

The night was magical, though I didn't notice. Crickets chirped in the distance as a steady breeze blew around us, keeping the mosquitos at bay. String lights dangled overhead, twinkling against the dark sky.

We sat together in the quiet of the night.

Ben finally broke the silence. "Honey, please tell me what's going on with you? You've not been yourself over the last few weeks. I know that Teddy running away really hit you hard, but I am concerned about you. I want to help." His voice soft and pleading.

"What do you mean, what's wrong with me?" I snarled.

I wasn't mad at him. I knew that, but the emotional twister was touching down, and he was in the path of the storm.

"If you're feeling overwhelmed…we could hire some household help. We could afford it. Maybe somebody who could come in a few times a week. Help with the house. Help with the boys…" he trailed off.

"What are you saying, Ben?? That I'm not a good mother? That I am not taking care of your house?" My voice unrecognizable, even to me.

"God, no…I just want to try to help you feel better…" His voice was still soft, but I could see I was pushing him too far. His face flushed with anger, but I couldn't stop myself.

"You want me to feel better? Really?! That's the most absurd thing I have ever heard! You don't give a damn, Ben! You're never here. You are always working! When you are here, you're not really here! Why don't you just put in a bed at work and stay there?!"

I knew none of that was true, yet it was spewing out of my mouth uncontrollably. I wanted him to be angry too. I was angry. Angry at what was happening. Angry at how I had no control over my life. I wondered if I ever had any choice at all!

Was this God's cruel plan? To force us to walk footsteps that we didn't choose?

Leave us helpless?

Resentment seethed out of every pore.

"Are you kidding me right now?" His face twisted, anger unleashed. "After all I do for you?! This is how you're going to treat me? I bust my butt for this family. I give everything to you and I ask for nothing in return. How dare you, Claire? Who the hell do you think you are?"

He stormed inside the house and slammed the door behind him, silencing the crickets.

The late spring moon was high in the sky, with only the sound of night lark calling nearby.

My heart sank, the slamming door echoing in my mind.

Well aware this was completely my fault.

He didn't do anything wrong.

I was just so angry.

At myself.

At everything.

The tears started to fall, and when they did, they didn't stop for an hour. I cried for Teddy, I cried for Ben, I cried for the boys, and I cried for myself.

June 3rd was only two weeks away.

The dream that was unfolding right in front of my very eyes, and I was incapable of stopping it.

I yelled up at the night sky, at God or whoever was listening.

"How dare YOU!" I screamed.

My words echoed in the night. No one answered me. Not that I expected anyone to.

I sat under the string lights alone and looked at the untouched glasses of wine. Guilt swiftly coursed through me. He was only trying to help…

I heard the backdoor click open, and soon after footsteps followed.

Ben came over and pulled his chair closer to mine. He reached out, grabbing both of my hands in his. He pulled them up to his mouth and kissed them.

"I'm sorry I lost my temper, Claire." His eyes were sincere.

"No…Ben, it's me…it's my fault. I shouldn't have said those things. They weren't true…you're a good man…" My words were cut off by my sobs.

"God, Claire…what's going on? Please…let me help you." The strain in his voice distinct.

I couldn't tell him. Even now, I couldn't tell him the truth.

"I'm just tired…I think…I haven't been sleeping well, for some reason…"

He looked at me for a moment and then reached in and hugged me.

"It's okay. Let's get you inside, so you can get some rest…" He lifted me up by my arm and we walked together inside.

He stayed close to me in the bed throughout the whole night. His way of trying to provide comfort. I knew he didn't quite believe my lack of sleep as the answer to all of this, but he chose to let it be…and I actually slept through the night without waking once.

The next morning Ben got up and made coffee. I stayed in bed, not wanting to get up. My body craved more sleep, and my mind craved more escape.

He appeared in the doorway holding my favorite mug. A chunky blue and white, glazed, hand-made mug that we had bought on our honeymoon in Rio.

It was our honeymoon destination by happenstance. His mom had won a trip for two to Brazil, in a raffle, and had gifted it to us for our wedding.

It included a full week at a five-star resort right on the beach in Copacabana with our own private veranda. We spent the days on the beach, basking in the South American sun and splashing in the crystal blue waters of the ocean. Our nights were spent dancing to live Brazilian music in the streets. The beat of the music, coursing through our bodies.

We purchased the mug on our last full day in Rio. After perusing a small marketplace for souvenirs, we met an elderly woman who was selling her handmade pottery out the back of an old rusted pickup truck. She didn't have any teeth, nor did she speak English, but her kindness transcended language.

On our way back to the hotel, we purchased a bottle of spiced rum, sharing it that night out of that very mug. We made love on the beach, under the stars, then stayed up talking until dawn. One of the best nights of my life.

As he handed me the warm mug of coffee, I wondered if he had chosen it specifically as another way to reconnect with me.

I sat up and smiled weakly.

"Thank you..." I offered.

He smiled softly. "Listen, I have an idea. Why don't we get your mom or your sister to watch the boys this weekend, and let's go on a little trip together. Get you out of the house?"

I looked back at him, not responding. His face so full of hope and expectancy.

It was impossible to say no. Not to mention, a change of scenery might do me some good.

"Yeah." I nodded. "I'm sure my mom could do it."

He let out a sigh of relief. "Well, it's settled then. I am taking the whole weekend off and making plans for us! Pack your bags, little missy!"

He kissed my forehead and headed downstairs to take the boys to school.

I knew this was more of him trying to make things better. The only way he knew how. I loved him for that. I just wished I could appreciate this moment, but the knowledge of June 3rd being one day closer filled me with trickling terror.

I had only one thing going in my favor.

He didn't take the train. He's never taken the train.

I repeated the mantra to myself…*he can't be killed on a train that he doesn't take.*

Maybe fate really did have things wrong after all.

CHAPTER 15

I woke up early on Saturday morning to glaring sunshine. I grabbed an overnight bag and began packing. I threw in a green, strappy, summer dress and a pair of white shorts and a gauzy purple top with bell sleeves, along with a pair of comfortable sandals. They seemed to be appropriate choices for the locale.

Ben had chosen New Bern, a beautiful and romantic waterfront city near the coast, for our weekend getaway. As I packed, I could feel myself relaxing. The distraction was good for me. Maybe Ben was right, after all. I needed a break.

Soon after I was packed, we loaded the boys in the car and drove them to my mom's house. They were so excited because they didn't spend many nights at Gammy's house. I only hoped that they wouldn't be too much for her to handle. It had been a long time since she had to care for children for an entire weekend.

She came out the front door when we pulled up, meeting us on the walkway.

"Boys!! I missed your faces!" she called out.

They ran and hugged her, almost knocking her down. I looked over at Ben, and I could see he had the same concern I did.

"Boys, take it easy on Gammy, now," he laughed, but I knew by his tone that he meant business. The boys did too. They both looked back at him and nodded.

After a quick hug and kiss goodbye, the boys ran inside to where Gammy had promised there would be chocolate chip muffins waiting for them.

Mom came up and hugged me. "Honey, have a great time. Don't worry about us. The boys will be fine."

As I looked at her, I noticed she was wearing makeup. She hadn't worn makeup in years…and she was smiling. Something else I hadn't seen in years, either. It was strange behavior, but I took it as a good sign.

Mom seemed confident about the boys staying, so I let my worry go. Figuring she was probably glad to have the company.

I kissed her cheek and we were off to New Bern.

As soon as we pulled into the city limits, I was caught up in the magic of New Bern.

As the afternoon sun filled the sky, I gazed out at the picturesque streets lined with Spanish moss draped trees and fragrant flowering bushes. Breathtaking historic homes lined the sidewalks of the charming city. My face pressed close to the window as we drove past Georgian style houses, Victorian and Colonial homes, and Neoclassical style mansions with their towering columns, all with wide and inviting lawns.

We finally came to a stop in front of a Victorian Style home with white scalloped shingle siding. There were wide double porches, ornate with intricate wood trimmings. A large tower with a pointed roof stood on the right side of the house. The architecture was exquisite. Taking my breath.

I looked over at Ben with wide eyes, hoping this was the inn we were staying at.

It was.

We got out of the car, and with luggage in hand, walked past a wooden sign hung on a stake and squeaking as it swayed in the wind.

It read The Theodore House: 1885.

Ben led me down the inviting walkway lined with petunias and straight up onto a broad wraparound porch. Eight large, black rockers sat along the span of the porch with potted flowers on stands sporadically placed around them. Overflowing green ferns hung from the porch eaves. The sound of bird songs surrounded the property and mixed with piano music that seeped lightly out of an outdoor speaker.

Ben opened the front door and we stepped inside the open foyer.

We were greeted by an older woman.

"Hello and welcome to The Theodore House! My name is Edda and I am the overseer of the property." She was beautiful, her silver hair twisted up in a bun. She spoke with the most distinguished southern accent I had ever heard, reminding me of *Gone with the Wind*.

Ben stood beside her while she did our paperwork, and I wandered off into the parlor, a large room just to the right of the foyer. I walked inside past several couches centered around a large fireplace. I ran my hand along the edge of an antique Steinway piano. A grandfather clock stood against the wall, ticking softly. Two tables flanked the clock, each with a small Tiffany lamp. The room was filled with the same music I had heard on the porch. I imagined the coziness of cuddling up by the fire in here with a hot cup of tea.

After Ben got us checked in, an older gentleman, who introduced himself as Frank, led us up the curved wooden staircase to the wide hallway of the second floor.

We walked past rooms with gold-plated signs on them. Each the name of a tree. We passed The Oak Room, The Maple Room, and The Magnolia, before he opened the door to The Dogwood Room.

The door swung open, giving us a view in to the splendor. As we stepped inside, Ben tipped Frank five dollars and closed the door.

I scanned the room, taking it all in.

There was a large canopy bed covered in luxurious linens and a fireplace with an intricate hand-carved mantle. Two French leather chairs sat in the corner with a marble topped table situated between them and a bottle of complimentary wine on top. I stepped over to the large window on the far wall and saw it overlooked a brick-tiled courtyard garden filled with flowers, several benches, and a flowing fountain in the middle.

I left the window and went to explore the large bathroom, my shoes echoing across the white marble floor. The centerpiece of the bathroom was a porcelain clawfoot tub with a glistening British telephone style faucet.

I came out the bathroom, smiling. Ben smiled back, knowing he had done well.

"Do you like it?" he asked, though he already knew the answer.

"I couldn't be happier, Ben. This is exactly what I needed," I answered, as his eyes twinkled with the joy of success.

After we unpacked, we walked to Middle Street to explore New Bern's downtown, situated on the sparkling Neuse and Trent Rivers. We strolled the city streets, hand in hand, popping into any shop that sparked our interest. A breeze blew around us, encircling us, smelling of fresh river water. After a few hours we stopped grab dinner at a quaint corner café just off the main strip.

When we walked out, we found the afternoon had fully slipped away. The evening consumed us, as a light wind blew soft and sweet. We walked hand in hand down the sidewalk back to the inn, passing by porch lights putting off a warm and inviting glow, and homes with open windows, with the chatter of families drifting out.

I walked closer to Ben, the sky above us colored in an inky plum and filled with dazzling starlight. Ben stopped mid-step and took me in his arms, kissing me under a streetlight as a palmetto leaves rustled in the trees around us.

When we got back in the room, Ben lit the gas fireplace for ambiance and opened the bottle of wine.

"Don't you think we've had enough?" I laughed, still feeling a little buzz from the beer.

"A little more won't hurt," he said as he poured us both a generous glass.

With my wine glass in hand, I wandered to the bathroom and exclaimed, "I feel like a bath," as I eyeballed the magnificent tub.

Ben followed in behind me, turned on the water and lowered the lights. The bathroom filled with the roaring sound of the water as it filled the tub. Foggy steam rose up and fogged the mirror as I dropped my clothes to the floor.

Ben watched me intently, leaning against the sink, admiring the view.

I stuck one foot into the water slowly, letting out a small scream from the shock of the hot water, then followed it with my other foot. Once inside the tub, I lowered myself slowly until I sank all the way down into the deep basin. The hot water enveloping me.

Ben came over and handed me my glass of wine, taking a seat on the edge of the tub. He dipped his hand in and let the drips of warm water run down his fingers onto my chest and over my breasts. His eyes shimmering in the low light.

"You want to get in?" I offered.

"I'd rather you get out," Ben answered as he ran his fingertips across my jawline down my neck to my collarbone.

"I will, in a few minutes…let me finish my wine and I will be right there." Enjoying the power that I had over him. Making him wait.

He leaned over and kissed me, slipping his warm tongue in my mouth. I could taste the wine in his mouth, and I kissed him back. He slipped his hand down into the water and put his fingers inside of me. I groaned as delicious feelings ignited.

He pulled his hand back out of the water and splashed me.

"You better hurry up with this bath, young lady!"

"But, wait, you're stopping already?" Wondering, who had the power now?

"Oh, that was just a sneak peek of what's to come after your bath," he said as he winked at me.

He went out into the bedroom and closed the bathroom door behind him.

I sunk down deeper in the water, all the way up to my chin. Enraptured.

It felt so good to be here. To just relax.

Nothing on my mind except getting out and going to where my sexy husband was waiting for me.

I finished the last sips of my wine and got out of the tub. Feeling rather tipsy, I slipped on one of Ben's t-shirts without panties and opened the bathroom door.

Once I stepped out, I was met with the sound of light snoring. Ben's empty glass on the night table.

I sighed and crawled into bed beside him, thankful to have this weekend with Ben. With no anxiety. No fear. Just the two of us here. Safe from Charlotte and the dream.

Before I could count to ten, the fluffy pillows and comforter engulfed me, and I fell into a deep sleep.

When morning came, I tossed and turned, caught in a dream about the old man next door.

I ran as he chased me through endless mazes of tall green hedges. Running faster and faster, but he was always there, right behind me.

Stumbling, falling, trying to escape. Meeting dead end after dead end. Endless green swirled around me. Suffocating me.

My strength dwindling as I was caught in another dead end. I turned... and he was there, his crystal blue eyes ablaze.

Right before he grabbed me, I jolted awake.

With eyes still closed, I reached desperately for Ben in the bed and found only empty space.

Just as the panic began, I heard a sound I didn't recognize.

Loud lurching and groaning.

My eyes flew open, looking around in bewilderment.

Disoriented.

Suddenly it came into focus. The Theodore House Inn.

The menacing sounds were coming from Ben's shower as water rushed in old pipes.

All at once, relief flooded me, and I let out a long exhale.

I was safe.

Ben was safe.

And nothing here could hurt us.

Before long, the shower turned off, and Ben came out with a towel wrapped around his waist. The sight of him reminded me of last night and instantly stirred me. Water was still running down his face as he searched for the clothes to wear.

Still dripping, he came over to the bed and gave me a long kiss.

"Good morning sunshine." His eyes had a spark in them. "You ready for our day?"

We had a full day of activities planned, otherwise I would've pulled him straight into the bed with me, and from the look in his eyes, I was sure he was thinking the same thing.

I got up and put on the dress I had brought with me and applied a little bit of makeup. I tucked my blonde hair, already lighter from the spring sunshine, behind my ears and came out of the bathroom.

As soon as Ben saw me, he smiled.

"Let's go beautiful." He took my hand and led me to the door.

We emerged from our room and instantly heard the sounds of morning and of the other guests downstairs.

Edda met us at the bottom of the stairs and led us out onto the veranda, where a live harpist played her melodies. We sat at a small garden table sipping on mimosas and nibbling on fresh pastries. Ben and I sat together, our fingers entwined across the table. Butterflies flitted and flew around us, dancing with the music.

I looked at Ben and playfully said, "You know you passed out on me last night..."

"Oh, well I guess I owe you then?" He had a laugh in his voice. "Maybe even owe you double..." He winked at me and we both laughed out loud. A few people turned toward our laughter. I felt my face redden even though I knew they had no idea what we had been talking about.

Our first activity of the day was a historic tour of New Bern. We arrived at the tour depot about five minutes early. A small crowd gathered by the parked trolley, so we joined them. Not long after, the tour guide came around the corner smiling, wearing a white shirt, red tie, and black pants. His greeting lively and energetic. His part well-rehearsed, and he was ready to entertain and regale us with stories of the past.

As we rode around the city, the guide told us stories about many of the historic homes and places we passed. He even told tales about some that were haunted. I shivered, remembering the old man with crystal blue eyes, and scooted closer to Ben.

The last stop was The Christ Episcopal Church. We climbed out of the trolley and stood under large overhanging trees with draping Spanish moss, staring up at the magnificent brick structure. The church was built in a Gothic Revival style with enormous stained-glass windows. Ben and I walked together inside and gazed at the stunning interior of the church. We lingered long after the rest of tourists had exited.

There was something surreal but safe about being in here. A comfort I couldn't explain.

After the tour was over, we grabbed a quick lunch at a little café that overlooked the Neuse River specializing in French cuisine. We sat outside on the deck, inhaling the smell of gardenias. Soft French music played from the outside speakers. Soothing us as we ate a lunch of chicken Provencal with white wine. We made small talk as the river moved below us, dark and silent.

I always marveled at the power of rivers. Above the surface, the water so calm and serene, and below, in the depths, the current was pulling and ripping at anything in its path.

Once we were finished, we headed back to the car and drove to the marina in Beaufort.

I got out of the car and stretched my legs, looking over at all the boats that were docked in the large marina. Sea gulls called out as the boats bobbed up and down in the water. I watched as the tourists bustled back and forth. Some leaving, some arriving. As I looked at the flow of people moving, I saw a man that looked like Lewis, with a long-legged brunette on his arm, walking toward the docks. Ben was locking the car and I yanked on his shirt.

"I think I just saw my sister's husband down by the boats. He was with some woman!" I exclaimed.

"Don't be ridiculous! I am sure that wasn't Lewis," he answered.

I could still see the top of the man's head as we headed down to the docks, but soon lost sight of him.

"Stop worrying about it!" Ben said, sternly. "Why would Lewis be all the way down here with some other woman?"

I shrugged and reluctantly agreed. Ben was right. Anyway, Lewis was so wrapped up in Mandi, it was impossible that he would stray.

Ben took my hand as we walked the rest of the way down to the docks where the boat was waiting for us. We chose a seat near the back, and Ben put his arm around me as the boat glided out onto the water.

We took in a lush landscape of flowering Crepe Myrtles and wild growing Mimosa Trees bordering the open waters. Birds flew just above the water line, and herons with long legs and long beaks hunted in the low-lying water areas. Along the way, we passed by Shackleford Banks and saw wild horses grazing on sea grasses. They stood majestic as the wind blew through their manes and tails, completely oblivious to our presence there.

We finally hit the edge of the open water and I stood up, looking over the railing at Onslow Bay. Ben stood up behind me, and I leaned into his strong frame. The sea breeze whipped my hair as I inhaled the salty mist. The sun shone down on the water, giving it the sparkle of millions of diamonds. Sea gulls cried overhead in the crystal blue sky as water splashed against the side of the boat. We bounced gracefully over the waves as dolphins came and swam along beside us, jumping in and out of the wake.

The captain told us tales of pirates and merchants that had once roamed in this very bay. Of sunken ships and tales of lost treasures.

He said that no one was allowed to jump in the water and check out his story.

Everyone laughed.

Once we got back into New Bern, we began looking for a place to have dinner. As we drove down the street, we saw Middle Street Oyster Bar & Grill. The sign weathered and old, but there was a crowd filing in. A sign of good food.

When we walked in, we immediately realized that we had made a good choice. The atmosphere was upbeat, and there was a live saxophonist playing in the corner.

The server sat us down at a table, right in the middle. The only table left in the full restaurant. Ben ordered a bottle of wine, and as the server walked away, I said, "Don't drink too much now…remember you owe me!" I gave him a serious look, trying not to laugh.

"Oh, don't you worry about that. I have not forgotten. Trust me…" With that, he gave me a sly smile.

When the server came back with our wine, we ordered a bucket of oysters with hushpuppies on the side. While we waited for our food, we sipped on the wine, enjoying the saxophonist's music as it whined soulfully across the restaurant.

Ben looked over at me and smiled. "Would you care to dance?"

I looked around nervously.

"Ben, this isn't a dancing place…"

He laughed and said, "Well, it is now."

He stood up, walked around the table, took my hand and led me into the main aisle that ran between the tables. He pulled me close as we began to sway back and forth with the flowing melody.

The entire restaurant grew quiet, all eyes were on us.

I didn't see them; it was just him and I, moving together with the music.

Ben whispered in my ear, "Claire, I don't know what you're going through because you won't talk to me, but I want you to know how much I love you, and I will be there on the other side when you come out of it. I would do anything for you. You are the reason for my every-thing. I just need you to know that."

I buried my face in his shoulder, fighting back tears.

When the song was over, everyone clapped and cheered.

After we sat back down, the server came over with two glasses of champagne. Apparently sent over from a secret admirer, who had been moved by our dance.

I looked over at my husband. "I love you too, Ben, more than you know."

His hand came across the table and grasped mine.

"I know you do…"

When we walked into the inn, it was quiet. Not much seemed to be happening on a Sunday night.

As soon as we got back to the room, I went into the bathroom to freshen up.

When I came out, Ben was sitting in one of the chairs across the room. He motioned for me to come to him.

I walked over, knowing exactly what was on his mind.

It was on my mind too.

Twenty-four hours of foreplay had reached its peak. I stood in front of him as he leaned forward, running his hand up my inner thigh and under the skirt of my dress. I stepped back from him and slowly undressed. He watched, his eyes filled with lust, as I slipped off the dress and my panties.

I stood in front of him, completely naked, and for just a moment, he didn't move, taking the moment in. With swift movements, he stood up, slipped off his clothes and sat back down in the chair. I moved toward him again. He ran his hands over my butt and pulled me closer still. I climbed onto the chair, straddling him. He slipped himself inside of me and I groaned, feeling the fullness of him inside of me. Tilting my head back with pleasure as he tickled my nipples with his tongue. We moved together slowly in unison, not breaking our locked eyes. I began to move faster on top of him, and he moaned with pleasure. I grabbed onto the back of the chair to steady myself. He ran his tongue up and down my neck, sending jolts of electricity through my body. He grabbed my butt and moved my hips back and forth on top of him faster and faster, until I could no longer hold back. My body exploded in ecstasy, and I cried out so loudly, I was sure the neighboring room heard me. When it was over, I collapsed on him, and he lovingly caressed my back with his hands.

I was overcome with love for this man.

He was my heart, living outside of my body.

He was everything to me.

Without warning, my emotions escalated. The dream, invading the moment.

My sensibility faltering.

Fighting against fear as it steamrolled me.

It was too much, more than I could bear.

My thoughts, unhinged, as I fell into a restless sleep.

CHAPTER 16

─⌒⊙⌒○─

The days after we returned from New Bern were a roller coaster.

My emotions completely out of balance.

Negative thoughts prevailing.

My imagination filled with endless suffering. My days, endless anxiety.

I knew Ben was worried. I saw the pained way in which he looked at me.

Who was I becoming?

I was a stranger even to myself.

I started marking the days off the wall calendar with big red X's as June 3rd rapidly approached. In some way, I thought the act of marking off the days, one by one, would somehow prepare me for what was coming. But in reality, it was only making me feel more helpless.

The morning of my art class came and I was tempted to skip it, but the thought of sitting at home another day thinking solely about the dream stirred me to the point of getting up and moving. I got in the shower and washed my hair. When I got out, I wiped the steam from the mirror, seeing my face for the first time in a week. I was shocked at what I saw. I looked like I had aged ten years. Dark circles and bags had taken residence under both of my eyes. My lips dry and cracked from repeatedly biting on them. I put moisturizer on my face and lips, but it didn't help much.

I went to the dresser, staring off into space for several minutes before I began searching for something to wear. I dug through the drawer and found one of Ben's old t-shirts. Blue with yellow lettering that read Rowing Team across the front. I didn't think he'd ever rowed in his life, but it was one of his favorites. Soft and broken in from years of wear. I put it on for a sense of comfort, along with a pair of grey running shorts.

I threw my hair into a ponytail and looked in the mirror.

I definitely wouldn't be winning any beauty contests today.

It was a clear day, but clouds were gathering on the horizon as I drove to class. I parked in my usual parking space and walked into the studio a few minutes early.

Mr. Thompson was already in his seat. He was wearing a blue leisure suit that I am sure he must have worn in the seventies. His hair was combed and he was humming to himself.

"Good Mornin' there Missy!" he greeted me with a broad smile.

I wondered why he was in such a good mood.

"Hi there, Mr. Thompson…." I offered back, reluctantly, not feeling like conversation.

"Yes, indeed, it is a good morning…" he added.

Was he talking to me or himself? I wasn't sure.

I set up my brushes, one by one, along the side of the easel to pass the time until class started.

I could feel Mr. Thompson's eyes on me, and I knew he wanted to talk.

My guilt over ignoring him won out and I looked up, giving him a forced smile.

"How are things going for you?" I asked.

"Oh, well they are just great. I've made me a lady friend. Her name is Sophia and let me tell you, she is a looker. She might be in her seventies, but you wouldn't know it. She doesn't look a day over sixty. And boy, does she know how to cook. I haven't eaten this good since the last time my Lola fixed a meal, right before she got real sick." His voice trailed off a little.

"I'm happy you've made a friend. I am sure Lola would be pleased. I don't think she'd want you to spend the rest of your life alone... Would she?"

He looked up at me with grateful eyes. "You know what, young lady? I needed to hear that. You're alright, you know it?"

I nodded back, glad to have helped.

Then my mind started to spin.

There were questions I wanted to ask him.

I wanted to talk to him about what it was like knowing Lola was going to die, but at the same time, I didn't want to push him. Especially when he seemed so happy now.

But it still came out of my mouth. Word vomit at its finest.

"What was it like for you when you knew she was going to die?" I stuttered, wishing I could shove the words back inside.

He paused and looked out the window across the room, lost in thought.

When he answered, he looked directly in my eyes.

"It was scary, confusing, and painful knowing I couldn't save her. I was filled with regrets from our years together. I wished I had made more of the time we had. But mostly, I felt cheated. Like, life was stealing my most precious gift right out from under me, and I was helpless to stop it. As her days grew shorter, I did the only thing that I could do, and that was to be with her. I spent my time right up until the moment she passed loving her. Making sure she knew how much she meant to me. I wouldn't trade one moment of those last days with her for anything. Well, except being able to get her back, that is..." he trailed off, his eyes misty.

I reached out and touched his arm.

"Thank you for sharing that with me..." I could feel the tears forming in my own eyes.

"Yeah...I sure would give anything to have her back, but I will tell you, this new girl, she has given me back my smile and put a little pep back into my step..."

"She sounds wonderful. She's one lucky lady to have you, Mr. Thompson." I smiled, gently.

With that, he started humming again, a tune I didn't recognize. As his words rolled around like thunder in my head.

After class was over, I stopped by the coffee shop. I was in dire need of some caffeine. I ordered my usual vanilla latte and waited, watching the television in the corner of the room as it broadcasted the local channel.

My eyes were glued to the television when the barista came up with my latte in hand.

I stared at a face that appeared on the screen. One that seemed familiar to me.

I turned and walked away from the counter without looking back. The barista stood holding my drink in the air, her face poised with confusion.

I was helplessly being pulled toward the TV.

Toward the man speaking. I needed to see him better.

And as I got closer, certainty washed over me.

I knew that face.

A face I would never forget.

The face of Detective Anderson.

He was giving a news flash interview about an attempted bank robbery downtown that had happened earlier in the morning.

As he spoke, a cold chill went down my spine.

I had heard that voice before.

The voice from my dream.

The voice that told me that my husband was dead.

I ran straight out of the coffee shop, never stopping to get my latte. The door slammed behind me as I ran through the parking lot. Tears streaming down my face.

He was real. I didn't imagine him after all.

Detective Anderson was a living, breathing person. But, how could I have known him? How could I dream of someone I've never met?

All at once, a rush of despair threatened to swallow me up

It all had to be true. Every bit of the dream had to be true. How else could any of this be happening?

Later that day, I sat outside the boys' school. My tears dried up.

Numb.

A flood of weariness rushing over me like a flowing river.

The clouds that had threatened to gather earlier this morning had moved out and given way to the afternoon sun. As the boys climbed in the car, I told them the news. I had decided to take them to the park on the way home from school. Truth being, I couldn't face going home right then. Not to mention, it had been months since I had taken them to the park, and I was way overdue.

We arrived at the park to see it was already bursting with activity. The happy shouts of children rose above the squeak of the swings in motion. Beyond the playground sat baseball fields filled with Little Leaguers running around the bases as their teammates cheered them on. Soon, Grayson would be one of them. He had been asking Ben to sign up for months, and Ben had finally conceded.

Would Ben be here to take him?

The boys ran across perfectly manicured grass and onto the sandy substrate of the playground. Oliver climbed the rock wall, and once at the top, yelled for Grayson to follow. When Grayson didn't come, Oliver slid down the slide, his bangs blowing in the wind. He smiled, pleased with himself, repeating the pattern again and again. Up the rock wall, down the slide. Yelling for Grayson each time he mounted the top of the rock wall.

Grayson ignored his brother. He was busy playing chase with a group of boys his age. He ran, cheeks flushed with the determination to win. A look I often saw on his father's face.

Soon, Oliver grew tired of his trek and turned his attention to a puddle near where I was sitting. He crouched down at the puddle, poking the water with a stick.

"Look, Momma, I'm fishing!" he exclaimed, bent over the tiny body of water poking his stick in and out, stirring up clouds of mud. I watched him, so serious and absorbed in his task. I looked as the sunlight glimmered in his dark hair, thankful for his still vivid imagination.

Soon, he ran off again to try out the swings.

I rested in the warm sunlight, watching him play.

The air was filled with the sights and sounds of spring in motion. Bees buzzed around freshly bloomed azaleas as the park continued to fill with children just released from school.

I watched the crowd filtering in from the parking lot and suddenly saw a face that I recognized. It was Mr. Thompson, now wearing a button up shirt and shorts. He was walking toward me, with a woman on one side and a little girl on the other, and a broad smile on his face.

"Fancy meeting you here!" he exclaimed.

I smiled in return.

"This here, is the beautiful lady I was telling you about, and my vivacious, granddaughter, Lauren." His face beamed with pride.

"Nice to meet both of you!" I said, holding my hand out to Lauren. She stepped back behind Mr. Thompson.

"Oh, don't mind her, she's a little shy," he told me. "Run along and play, Lauren. There's lots of kids your age here!" he whispered in her ear. She turned and ran straight to the rock wall and began climbing, taking the same journey Oliver had taken earlier.

I looked at over at Sophia, who had not taken her eyes off of Mr. Thompson. She was definitely in love.

He had been right when he said that Sophia looked younger than her age. I would've never guessed her to be in her seventies. Her honey blonde hair was long and her figure petite. She was wearing white cropped pants with a vibrant blue top and gold sandals with painted toes to match her shirt. She looked at me and smiled, her eyes sparkling. I could see why Mr. Thompson was so crazy about her.

"I'm Claire," I said, holding out my hand to her. She shook it gingerly.

Lauren's voiced echoed out across the playground. She called to her grandfather for help. Her shoelaces had come untied.

As he went to her aide, Sophia and I got caught up in a burst of conversation.

I was surprised when she told me she was widow.

"My husband died of pancreatic cancer. Two years ago, now. It happened so fast, that I barely had time to prepare. Hit me hard," she said as she looked back at Mr. Thompson tying Lauren's shoes.

She looked back at me. "I spent the first year after he was gone in the house not wanting to go anywhere. Not even the grocery store. Got all my groceries delivered. As time went on, I realized that I was wasting away. My husband would've not wanted me to live this way. So, I signed up for a wood burning class. I wanted to do something that was mine and mine alone. Something that didn't relate to my husband. And that's where I met Harry."

Harry? Mr. Thompson's first name. I never knew. Apparently, acrylic painting wasn't the only class he was taking at the Arts Center.

I looked over at the playground. Mr. Thompson was headed back this way, and Oliver was now playing with Lauren. They were racing up the rock wall and down the slide. Grayson was on the swings with the same group of boys from earlier. His head tipped back to the sky, a smile on his face, as he swung through the air. He was growing up so fast. Too fast.

I looked back at Sophia, who was still talking.

"At first, we were just friendly in class. Nothing more. But I always thought he was funny and so handsome. When we both signed up for part two of the wood burning class, I decided to ask him out. I thought, what the hell? Why not? I knew I had to get on with living or get on with dying, so I chose the former. We had coffee on our first date and have barely been separated since." Her eyes sparkled with the glow of a teenager. It warmed my heart that she was able to find love again after such a loss.

And Mr. Thompson, too.

The beauty of second chances.

He came up and put his arms around her, kissing the top of her head as she giggled.

"And the rest is history," she said, looking up at him.

After dinner, Ben took the boys outside to toss the football around, and I disappeared upstairs. I sat against our bedroom wall with my knees pulled to my chest, rocking back and forth, crying. With the realization that the dream was in fact coming true, all the walls I had barely held up were coming down around me.

Seeing Mr. Thompson and Sophia together had warmed my heart, but mostly it made me feel worse. I didn't want that for my life. I didn't want to have hope for a new love. Or for a new life. I wanted Ben.

And I didn't know how I was going to survive without him.

Heartache and distress filtered through me again and again.

And I was tired.

I was tired of being scared all the time. Tired of feeling so helpless.

Weariness and fear were tearing me apart, bit by bit.

I listened as voices and laughter floated in through the open window.

Numbly, I got up and walked over to the window, gazing out over the yard just as Oliver caught a football for the very first time.

Oliver's face lit up like sunshine as Ben and Grayson ran over and gave him a high-five.

And I had almost missed it...

All at once, it came into focus, what Mr. Thompson had told me about the last days with his wife.

The realization washed over me like a tidal wave.

Ben was alive and well in the backyard. He wasn't gone, he was here now and I was missing out on life with him and the boys. All I had was the present moment. Today, right now, was mine. I had been so consumed with death, that I had completely forgotten about life.

I ran downstairs as fast as I could and out the back door to where my guys were waiting.

When I stepped outside, Oliver and Grayson spotted me and instantly cheered.

Ben looked up at me and smiled.

I smiled back as he tossed me the football.

CHAPTER 17

Unfortunately, my newfound appreciation for life only existed when Ben was home.

And my days had taken on a new ritual. Each morning after dropping the boys off at school, I would come home, drink my coffee, and just sit.

Sometimes on the porch. Sometimes in the kitchen.

Staring at nothing. Depleted of emotion.

The house quickly fell into chaos. Laundry and dishes backed up. Sweeping undone.

With June 3rd so close now, housework seemed unimportant.

I was simply existing. Floating through my days in a mental coma.

But when Ben came home, I would come to life again.

Momentarily.

Relishing in my time with him. As the days quickly faded away.

This morning, I stood in the kitchen, gazing out the window as leaves rustled on trees, and the sunshine played peek-a-boo with the clouds. Suddenly, a cardinal landed on a nearby branch, its red coloring contrasting to the green. Startling me to alertness.

My coffee had grown cold while I stood there.

Time disappeared when I was lost in moments like this.

The world consisting of only me and nothingness.

Just like my mother.

I remembered one particular morning, when I was in middle school. She hadn't been out of bed in three days. I came down the stairs for school and she was up, coffee in hand, sitting at the kitchen table.

Looking but not seeing.

"Hi, Mom," I offered.

She didn't answer, so I went about making my breakfast.

I sat at the table with her and ate my cereal. The silence deafening.

Looking at her.

Watching for signs of life.

Eyes glazed over, sipping, breathing.

After I finished eating, I put my bowl in the sink and just as I left the kitchen, she called out, "Have a good day, Claire."

I turned, rushed back in, and kissed her cheek.

Her face unchanging.

Had she spoken? Did I imagine it?

I couldn't understand her back then.

My mother, lost in a world of despair.

But now, I did.

The loss of hope. The disappointment.

I set my coffee cup down.

I should call her.

I picked up the phone and dialed her number.

The phone rang six times before she answered. And when she did, she sounded out of breath.

"Mom? Are you okay?" I asked nervously.

"I'm fine," she laughed.

"Is something going on?" I pressed, not convinced.

"Nothing! Why would you ask me that?" she retorted.

"You sounded winded, that's all," I offered, not wanting to push her too much.

"Good lord Claire, I'm fine. Don't you have enough going on there than to be concerning yourself with whether I sound winded or not?" Her tone, hostile.

She had been softer in her later years, so this sharpness stunned me. *Maybe she was mad that I haven't been calling her much lately?*

I could hear something in the background but couldn't make it out. She covered the mouthpiece and mumbled something I couldn't understand. Soon after, she came back on the phone. "Claire, I'm kinda busy right now. How about we chat later?"

She never has anyone over at her house!

"Mom, who's there with you?" The sound of my voice came out high-pitched with mounting concern.

"Young lady, stop asking me so many questions! I am a fifty-eight-year-old woman, and I think I can take care of myself! Have a good day, dear."

Without a goodbye, she hung up.

I stood there, my thoughts swirling. Offended... and worried.

The phone was still to my ear when it began ringing. Assuming it was Mom calling back, I answered immediately.

It was Mandi.

I groaned silently, wishing I had checked the caller ID before answering.

I was in no mood for Mandi. I had enough on my plate to deal with.

"Hey there!" she exclaimed enthusiastically. I pulled the phone back from my ear.

She was in a great mood and apparently had amnesia about our last interaction.

"So, have you talked to Mom lately? She's acting kinda weird, if you ask me," she spouted.

"I just got off the phone with her, actually, and I couldn't agree more. She was talking to someone in the background. Does she have a boyfriend?"

Mandi laughed loudly. "Hell, I highly doubt it. That woman is as frigid as the arctic."

I knew she was right. Mom had not shown interest toward any men since Dad left her. It was as if she held every single man on the planet responsible for what he did. And Dad was forever guilty; there was no forgiveness to be had.

"You talked to Dad?" Mandi asked, as if she could read my mind.

"No, I usually am so busy when he calls, I don't have time to talk," I lied.

"Yeah, right!" Mandi scoffed. "God! Why can't you just let the past go, Claire?"

I was instantly irritated by her self-righteous tone.

"Mom says that you've been acting weird lately. What's going on with you?" I asked, quick to change the subject.

"Oh Lordy, I'm fine. She's just a worrier, that's all." She laughed. "So, I'm going to be in the Arts District around lunchtime. Feel like some company?"

I could hear the pleading in her voice, and instantly a tug-of-war began in my mind.

Every cell inside of me wanted to say no, but the expectancy in her voice broke down my will, and the word yes spilled out of my mouth.

I immediately wondered why I did things like this to myself.

Seeing Mandi was the last thing that I wanted to do right now.

After we hung up, I took one look around and began to panic. The unkemptness of the house, glaringly obvious. And I didn't want to hear any comments from Mandi. Her house was always in pristine order. Not only did she not have any children to leave a trail of toys everywhere they went, she also had a maid who came in three times a week.

What did that maid do with her time?

Dusted the lightbulbs? Shined the door handles?

I mean, the house was already clean when she got there.

I had often imagined what it was like to live Mandi's life. Everything about her was so perfect. Her life, like a dream. She had a charmed life. She and Lewis owned a mansion on Providence Road. The house was so big that she didn't even use half of the rooms, keeping most of them closed up.

She drove a black Jaguar, wore a Rolex on her pencil thin wrist, ate at the finest restaurants, and shopped at the best boutiques. She was wealthy, beautiful, and vibrant.

Had she ever had a bad day in her whole life?

If she did, she never told me about it.

Envy rose up like a wildfire, burning my insides.

Yes, I was jealous. But deep down inside, I didn't really want her life. I had always been happy with Ben and the life we had together.

Ben, this house, our boys…it was my dream come true.

I didn't know why I let Mandi get under my skin. But she always had. As far back as I could remember.

Maybe Ben was right. I should just let her behavior go.

Give up on trying to figure out who's at fault in all this.

But mostly, I wanted to stop living my life in her shadow.

Despite my resolve, it still irked me that everything was so perfect for her.

And now look what I was going through.

My life was unraveling in front of me, and there was nothing I could do to stop it.

Mandi arrived at close to one o'clock with a bag of pastries from Des Floure, a French bakery in downtown. I had just finished cleaning the house when the doorbell rang.

She waltzed in the door smelling of Dior and looking as fabulous as ever.

Did she ever age?

As soon as she stepped inside, she kissed my cheek and shoved the bag of treats into my hands.

"Save some for the boys," she said as she eyeballed my waistline.

"Lord, Mandi! I might not be as skinny as you, but I'm perfectly fine the size I am. Why do you always have to make me feel like a beached whale?"

She gasped. "Claire, I didn't say a word about your weight! Your body is cute!"

I noticed how she accentuated the word *cute*. That was just like her to turn something around that was meant as a put down and turn it into a passive-aggressive, pseudo compliment.

I could feel my cheeks burning as I followed her into the kitchen. "Can I get you something to drink?"

"Do you have espresso?" she asked as she took a seat at one of the counter barstools.

Do I look like a coffee shop?

"No, just regular old coffee…you know the kind that gets served in ceramic mugs?" The sarcasm slipping out.

"God, what's with you today, Claire? You're being snappy."

I took a deep breath. *She was right.*

"I'm sorry. I've just been a little stressed out lately," I said as I warmed the leftover coffee in the pot.

Her mouth dropped open in shock. I wasn't certain if it was my apology or my stress that surprised her.

"What could you possibly have to be stressed out about? You have the perfect life, for god sake!" She averted looking in my eyes as she turned her barstool and looked out toward the foyer.

"I have the perfect life?" I asked, not sure if I had heard her right.

She turned back around and looked at me. "God, yes. You have the life every woman dreams of. You have Ben, who is absolutely in love with you, and you have those beautiful boys. I will admit that sometimes I'm a little jealous."

I was stunned.

Jealous of me? Mandi? I knew she was competitive, but never jealous. It seemed impossible to me.

Before I could speak, she quickly changed the subject. "So, what's going on with you that's got you so stressed out?"

I poured us both a cup of coffee and then came and sat down on the stool next to her.

She waited patiently for me to speak while her red lipstick made prints on the coffee cup that she was sipping from.

I turned my body around, so I was directly facing her.

"Ben's going to die..." A sob caught in my throat.

"Oh my God, what!? What's wrong with him? Does he have cancer? This is just terrible!" she exclaimed.

"No...he doesn't have cancer..." I answered quietly. Wondering if starting this conversation with her was actually a good idea. She was already getting into hysterics.

"Well then, what's wrong with him!?" Her eyes on mine as she reached over with long maroon colored nails and patted my arm in a frail attempt to comfort me.

"He's going to die in an accident on June 3rd." My voice cracked as I said it.

Her face was blank and she blinked rapidly, looking at me, trying to figure out what I meant.

"What the hell are you talking about? You're scaring me, Claire..." Her eyes were wide with fear.

"I had a dream. I think it was like a premonition or something," I responded.

Suddenly she began to laugh. "Oh my god, Claire. You terrified me! Lord, I thought something was really wrong for a minute!"

"Something IS WRONG!" I shouted.

"Stop being so dramatic! It's not becoming! It was just a damn dream. Get over it!" she yelled back.

I stood up too quickly, and the barstool that I had been sitting on turned over and landed with a loud thud on the floor.

"How dare you talk to me that way, Mandi! I have had enough of it! You think you are the most perfect thing that ever walked on the face of this planet, and the rest of us should just fall in line behind you. Well, I'm DONE with falling in line behind you!" I shrieked.

"What the hell are you talking about?" she bellowed. "I have NEVER thought I was perfect! My life is FAR from perfect! God! You always do this. Little miss innocent Claire, sitting in the corner. Poor Claire! You always want people to feel sorry for you! And I always have, but I'm done with it now! You have no reason to be falling apart! Because of some dream? Why don't you try living my life for a while? Let's see how perfect you think I am then!"

"God, Mandi! Oh yes, it's such a hardship to be a rich housewife! Go where you want, buy what you want, do what you want, whenever you want! Poor POOR MANDI!" My voice echoed out into the foyer.

When the echo faded, it was quiet, and I instantly regretted yelling.

When I looked back at her, I was stunned to see her face red and her eyes filling with tears.

"You just don't get it, do you?" she choked out. Tears now streaming down her face, making troughs in her perfect makeup.

I walked to bathroom to get her some tissues.

When I came back into the kitchen, she was sobbing.

I held the tissue out to her, and she took it and blew her nose. Beige foundation and mascara smeared carelessly all over it, reminding me of Amanda's painting rag at art class.

"Claire, my life is far from perfect," she hiccupped.

I felt awful for starting this and I didn't know what to do.

I had never seen her this way.

The last time I saw her cry was when she was fifteen, and she was throwing a fit to go on a beach trip with her friends and Mom had said no.

I said the only thing I could think of, "You have Lewis and he adores you..."

"You think Lewis and I are in love? God, you are more naïve than I ever thought! I didn't marry him for love, Claire! I married him for security. For money. I saw what Dad did to Mom, and I didn't want to put my heart on the line. Take a chance of getting hurt, like she did. I just wanted someone rich to take care of me." She blew her nose again.

"But he seems to love you so much..." I offered.

She laughed, sudden resentment appearing in her eyes. "He loves the way I look, Claire. I'm his showpiece. Nothing more."

"I find that hard to believe," I offered.

"Well, believe it. He's actually having an affair. I thought my looks were enough to keep that old man faithful, but hell no, he still went off and found somebody else. And...and she's not even that pretty!" She began to sob again.

Oh my god, it was him in Beaufort! The image of him so clearly coming back to me.

I was stunned and had no idea what I could say to comfort her. And I couldn't bring myself to tell her that I had seen him weeks ago with that brunette.

I walked over and wrapped my arms around her shoulders while she cried. Her body curled around itself as I held her close.

When she had finally spent all of her tears, she blew her nose again and looked at me.

"Claire, you don't know how much I look up to you...I always have. Even when we were little girls. You are the most amazing person that I know. You're such a generous and kind person. A great mom and wife. You know, I would kill to have your life. I wanted to have children, you know...I tried and I couldn't get pregnant. We even went to a fertility specialist. Come to find out, all the money in the world can't make you get pregnant."

A deep sense of sadness came over me.

I had no idea.

"I'm so sorry, Mandi. I wish you would've come to me, so I could've been there for you. You made it seem like you didn't want children…"

"That was my coverup. So, no one would know how much I was hurting. We spent tens of thousands of dollars on Invitro fertilization, and every time I took a pregnancy test, it was negative. All those hormones they injected me with nearly made me crazy. And God, talk about feeling like a failure. Try living with the fact that you can't do something that every other woman on this planet can do. I can't make a baby. I have always felt insecure around you, and this made it worse. I have never felt good enough. That I could measure up to you. I have lived my entire life in your shadow. Wishing I could be just an inkling like you. Everything you do is perfect. And everything I do…well, is not. It's no excuse and I know it's wrong, and I'm sorry that I am that way… but that's why I flirt with Ben so much. Because I thought maybe, if he wanted me, that would make me worthwhile too, but I'm not going to flirt with him anymore, I promise. I know that Ben isn't the answer, and I know Lewis isn't the answer either. No man is. I just have to figure out how to do me and stop hurting others in the process."

She paused and blew her nose. "And just so you know…I'm leaving Lewis…I can't stand by any longer and be his second fiddle. God, that's so humiliating! I know the women at the country club have already heard the rumors. I can't even show my face there." She laughed, but I knew it was masking deep pain.

"What are you going to do?" I asked, not knowing what else to say.

"Oh, don't worry. I will be okay. I leased a loft apartment downtown today. Not far from here, in fact. On the bright side, this will give me more time to be a better aunt to the boys." She smiled softly. "Lewis doesn't know it yet, but I will be out by the end of the week." I could see a glimmer of pride in that statement.

I stood the overturned bar stool back up and sat down on it. I was stunned. I never expected anything like this. I had been misguided by my own insecurities.

I looked at Mandi as she pulled a mirror out of her purse.

"God, what have I done to my face?!" She took her bag and went into the bathroom. When she reappeared, all evidence of her breakdown was gone and her makeup was back in place.

She took her coffee cup to the sink and dumped it. I didn't think she had taken more than a couple of sips. Not her usual European brew.

She walked over to where I was sitting. "Look, whatever is going on with that dream of yours. Let it go. Don't let it have power over your life."

"But some parts of the dream have been coming true. Mandi, I'm terrified all the time. So much so that I can't even live a normal life," I whispered.

"Talk to Ben about it. Tell him your fears. Hell, keep him home for a few days. Can't he take some time off for vacation or something? June 3rd isn't that far away."

"Honestly, I don't think I can tell him. You know how he is about anything spiritual. He will never listen to me..." I trailed off.

"Trust in your husband, Claire. He really does love you. You guys can work through this." Her voice soothing.

I knew she meant well, so I didn't contradict her. But I knew Ben better than that. He would never buy into a premonition type dream. And I also knew he wouldn't be willing to take vacation time, right now. He had just reeled in a big client and wouldn't be able to just disappear. He would never agree to it.

I walked Mandi to the door and hugged her tightly. "Let me know if you need anything. I am your sister, you know? Let me help." I meant every word.

She nodded, but I knew she wouldn't take me up on the offer.

We still had a long way to go yet, but we had at least made a step in the right direction.

As her Jaguar disappeared down the road, I closed the door.

CHAPTER 18

M A Y 2 9 T H

The Saturday morning sunshine fell softly through partially open blinds. I pulled back the covers and stretched. I could hear that Ben was downstairs in the kitchen with the boys.

He was making pancakes, of that I was sure. Another of his specialties. Chocolate chip pancakes with whipped cream.

I slipped down the stairs and peeked around the corner so I could watch them.

The sound of the boys' laughter filled the downstairs as he flipped pancakes in the air. They were sitting on stools, pulled up next to the stove where Ben was cooking. Still in pajamas and the hair on the back of their heads matted and messy from sleep.

As Ben flipped one of the pancakes high in the air, he saw me and missed it when it came back down, landing on the floor with a thud as the boys roared with laughter.

"Well, hi there! Care to join us?" he offered.

With that, the boys turned around and saw me too. Oliver climbed down from his stool, ran over and wrapped his arms around my legs, squeezing me with all of his might. I squatted down to get a real hug. I walked over and kissed Grayson on the top of the head as Ben picked up the fallen pancake from the floor, tossing it into the trash. He came over and took me in his arms, kissing me deeply.

While still in our embrace, the boys starting screaming as smoke plumed off the frying pan.

"Four more pancakes lost in battle!" Ben yelled as the smoke detector blared.

After breakfast, Ben left to take the boys to the batting cages. Since Grayson would be joining Little League soon, Ben wanted him to start learning how to hit a baseball.

After they left, I cleaned up the breakfast dishes and the table. Another casualty, covered in syrup and grease.

After I finished cleaning, I threw the dirty dishrag onto to the edge of the sink basin and sighed.

This morning had been perfect. I had been able to enjoy every moment.

Not thinking about the dream.

Listening to chatter of Ben and the boys, not minding the sticky mess as they fully embraced life. Pancakes and all.

But now that it was quiet…and I was alone. Despair came knocking on my door again.

I went upstairs to dress for the day, trying to pretend like June 3rd wasn't four days away. But despair had its way with me. The countdown haunting me as I brushed my teeth.

The one thing that gave me pause. The one thing that gave me hope. Was that Ben still didn't take the train.

How could the dream have that part completely wrong?

I was sure it didn't.

If I could just make him promise to not take the train anywhere on June 3rd, then everything would be okay!

Could it be that easy?

He'd have no reason to take the train, anyway. So why not?

Suddenly, I heard a loud bang coming from outside. I ran over and looked out the tiny bathroom window and saw what looked like a grey cat, rummaging through the trash. The lid had fallen onto the ground.

"Teddy!" I screamed as I ran down the stairs, flinging open the back door, calling out his name.

I rounded the corner, only to scare a stray cat as it hissed at me and darted away.

It wasn't Teddy.

Before I made it back inside, I heard another sound. This one, coming from the other side of the hedge.

My heartbeat instantly quickened.

The old man...

I listened as someone walked down the other side of hedge. I quietly followed along beside them, just out of sight. When we got to where the hedges ended, just before the sidewalk began, they turned and walked away to the middle of the yard.

Right afterwards, I heard hammering.

I jumped around the hedge, refusing to let him get away this time.

Only it wasn't the old man.

It was a middle-aged woman with chestnut brown hair pulled back into a ponytail, wearing a grey pants suit. She was hammering a sign in the front yard right next to the walkway leading to the house.

The sign read: Holloway Realty – FOR SALE.

When she saw me, she jumped.

Apparently, jumping out from behind the hedges like a maniac startles people.

"Good morning," she nervously offered.

I walked in closer, looking at the sign.

"The house is being put up for sale?" I questioned.

She nodded her head. "Yes! Finally! The owner, Ed, died years ago, and his brother refused to let it go. Felt like he was betraying him or something. Finally decided it was time. So here I am," she said as she continued her hammering.

"No one lives here?" I stepped closer.

"No. No one has for a very long time. I'm an old family friend and a realtor. They asked me to put it up for sale. I thought I better get over here and at least put the sign in the yard before they changed their minds." She laughed to herself.

"I live right next door, and I could've sworn that someone lived here." I waited for her response, studying her face carefully.

"No, definitely not. The last guy that lived here died ten years ago. I guess you never heard about the scandal then?"

I stepped a half a step backward, not sure if I wanted to be in on the neighborhood gossip.

Her voice lowered to a whisper and her eyes glimmered as she spoke. "Well, it turns out that that Ed was an old sly dog. He was having an affair with the lady across the street, both still married, no less! Mrs. Parks, I believe her name was…is, actually. I think she still lives over there. They used to meet at midnight when everyone else was asleep and well ummm…you know…in his car parked right here in this drive-way. Can you believe that? They would've gotten away with it, for god knows how long, but somebody saw them one night getting out of the car. Well, the rest was history. Split both marriages up. The crazy thing is that they never spoke after that. At least, not that any of us knew. I mean, I was a kid back then. It's incredible. That affair went on for five years before they were found out. Then they were single and living right across the street from each other…and never spoke again. So strange, isn't it?"

I stood looking at her. I didn't know what to say. It was strange…but not as strange as seeing that man here.

"You want to see the inside the house?" she offered. "That way you know what it looks like. In case you know anyone that wants to be your neighbor."

I followed her up onto the steps past vibrant yellow daffodils swaying in the breeze. Flowers that were planted years ago, giving return on investment, year after year.

She led me into the white bungalow with green shutters. We walked through the front door with frosted glass panes and into a small foyer. We passed the living room as she rushed us from room to room, as if she were on a game show version of "show this house." The floor underneath us creaked with every step. The threadbare carpet under our feet was badly in need of replacing. Dust filtered off of the large windows with olive green drapery, drifting down through strips of sunlight like snowflakes. In the kitchen, fluorescent lighting poured across ugly linoleum and outdated appliances.

She led me through the three bedrooms in a flash and into the single bathroom that was wall to wall green tile. The faucet dripped in the sink with a large rust stain underneath it.

There was an emptiness in the air. A loneliness reflected back, by empty closets and plain walls.

We ended back up in the living room again. The furniture, covered in protective plastic. There was an ornate mantle around the fireplace, and I could see that it had several framed pictures sitting on it. I walked toward them, out of compulsion.

I had to see.

As I got closer, I could see that they were family photos. There was one of a group of kids sitting on this very porch. One of a blonde-haired lady with a bouffant hairdo and a pretty smile.

I spotted a wedding picture and stepped closer. It looked to be from the fifties or early sixties. I couldn't tell.

The realtor came up behind me. "That's Ed and his former wife. The one he cheated on. He must've felt pretty guilty to leave this picture up all this time. Don't you think?"

I could see right away that the bride was the girl in the picture, with the pretty smile.

And the groom, he had the most distinct crystal blue eyes.

The same crystal blue eyes I had seen that day on the other side of the hedge.

I looked back at the realtor for a just a moment and then ran out the front door without looking back.

She called out behind me, "Hey! You want to take some of my business cards?"

I didn't answer her. I just ran as fast as I could back to my house and slammed the door shut behind me. My head spinning. Thoughts racing.

My suspicions had been right. It was Ed that I saw that day.

I had no explanation for it, but I knew that it was him.

Who else could it have been?

And those eyes…there was no mistaking those eyes. I'd know them anywhere.

I looked out the window and saw the sky had turned an ominous slate grey. And the wind began howling as the trees and bushes swayed hard to the right. A storm was headed this way.

Just as the sky opened up with rain, Ben and the boys pulled up. By the time they got inside, they were soaking wet. I met them at the door with towels.

"Man, it's really coming down out there!" Ben exclaimed.

The boys were laughing.

"Mom, can we go back out and play in the rain?" Grayson asked.

Before I could answer, lightning cracked right outside the window and was followed by a loud boom of thunder.

"I think that would be a no," I answered.

Ben chased them up the stairs to change clothes as they squealed with delight.

The storm grew stronger as I made the boys a lunch of grilled cheese sandwiches and tomato soup. I let them eat it in front of the television. By the time I came back into the living room, I found them both passed out on the couch. Worn out from their day. I turned the TV off.

The lighting in the house was darkened from the storm. Ben walked around the corner and smiled.

"Hi…" he said softly.

I smiled back and walked up to him. He put his arms around me and I snuggled into his chest.

"So, is my wife back? I sure missed her…" he said softly.

No sooner did the words come out his mouth, thunder shook the house, and another crack of lightning hit in the front yard, followed by a loud smashing sound.

We looked at each other, confusion in our eyes.

Ben ran to the front window to investigate.

"Shit!" he yelled as he turned and headed to the front door.

"What is it?" I said, as he swung the door open wide. He stood in the doorframe, looking out through the rain into the driveway.

A large branch from my beloved oak tree was lying on top of his car. The entire roof collapsed under the weight of the limb.

He shook his head in disbelief and looked at me. "Looks like I'll be taking the train for a while…"

My entire world swirled in flashes of white light.

I couldn't see. I couldn't think.

The next thing I remembered was waking up with Ben crouched over me.

"Claire, are you okay? Should I call 911?" His face, strained with panic.

I attempted to sit up but my head was still spinning, violently. Apparently, Ben had caught me in his arms just before I fell to the floor.

"I'm okay, now…" I said hoarsely as Ben helped me into the living room where the boys were, surprisingly, still asleep. They could sleep through anything. He seated me in the recliner before he disappeared. Reappearing a moment later with a glass of water.

"Are you sure you're okay?" He squinted, studying my face.

"Yes, I'm fine…" I lied. Well, I was okay physically but mentally…not so much. "Ben, you can't take the train," I stated bluntly.

He looked at me strangely. "What do you mean?"

"You just can't take the damn train, okay? Just take my Yukon instead."

"I'm not taking your car. You need that car to take the boys to and from school. You've got your art class, and not to mention, you have to have a vehicle here in case of an emergency." His voice, firm.

"No! I don't need the car! You need the car! God, Ben, please." Tears threatened to spill over.

"What the hell is going on, Claire? Dammit, this is getting old. You have been an emotional basket case for weeks on end, and you refuse to tell me what is going on. And now you don't want me to ride the train? I mean, what the hell?" His face strained with frustration.

"Please just trust me, Ben. Don't take the train…I'm begging you…" My voice thick with despair.

He paced back and forth across the floor.

"Look, Claire, I don't have a choice in this matter. I have to take the train. I have to go to work and I have to have a way to get there. I am not taking your car. You need it here. I mean, for crying out loud, we wouldn't even be in this situation if you had let me cut back those damned branches. I told you something like this would happen!" His voice echoing, causing the boys to stir.

My blood ran ice cold. Oh God…if I had let him cut them back…a sob escaped from me.

"I'm afraid, Ben. Please…"

Ben's face immediately softened. He came over and kneeled down next to me. "There's no reason to be afraid, Claire…" His tone was soft now. The heat of the argument, over.

After the surge of the storm passed, Ben called the insurance company and asked if they would cover a rental car, to appease my worry. Much to my dismay, the answer was a definitive no, and Ben refused to pay for one out of pocket. Saying it was a waste of money.

The rain was steady and soft as he called around looking for a tow truck to pick up his Honda out of the driveway. He had a lot of trouble finding someone to come out because of the holiday weekend. Finally, a guy showed up and together they pulled the limb off of the car.

As the man towed Ben's Honda away, the boys watched from the window in complete awe.

I went into the kitchen and opened a bottle of wine. I had finished nearly half of it by the time the tow truck had pulled away. I sipped from my wine glass, refilling it again and again.

Ben fed the boys dinner and got them in bed while I finished another glass.

By the time Ben came back, I was feeling drunk, sitting at the table. Staring off into space.

"You want me to fix you something to eat?" he offered.

I shook my head.

He sat down at table with me and I looked him in the eyes, covering his hand with mine. I half expected him to pull away, but he didn't.

We sat together like that for a while. Neither of us saying a word.

The kitchen light reflected off of the table where we sat as the rain continued to come down outside. Small traces of thunder could still be heard in the distance.

Finally, Ben broke the silence.

"What the hell is going on with you, Claire?" His voice, unsettled by frustration. His face, worn with exhaustion.

I could feel that same exhaustion on mine. I didn't want to fight with him anymore.

I just wanted everything to be okay again.

"I had a dream you were going to die." I couldn't bring myself to look at him when I said it.

"Ah, honey, it was just a dream..." he said, looking at me sympathetically.

I yanked my hand away from his.

"It wasn't just a dream, Ben. It was a warning!" I nearly shrieked.

He began shaking his head. I knew I was losing him.

"Things came to pass from this dream..." I pleaded.

"Like what?" His face, becoming agitated.

"I knew Teddy was going to run away!" My voice, shrill.

"Then, why the hell didn't you stop it?" His eyes were glazed with anger.

"I tried. I did! But the things that are happening from the dream… they're unstoppable. Nothing I do changes what is going to happen. It's like it's meant to be." Tears slid down my face even though I was trying to hold them back.

"That's a bunch of nonsense. I'm sorry that the dream shook you up. I really am. I hate to see you like this. But you're not going to get me to believe that a bad dream can predict the future. You just need to calm down. I am going to be just fine. Stop worrying about it. Seriously! What's going to kill me is the stress of worrying about you!" He laughed after he said that.

He just didn't understand. Just like I knew he wouldn't.

"Ben, this is serious!" I pleaded.

"Why are you trying to cause a fight, Claire? Dammit, just leave things alone. It seems like you just want to find things to worry about. How can you feel sorry for yourself if everything is going well?" His voice low and harsh, a tone I rarely heard.

His words stung, but there was a thread of truth.

I pressed my lips together, still undeterred.

"Please don't take the train…" I asked again.

He looked at me with such an intensity, that it made me draw in a sharp breath. He was to his breaking point.

"Now, that's enough!" His fingers were woven tightly together, making his knuckles white.

It jolted me to hear the anger in his voice.

He stood up quickly from the table.

I looked at him, and for a moment he seemed unrecognizable to me. Like someone I knew long ago. His face pursed with anger and a stubborn refusal to listen.

He looked at me like he wanted to say more, but instead, he turned and went upstairs. I could hear him mumbling to himself and his footsteps in the bedroom just above me.

Suddenly, the realization dawned on me. I could lose him. Not just from an accident, but he could leave me. I closed my eyes for a moment and thought of the fight. The look on his face. A look I wasn't accustomed to seeing. A look that said that he had had enough. But I knew him better than that. He wouldn't leave me. *Would he?*

I was pushing him away.

And why? Because of a dream...

A dream that I could barely remember now, but somehow had become a part of me.

When I finally went upstairs, the lights in the bedroom were off, and I could see he was already in the bed. I put on pajamas and slipped in beside him. Quietly, as not to wake him, but as soon as I settled in my spot, he spoke.

"I'm sorry, Claire. I don't know why I was so harsh with you. I just get frustrated sometimes with the hocus pocus stuff. You know how I am. Especially after what happened with my dad. I just don't buy into that stuff." His voice was choked with sleep.

"I understand. I'm sorry too. I just wish you believed me," I whispered.

I listened in the silence for his response, but he was already sleeping again.

He was unreachable to me now. Inches away, but it might as well have been miles.

I laid on my back staring at the dark ceiling, listening to the rain falling, sputtering and spattering against the window pane.

When I finally fell asleep, the rain had stopped, and the only sound was the occasional creak and splash as water dripped from the gutters.

CHAPTER 19

The next morning, I drifted silently down the stairs, the world around me unsettled. I slipped out the front door to get a look. I wanted to face the catalyst that had cemented my fate.

The door clicked shut behind me as I walked out onto the porch.

Everything was still damp with leftover rain. Water droplets pooled on bushes and blades of grass with the occasional splashing dripping from the roof. The sky was dusted in a hazy mist, as I stared out at the fallen limb.

A chorus of bird songs surrounded me as I closed my eyes, the limb looming in front of me, foreboding.

When I opened them again, my eyes were on the now empty spot in the driveway.

My heart in turmoil.

Despite everything, the dream was having its way with my life. Nothing I had done or not done had made any difference at all.

No matter how careful I had been.

No matter how desperately I had hoped.

No matter how hard I had tried to believe that all of this was just a result of my over-zealous imagination.

Nothing changed the events…they just kept unfolding and leaving me a powerless spectator.

And now the final act was upon me.

When I came back inside, Ben met me at the door.

"Good morning!" he said as he took my hand. Relief flooded over me. Nothing had changed between us. He was still mine.

I didn't respond, only nodded, still not trusting myself to speak. Not wanting to argue again.

Not when so little time was left.

He kissed my cheek, softly.

"I'm sorry about last night," he whispered. His breath warm on my neck. His body close to mine.

"I'm sorry too…" I stopped myself from saying more. The words were bubbling up and I pushed them down.

He put his lips on mine. The warmth of love and desperate longing, mingled together in an abundant cocktail and spread throughout my entire body.

"Your mom called while you were outside," he said, walking away and taking a seat at the table in front of his laptop.

"What did she want?" I asked.

"She didn't say. Just said for you to call." Ben's eyes already on the screen in front of him, giving him a soft glow.

I walked into the living room to check on the boys. They were still in pajamas, watching The Disney Channel. I'd let it slide and not make them get dressed just yet.

I'd call my mom back first, while it was still quiet in the house.

I dialed her number and the phone rang and rang, no one answering. Her voicemail came on and I hung up, repeating the sequence.

Strange, Ben said she had just called. Why wasn't she answering?

Coupling it with her strange behavior yesterday, darts of panic lit inside of me.

Something wasn't right and I knew it.

I looked over at Ben, still working at his computer. "I am going to go run and check on my mom." He quickly looked up. "Want me to go with you?"

"No, I won't be gone long," I answered. Panic prickling at the back of my neck.

Ben got up and walked over to me. "Is everything okay?"

I stifled the words; *everything was NOT okay. And it wasn't going to be okay. Not now! Why can't you just not take the damn train? Is it really that hard?*

Instead I looked at him and smiled weakly. "She's just been acting weird, and she didn't answer the phone just now."

Ben laughed. "Stop worrying so much, Claire! I am sure she's fine. Why don't you just wait and try again in a little bit?"

As he walked back over and sat down at his computer, I grabbed my keys and headed out the door.

I turned onto Evergreen Street and passed by two morning joggers, waving enthusiastically. I didn't wave back; my eyes were on the driveway, just ahead.

I pulled in and parked next to my mom's white Volkswagen Passat with a bumper sticker that read: *Grandma Life.*

I got out of the car and walked up onto the porch as the breeze flowed through two potted hibiscus trees covered in vibrant coral flowers flanking the front door, one on each side.

I was surprised to see them there.

Mom had always had lots of plants around the house when I was young. She spent hours in the mulch beds, working on her hydrangeas, lilies and other plants. There was even talk of her putting up a green-house in the backyard. But after Dad left, that all changed. All her plants died and were never replaced. It seemed, as if even plants reminded her of what she had lost.

Reaching out, I touched one of the coral petals. Silky soft and moist under my fingertips.

I reached up and knocked softly on the door.

When she didn't answer, I knocked again.

When she still didn't answer, I knocked vigorously.

And when she still didn't answer, my body filled with adrenaline.

I had to get inside!

She didn't answer the phone.

She didn't answer the door.

And her car was in the driveway...

I ran back to my car, grabbing the spare key to her house.

Back up on the porch, I put the key in the lock and twisted until it clicked.

Tentatively, I walked inside. The shades were drawn, giving everything a shadowy appearance.

The house had the faint odor of cigar smoke. Something I hadn't smelled since I was a little girl.

I could still see my dad now, sitting in his recliner, newspaper in hand, cigar in his mouth. He quit smoking them years ago, but the smell of it still reminded me of him.

"Mom?" I called out into the darkness of the house.

She didn't answer.

I walked into the kitchen. The sink was full of dishes, as if she had cooked a big meal.

Who would she be cooking for?

On the counter was a wine bottle, completely empty of its contents.

A Chardonnay.

Suddenly it occurred to me that maybe she had started drinking heavily.

That would explain her strange behavior. But it didn't explain where she was.

I walked through the dim lighting of the living room and stopped suddenly.

Soft music drifted in from the hallway where the bedrooms were.

"Mom?" I called out again, a little louder.

But there was still no response.

With my heart beating in my ears, I walked to her bedroom door. The music becoming louder as I approached.

As I knocked, I was met with a shuffling sound from behind the closed door.

Suddenly there was a loud thud, followed by quick footsteps.

Rationality went out the window, as visions of her being attacked flooded my mind. I flung open the door and saw my mom standing in the middle of the room, completely naked. And a man with his back to me was trying to cover himself with the quilt from the bed.

Mom and I both gasped at the same time.

The music that had been coming from an old record player was now skipping.

"What is going on here?" I shouted.

Mom didn't answer, still scrambling, trying to find something to cover up with.

I looked over at the man. His back was still to me.

But even in the dim lighting, I sensed something familiar about him. Something I couldn't quite put my finger on.

I stepped all the way into the room.

"I said, what is going on here!" My voice shrill, demanding.

Mom scooted past me and grabbed her robe from the bathroom door as I flipped on the light switch to see the man better.

He turned around and faced me, and the world became swirly.

"Dad?!" I called out in shock.

I whipped back around and looked at Mom fastening the belt around her robe.

"How dare you barge into my house, like this." Her voice thick with anger.

I stepped backwards, feeling dirty, as the realization of what had just happened dawned on me.

I just caught my parents doing it.

"What the hell, Mom?" I looked past her, suddenly unable to look at her face.

Dad spoke up, "Why don't you let us get dressed and then we can talk. Go wait in the living room and we'll be right out."

I couldn't respond. *What could I say?*

Quietly, I stepped out of the room as they closed the door. Their whispers trailing behind me as I walked away.

I went into the living room, trying desperately to delete the image of my parents' naked bodies from my mind. I had a feeling that image was going to stick there for a while, and I shuddered.

Nervously, I sat down on the couch.

A few seconds later, I moved to the arm chair.

And then to the recliner.

I couldn't find a comfortable place to sit.

After several long minutes, they emerged from the bedroom, holding hands.

They sat together on the couch, side by side, staring at me. Bringing me right back to childhood, waiting for a lecture from my parents. I glanced at the front door, wondering if I should just run out.

Mom was the first to speak up. "You have a lot of nerve to bust in my house like this…"

Dad looked at her with pleading eyes. "Let's not make this a war with her."

He looked back over at me. "Claire, we were going to tell you kids about us, but your mom wanted to give it some time to see how things went first. Then, we kind of enjoyed the sneaking around. Made us feel young again. So, we decided to wait just a little bit longer before we spilled the beans."

"Spilled the beans…about what?" I said, feeling defiant.

"We are getting back together." My mom glared at me, ready to fight.

"What? Why?" I stammered.

Dad laughed a little. "It might be hard for you to understand, but I have always loved your mother." He looked over at her and smiled gently. "I made a terrible mistake when I left, and I have regretted it every day since it happened. All I want to do is be with her. Every day for the rest of my life."

"Yeah, I'm sure! The real reason that you regretted is because that girl left you in the dust!" I scoffed.

"She wasn't right for me, Claire. Just because someone makes a mistake doesn't make them unworthy of love. I know you're angry and you have every right to be. But you also need to respect your mother's wishes about reconciliation with me. I hope in time that you will be able to forgive me for hurting you girls and your mother."

He paused and looked at Mom. "I will spend the rest of my life trying to make it up to you all."

When she looked back at him, her eyes returned nothing but love.

"Are you moving back to Pinehurst?" I demanded, looking at my mother.

Dad shook his head. "No, I am moving here. I've retired and my new business will be spending time with this beautiful woman right here."

Mom giggled.

I raised my eyebrows and looked at her. *She was giggling?*

It was strange to see her like this. I could barely remember what she was like before the divorce. When she actually had a personality.

She looked me directly in the eyes. "Just be happy for us, Claire. This is what I want. I want to be happy. Don't I deserve to be happy?"

"Yes, but…" I protested, feeling conflicted.

"There's no but. You don't get to decide what makes me happy and what doesn't. I love your father. I always have. Yes, I spent many years being angry, but that is all in the past now.

She paused, looking between Dad and me.

"We are in love and we are happy. Just, let us have this, okay?" She said it gently, almost pleadingly.

I looked at the two of them and realized I needed to stay out of it. If they could make it work, then so be it.

"I am happy for you. I am…" I said, looking at Mom. And I meant it.

Who was I to judge her decisions? If she could forgive him and move on, why would I stand in their way?

I got up to walk to the door and my dad followed behind me, catching my arm.

He cleared his throat before he started to speak. I yanked away from his grasp putting my hand on the doorknob, wanting to leave, not wanting to hear what he had to say.

"Claire, I am sorry that things haven't been good with us over the years. I want them to be better. I want to spend time with you and the boys. You don't know how happy it makes me to know that I am a grandfather."

"You have a fine way of showing it. When is the last time you came to see them?" I barked back.

"I haven't come because I didn't feel welcomed. I just want us to be a family again. Can we do that?" he said, his face strained.

I looked at my dad, beginning to go bald. The hair that he still had was turning slate grey. He was aging, but softly. His brown eyes, the same as mine, still sparkled with the fire of a young man. He had been handsome before and still was.

Sometimes when Grayson smiled, I could see my dad's smile reflecting on his face.

I broke away from his gaze. His desire for reconnection was not shared by me.

"Well, you should've thought about that a long time ago. I'm happy for Mom, but don't think you're getting the same welcome mat at my house." My words came out harsh. I was shocked at my ability to speak to him that way.

"You think you know everything about the world, Claire, and you don't. You shouldn't be so closed minded," he responded.

"Close minded?" I shrieked. The air was charged, and before I could say another word, Mom closed in.

"What's going on here?" she asked, looking between the two of us.

Pushing the door open, I stepped away from them both of them, calling back, "Nothing, nothing at all."

I walked out, letting the screen door slam behind me.

As I approached my car, I heard Mom calling from behind.

She met me out on the walkway.

I turned to look at her. She was blinking back tears.

"You shouldn't treat your father that way, Claire. He's a good man." Her voice trailing.

"A good man?" I scoffed. "You can't be serious?"

"There's things that you just don't understand and probably never will." She shook her head and stared off into the distance. A breeze kicked up and rustled the leaves on the trees nearby. We stood together silently for several moments before she spoke again.

"I am sorry for the shock it gave you by stumbling in on us this way. I wanted to be able to tell you myself. I'm sorry it didn't work out that way. I just wasn't ready yet. But I guess things have a way of working themselves out."

I nodded in agreement as a squirrel ran up the tree in front of her house, an acorn in its mouth.

"Listen, don't tell your sister or your brother yet. I want to be able to tell them myself. I promise I will do it soon. No sense in procrastinating, now that the cat is out of the bag." She half laughed.

"I promise..." I said.

She turned and walked back onto the porch where Dad was waiting for her. They both waved as I drove away.

When I got home, I told Ben about everything, leaving nothing out.

He laughed, hysterically. "I guess your dad's still got it!"

I shuddered, remembering the moment I opened my mom's bedroom door.

Ben approached me with a playful look in his eyes. "You think we'll still be doing it when we're that old?"

I couldn't answer; I was looking over his shoulder at the calendar. It had already been switched over to a new month.

A day early.

Ben must've done it while I was gone.

June.

A knot came up in my throat and I knew the tears weren't far behind it.

I ran to the bathroom, closed the door and turned on the fan. I sat down on the closed toilet with my hands in my face.

Ben knocked softly on the outside of the door. "Hey, are you okay in there?"

"I'm fine," I answered weakly.

What else could I say?

CHAPTER 20

MAY 31ST

The early mornings were the worst part of the day. That blissful moment of waking shattered as reality came crashing down around me and a deep sense of loss would rise up in my heart.

The realization jolting me forward, as if I was hearing the news for the first time.

This particular morning, I was given a pardon. The first thought to enter my brain, instead of June 3rd, was Jamie. Today was her annual Memorial Day party and I had completely forgotten about it.

I didn't want to go.

How could I go to this party and pretend that everything was great and normal?

Suddenly, the bedroom door swung open and Ben appeared, wearing a wrinkled Hawaiian button up shirt that I had never seen before. I imagined that he must've gotten it from the bin in the attic filled with his old college stuff.

"Who's ready for the party?" he shouted as he jumped on the bed, kissing my face all over.

"Where did you get that shirt?" I asked, trying not to smile.

"What? You don't like it? I was trying to be festive!" He laughed as he feigned offense.

"It's not a luau!" I rolled my eyes and laughed.

He jumped off the bed and strutted around the room, showing off his best Hawaiian dance moves.

I shook my head in defeat.

Maybe it would do us all some good to go to the party.

We arrived at Jamie's house right on time and parked behind a white Passat with a bumper sticker that read: Grandma Life.

I looked at Ben and grimaced. "My parents are here?"

He shrugged. "I didn't invite them."

I had to fight every urge inside of me to ask Ben to take us back home. I just couldn't deal with my parents right now.

I turned and looked back at the boys, their faces beaming with excitement, and their eyes glued to the top of the bouncy house peeking over Jamie's fence.

I couldn't do that to them.

I didn't want them to miss out.

With the boys leading the way, we walked through the thick grass of Jamie's perfectly manicured yard, and when we stepped around the back of her house, we were greeted with the mouthwatering aromas of grilled hamburgers and hot dogs.

Every year Jamie's Memorial Day party had gotten a little bigger, and this year she had gone all out, ordering the bouncy house, a balloon guy, a cotton candy stand, and a DJ.

There looked to be about thirty people here, not including children. I couldn't even begin to count all of the kids. They were running back and forth between the cotton candy machine and the bouncy house in a sugar rushed frenzy.

No sooner did we enter the backyard, the boys disappeared into the bounce house too, with Ben right behind them reminding them to take off their shoes.

The party buzzed with music and laughter. I moved through the guests wearing a mauve top with wide-legged white pants and my hair pulled back into a low ponytail, and passing people mingling. Their voices twirled together into a low hum.

I looked around and saw my parents by the beer cooler, talking. I moved away before they saw me and quickly spotted Jaime. She was surrounded by a group of people, queen of the hour. She saw me at the same time and waved as she slowly removed herself from the group.

She ran up and hugged me. She was wearing a pink polo shirt, white Bermuda shorts and a big smile.

"I'm so glad you're here!" she said as she wiped her forehead off with the illusion of sweat. "This party has nearly been the death of me!" she exclaimed.

She told me about the disasters that preceded everyone's arrival. Including the first batch of hamburger patties being rotten, and the party supply company trying to deliver a miniature carousel instead of the bounce house. Then the brewery was out of kegs, so she had to buy "umpteen thousand bottles of beer."

I laughed. She glared back at me. "You think that's funny?"

I nodded, and she laughed too.

"Yeah, maybe I will think it's funny too after I've had a few drinks. I haven't had time to do anything yet." She sighed. "I don't know why I plan these things!" She rolled her eyes sarcastically and laughed.

"Well, speaking of planning things, what are my parents doing here?" I asked.

She laughed in response. "Talk about a surprise! I invited your mom because you told me that she had been lonely lately, and then she shows up with a date! Your dad, no less! I nearly crapped my pants!"

I shrugged. "Yeah, apparently they're back together."

"That's a good thing, right?" she asked, her eyes on me.

I shrugged again, not wanting to get into it.

She went on, gossiping about this person and that person. Who came to the party and who didn't even have the courtesy to RSVP. I listened, but all the while my eyes were on Ben. He made his rounds, shaking hands with several of the men, putting his hand on their shoulder as they spoke. A comforting gesture that he had learned from dealing with his clients.

He looked up and checked on me every once and a while.

Our eyes would meet and he would smile.

Jamie had stopped talking without my notice. I was still watching Ben.

"What in the world is going on with you, girl? You haven't taken your eyes off of that man. Haven't you seen enough of him at home!?"

When I looked back at her, I laughed.

Just then, some of the guests spotted her and headed in her direction.

"Here we go!" she spouted back to me as she walked over to greet them.

I looked over and saw the boys climbing out of the bouncy house, their bangs wet with sweat.

"You guys been having fun?" I asked as I met them at the entrance.

"It's so fun! But Oliver keeps tripping me," Grayson complained.

"I'm hungry," Oliver said as he rubbed his tummy.

I led the boys over to the food table to let them pick what they wanted to eat. Seemingly out of nowhere, Ben was behind me, tickling me and startling me so much, I almost dropped the plate full of baked beans I had just made for Oliver.

"Hey, you're awful cute? Wanna go home with me later?" he said as he raised his eyebrows up and down dramatically.

I giggled. "That was the plan."

He started dancing. "Oh yeah, I'm gettin' lucky tonight."

Oliver looked up at his dad. "What are you winning, Daddy?"

"I'll tell you when you're older!" Ben patted him on the back and winked at me.

We got the boys seated on the grass with hot dogs, beans, and cans of Fanta orange soda.

Ben put his arm around me as "Billie Jean" by Michael Jackson blared out of the DJ's speakers.

Sitting close by was Annie and her family. She waved at me joyfully. I hadn't seen Jessica yet. I wondered if she had even come.

After the boys finished eating, I went to get Ben and me a beer.

As I walked toward the cooler, my dad spotted me and headed straight in my direction. I felt the muscles in my back tense up as I fought the urge to walk in the other direction, away from him.

"Can I talk to you for a minute?" he asked.

I reluctantly agreed as he led me to the side of the yard, away from the hustle and bustle of the party.

"I didn't like the way we left things yesterday," he started. "I know a lot of your resentment has more to do with Mandi than me leaving your mother. I know that you believe that I always favored her. I want you to know that I never favored her, but I did give her extra attention because I felt that she needed it. I never meant for you to feel less than." His were eyes low to the ground.

Mom suddenly appeared behind him, swaying, her eyes glassy with alcohol.

"Why don't you just tell her the truth?" she demanded, her words slurry and sticky.

Dad's face was silent. Cold.

"What truth?" I demanded.

"No!" Dad said, his voice stern as he looked at Mom.

"It's time. You've been the bad guy long enough," she said as she patted his arm. Her eyes filling with tears.

"I won't do it," he said harshly as he turned and walked away.

Mom took another long sip of the beer she was holding.

We stood together under a trellis of grape vines, tiny grapes forming overhead, silent for several minutes.

Finally, she spoke.

"You don't know the whole story about your father, and it's time you did. He's suffered long enough."

She sat down on the ground and I sat next to her.

"Before you were born, I did something that I am not proud of. I was young and stupid. Lonely. Bored. I don't know. There's no excuse, really."

She paused and then started again.

"Jonathan was in school and I had gone to the grocery store. On the way back, I picked up a hitchhiker wearing a backpack. He was a drifter making his way to Virginia when I saw him. I don't know what made me stop that day. There was just something about him. He was a beautiful man. Red hair, lean muscles. Sexy.

"Needless to say, we ended up at a motel and we made love all afternoon. By the time I got back in the car to go pick up Jonathan from school, the groceries had spoiled. I never asked his name and I never saw him again. And nine months later, Mandi was born."

My mouth dropped open. "Are you saying that Mandi isn't Dad's child?"

"Yes, that's exactly what I'm saying. I didn't tell your father until much later. But he knew something wasn't right. We had been going through a dry spell and had barely made love, so when I turned up pregnant, I could see the question in his eyes. Part of me wanted to believe that somehow the baby was his, but when she was born with that same vibrant red hair as the guy that I had the affair with, I knew the truth." Her face solemn as she spoke.

The wind kicked up and blew across my face as I looked down at the grass underneath me. Picking at it. Listening.

"And finally, one day, I just told your father. I couldn't hold back the truth any longer. He was devastated...but he didn't leave me. He said that he loved me—and he loved Mandi, just the same as if she were his own child. What more could you ask for?" she said as she shook her head.

"But the guilt was too much. I wouldn't let him get close to me. And that's the real reason that he left. I pushed him straight into Linda's arms." Her voice choked on bitter tears.

She took another sip of her beer.

"He wanted to come home. Put the family back together. He begged me, and I refused him. I wouldn't have it. I was too bitter. Angry at myself. Angry at him. I wanted to hate him for going off with Linda, but I knew it was me that pushed him away, and she had been just a band-aid to his pain. I spent many years in a literal hell, hating myself for what I did to him. To us. To our family. It was me that destroyed our family. All he wanted to do was put us back together again.

"And he never wanted you kids to know about what I did. He wanted Mandi to know him as her father. Her real father. He did everything he could to show Mandi how much he loved her. That's why it seemed he favored her, Claire. He was overcompensating. God love him for it. He did the best he could."

I sat beside her in silence. The words wouldn't come. I didn't know how to feel. I had so many questions but nothing came out.

After a while, I got up and walked away.

I searched for my dad and found him sitting alone under a tree. His face in his hands. I went over and sat down next to him. He looked up at me. His eyes worn with stress.

"Why did you do it?" I asked. "Why did you take the blame, all of these years?"

"I did it to protect your mother. And to protect you kids. Especially Mandi. Something like this has the potential to ruin everything, and I wouldn't have it." His voice was strained as he spoke.

"But, it kind of did anyway…I mean, look at us," I said bluntly.

He nodded. "Yeah, I suppose you're right. I guess I just didn't want to be found out as an imposter. I love Mandi. I really do. There's no difference between her and you and Jonathan. You're all my kids. The only thing I regret is that my misguided efforts ended up hurting you. I never meant for that to happen. I love you so much, Claire. And I'm sorry for not being the best dad I could've been." His head lowered in shame.

I scooted up closer to him and put my arm through his and leaned into him, fighting back tears.

"It's okay, Dad," I whispered.

We sat together like that for a while, and when I got up, I kissed his cheek.

"Dad, try not to worry too much. Everything will be okay. I know it," I told him.

"Are you going to tell Mandi?" he asked, looking up at me.

"No," I answered. "You and Mom will have to."

He nodded in response as I walked away.

I stood in the middle of Jamie's yard, as the evening drifted in, the sky turning purple and orange as the party dwindled and people drifted away. Suddenly, Ben was next to me. Arms around my waist, kissing my neck. His presence coursing through me like a river rapid as I inhaled his scent.

"You okay?" he asked, softly.

I nodded and leaned into him.

We left soon after, and the boys fell asleep in the car just five minutes from home.

Once the boys were settled in their beds, Ben went downstairs, and I stood in the doorway of their room looking in.

They were snuggled in their beds, wrapped up in sleep.

Safe and sound from anything that could harm them. Their futures unmapped and filled with possibility.

How I wished I could just protect them from pain.

Emotions rolled over me, thinking about Mandi and what my mom had revealed, but mostly I was thinking about June 3rd.

It was only two days away now.

If only I could stop what was happening. Ben told me not to worry about it. Jonathan told me not to worry about it. Even Mandi told me not to worry about it. But how could I not worry about it? When everything seemed to match the dream. How could I not worry when now he would be taking the train on Wednesday? How could I not worry when I wanted to spend the rest of my life with this man? He was part of me and I was part of him. I didn't want to be me without him.

I knew I would have to keep going for my boys. And I would.

But what I really wanted was to find some way to stop this from happening.

If I just had some way to stop fate... But fate was hell bent on destroying my family, and I didn't know why.

I walked out into the hallway and I could hear Ben downstairs, whistling. I walked down and sat at the bottom of the stairs and listened to him. I was trying to record this moment, taking every bit in that I could. While he was still there....

CHAPTER 21

JUNE 1ST

It was a sunny day, blue skies and perfect cotton candy clouds were in the sky overhead. I stood on the front porch, watering can in hand giving water to the ferns, when I heard a noise coming from the other side of the hedge.

I walked off the porch and into the yard, pausing, letting the sunshine warm my face.

I heard the sound again. The distinct thwack of a hoe into the ground. I walked closer to hedge and peered through.

All at once, a rush of terror and excitement pulsed through me.

I couldn't believe my eyes.

It was the old man!

Ed was there, and I wouldn't let him get away again!

I ran as fast as my legs would move and rounded the hedge, startling him, as he took the hoe to the ground. He looked up at me with his bright crystal blue eyes, and I had to stifle a scream.

But yet, it wasn't the man I saw in the photo…

Not the long-lost love of Mrs. Parks.

It wasn't Ed…or his ghost. But a living breathing man.

So similar in appearance to Ed, it was startling.

"Well hello there, young lady!" he offered as I stepped closer. His white hair disheveled and sweat running down his brow. "My name is Bob and I think I owe you an apology," he said as he offered me his hand. It was tinged black with deep, rich soil from the yard.

"But who are you?" I demanded, still not understanding.

"Oh, I'm sorry. I am Ed's brother. I have been the caretaker of this place since he died. Been here off and on, getting it ready to sell. Kind of like a last goodbye, so to speak," he said, with a soft smile and continued.

"I've been keeping an eye out for you. I wanted to apologize. I think I might have given you a scare not too long ago. You ran off so quickly that I couldn't rectify the situation, and quite honestly, I was too embarrassed to knock on your door. You see, I had been cursing at these darned weeds. Crabgrass. Don't know if you've had any experience with it, but it's the darnedest weed to try and kill. I'd been treating it for weeks with a powerful herbicide that I paid big bucks for. And low and behold, that crabgrass was holding on for dear life to keep living, and I was madder than a nest of bees. I was giving the weeds a what for when I heard you scream. I knew that you thought I was a mad man, and I had never been so embarrassed in my life. I had no idea you were over there, or I would've never spoken that way. At least not out loud." He laughed, shaking his head.

All at once, it all made sense. It was all a complete misunderstanding. I had been such a fool to believe he was a ghost condemning Ben to die. I wanted to laugh at the irony, but I couldn't.

And as I walked away, I wondered how my perception of reality had gotten so off track.

I had allowed the dream to alter the way I looked at everything, and yet, I remained powerless to change it.

When I got back inside, the phone was ringing.

It was Mandi. My heart thudded at the sight of her name.

Did she know about Dad yet?

When I answered, she invited me to meet her for lunch at Celia's Café downtown, and I agreed to go. Neither of us mentioned our parents.

She was waiting for me at a table inside. I was shocked when I saw her. Her long hair was gone and was replaced by a trendy pixie haircut. She smiled and waved when she saw me.

I sat down at the table for two next to a bright window as the afternoon sunlight poured in and warmed us.

"Oh my god, Mandi, your hair! It looks fantastic. I almost didn't recognize you!" I told her.

She had a glow about her. Something different. A look that I had never seen before.

She smiled and touched the nape of her neck.

"I just got it cut this morning. I got this moment of inspiration to do something different. Something I had never done before. Next thing I know, I was sitting in the salon telling the stylist to take it all off. Got ten inches cut off and I have never felt better. It feels so amazing!"

"It looks beautiful. You look beautiful," I said. It was incredible how the cut emphasized the elegance of her features.

The server came by and offered us wine, and Mandi refused. I was immediately struck by how strange that was.

Mandi never declined wine.

There was something different about her. Something I couldn't explain.

I looked into her eyes, and at once I knew Mom had told her.

"So, I guess, they told you?" I asked.

She looked down. "Yes, they did. Last night. I don't know how to feel about their revelation right now. It's going to take some time to digest." Her voice trailed off.

"I understand," I offered.

'But it doesn't change much, does it?" she said as she looked at me with questioning eyes.

"No, not at all," I answered, reaching across the table to hold her hand. "How are you? How are things with Lewis?" I asked.

"I'm good, Claire. Really good. Despite how it may seem like things are coming down around me, I don't think I have ever been better." She smiled as she continued.

"This morning, I found myself standing at the kitchen sink. My own kitchen sink, filled with my own dishes. A vase of daisies on the table, surrounded by soft cotton placemats that I had bought at TJ Maxx. Yes, I said TJ Maxx. Don't judge me." She laughed, still caught up in the memory as the waitress filled our water glasses.

"I realized then that I was happy. Truly happy for the first time in my life. I always thought I needed a man to complete me somehow, but it's not that at all. It's strange for such a little thing as dirty dishes to have such a profound effect on me, but it did. Like, life finally makes sense," she said as she tucked a stray hair behind her ear.

I looked at my sister with her short stylish hair, her face poised with satisfaction, and I saw a new person. A person I didn't know yet, but one that I would like to know.

"How are things with Ben and that dream of yours? Did you talk to him?" she asked.

"Oh, Mandi, you know Ben. Stubborn and willful. I tried to talk to him, but he wouldn't listen. I asked him to take my car and not take the train, and he refused outright."

"God, what a jerk! Can't he just get a rental car or something? Damned stubborn man!" she spouted.

I started to defend him, but she was right. He should've listened to me.

The waitress returned with our salads. Plated baby greens with goat cheese and walnuts.

"So, you want to hear a real plot twist?" she laughed. "I'm pregnant." Her face was beaming.

I gave a startled laugh. "Pregnant?"

"Yes! No IVF or anything, just happened on its own. Ironic, isn't it? I just found out yesterday. Took a test to be sure. Went to the doctor this morning and they confirmed it. I am four months along already. Craziest thing! I didn't even know. I knew my period was late, but they had been jumbled up since I took all those hormones months ago."

"Is it Lewis'?" I asked.

"God, yes! I might be a flirt, Claire, but I don't sleep around!" I could tell I had offended her, but she wasn't slighted for long.

"Are you going back to him?" I questioned.

"No way! I am doing this on my own. I know he will be a great father, but I have no desire to live with him again. I don't need him. Not to mention, I have a great sister to help me with the baby," she said, smiling, her eyes bright with joy.

I smiled back. "I'm so happy for you, Mandi!"

"I am happy for me too!" she said, her voice wistful and filled with a determination I had never heard before, and I instantly knew she would be okay.

We said goodbye at the door. She took my hand, hers light and soft in mine. We stood that way for several moments as people passed by us, coming and going, sharing a moment that I knew I would never forget.

And for the first time in my life, I knew that I had a sister.

I stood on the sidewalk watching her walk away until she disappeared completely out of sight. I turned and walked down the city street aimlessly. No destination in mind. Just wandering. My mind full of thoughts. Thinking about what Mandi had said about being happy on her own.

When had I changed?

When did being me become not enough? When had I morphed into something else?

Placing myself in Mandi's shadow.

Where was that lost version of myself?

I continued to walk as golden flecks of sunlight fell down around me, and I remembered when I was young.

When I was so full of hope and life.

When I stood on my own two feet.

How did I get to this point where I doubted myself?

What had happened to that girl that loved the feel of the ocean tickling her toes and could spend hours lost in a museum, all alone? One with fierce determination to make it on her own?

I was still her.

Suddenly, all the scattered pieces came into focus, and I really saw myself for the first time in a very long time.

I hadn't been seeing my own value until that moment.

I finally grasped my own worth.

Everything I needed in this world was right here inside of me. I lost myself when I let that first seed of insecurity take root inside of me.

Now I could set myself free. I let go of the old script and could feel the release flooding through my being. All the hurt and lost expectations, withering away. I stopped on the sidewalk and let the sun warm me as a train sounded in the distance.

When I arrived home, everything was the same it as was when I had left.

Same photos on the wall.

Same clock ticking in the kitchen.

Same reflection in the mirror.

Yet it felt different. I felt different.

And suddenly I knew that I would be okay. No matter what happened.

I started up the stairs, denying the pit of darkness rumbling against my bones.

CHAPTER 22

JUNE 2ND

As dawn emerged, tiny rays of orange pushed their way past the edges of the blinds. My eyes drifted over to Ben's dark figure still in the bed. I scooted over to him and put my head on his chest, listening the sound of his strong heart. Rhythmic and perfect with each beat. He wrapped his strong arms around me, pulling me tighter against him.

The illusion of safety.

"Are you okay?" he asked in a low tone.

I couldn't answer him. The emotional dam I was guarding threatened to break. The thought of tomorrow ripping at my heart.

He stroked my hair softly, and as he did, the dam began to spill over the edges as tiny sobs escaped and tears ran down my face.

He sat up with a jolt and turned on the lamp, still cradling me. "Honey, what's wrong?!"

I sat up and faced him, wiping the tears from my face with the corner of the sheet.

"I'm scared, Ben. So, so scared…" My voice cracking and choking on tears.

He scooted close to me again and put his arms back around me. Surrounding me.

Maybe now he would listen.

"Is this about that dying thing again?" he asked tenderly.

I nodded and began to cry harder.

"Honey, you have to stop this nonsense…" he spoke gently, but there was a hint of firmness in his voice. "I'm perfectly fine. I don't know what's gotten into you, but you have got to stop obsessing about me dying. It's not good for you, and honestly, it's freaking me out a little."

I pulled away from him and looked directly into his eyes. "Then please, don't go to work tomorrow…or today, for that matter. Please, Ben…Just stay with me…" I pleaded with every ounce of my being.

He huffed in response. "I can't just stay home, Claire! I have a very important meeting tomorrow with a client that is flying in from Charleston. I have spent months wining and dining this client to build trust, and if I am not there, it will destroy everything that I've worked for. In this business it's all about trust, and if I don't show up to a meeting, where's the trust in that?"

"Then reschedule it to Friday!" I offered, hopefully.

"I can't do that. He's flying in tomorrow morning, and I don't have a valid reason to change our meeting. And why would I? Because my wife thinks I'm going to die? I mean, come on, that's ridiculous!" he said, his voice now filled with irritation.

I hung my head in defeat. I knew there was no getting through to him.

He put his hand under my chin and lifted my head, forcing me to look him in the eyes.

"Hey, don't be sad. How about I take the rest of the week off, starting Friday? We will pull the boys out of school and we will take a long weekend trip up to the mountains. What do you say?" He smiled, proud of his compromise.

I shook my head. "By then, it will be too late."

He looked at me for another minute and got up without saying another word.

I laid back down and covered my face with the blankets as I heard the bathroom door click shut and the shower turn on.

After his shower, he came and sat on the edge of the bed. I refused to look at him. I was angry.

He could make all of this stop if he would just listen to me.

"I love you, Claire. I'm sorry that you're so upset, but I'm going to be fine." He patted my blanketed figure, then got up and walked out of the room.

I wanted to chase him, but I stayed put. I wanted to yell at him, but I didn't.

What was the use? He would never listen.

I heard him rushing around downstairs. He had to leave early to account for the time it would take him to walk the four blocks to the train station.

Why did he have to be so stubborn?

It was over now. I was out of options. I was going to lose him and I would forever be alone.

My heart was breaking in slow motion.

Shortly after the front door closed behind him, I heard the boys stirring and I reluctantly got up, to get them ready for school.

I got them dressed and fed them breakfast, lost in a cloud of emotion. I packed their lunchboxes with unseeing eyes and left to take them to school, still in my pajamas.

When we pulled up in front of Birchwood Elementary School, I handed them each a lunchbox and gave them multiple kisses. I watched through teary eyes as they ran up the walkway and into the tall brick school building. A rush of bitterness washed over me, and I couldn't help but wonder how the universe could deal out whatever cards it felt like?

It was unfair...More than unfair.

How could I be forced to sit back and watch it dismantle my family?

I drove back to the house in silence, without turning on the radio. The street flowed effortlessly in front of me as I drove home in a blur of thoughts. Weariness around me, thick and unpliable.

Overhead, streaks of grey were painted across the sky, reinforcing my despair.

Just as I pulled in the driveway, it began to sprinkle rain. By the time I reached the front porch, the sky had opened up and it was pouring down. The rain beat hard on the roof over me, making a rushing sound. My eyes fixed on the glimmering droplets falling in large dollops from the sky as they bounced on the walkway, quickly making small puddles.

Time ceased to exist while I stood there. Endless rain falling. Lost as a hurricane of emotion stirred inside of me. The sudden sloshing of wet tires on pavement as a UPS truck rushed by startled me, waking me from my trance, and I went inside.

I walked up the stairs to get dressed, my feet padding on the steps one by one, as I pushed myself forward.

I walked into the bedroom and stopped right beside the tall chest of drawers that held Ben's clothes. My eyes on an old framed photograph sitting on top of the dresser. Ben and I, taken before the boys were born. We were sitting on a grassy hill. Ben's arms around my waist, looking at me. My eyes closed, face tilted toward the sky, lost in laughter.

Now, I couldn't even remember who had taken the photo.

I had dusted it so many times over the years and never really looked at it. I hadn't for a long time.

I picked it up and carried it across the room, sitting on the edge of the bed with it in my hands, looking at the two people in the photo.

Who were they really?

Were we still those people after all these years? Or had time changed us?

I didn't know. Did it matter, really? Because now, there would be no more photographs.

I would be alone...

Suddenly, I felt depleted. I had nothing else to give.

I laid down on the bed, curled up in the fetal position with the picture against my chest.

I didn't wake up until hours later.

When I awoke, the rain had stopped, and the sun attempted to break through the clouds. I stretched and rubbed my neck. I left the picture on the bed and stumbled to the closet to find something to wear, throwing on a pair of jeans shorts and a white tank top. I picked up my pajamas and took them over to the laundry basket and dropped them in. Ben's t-shirt hanging precariously on the edge of the basket caught my eye. I picked it up and held it up to my nose. Breathing deeply, I inhaled the smell of Ben.

All at once, agony engulfed me. I slid to the floor, unbridled tears rushing.

I stayed there until the tears slowed and mind-numbing grief filtered through me. Weighing me down. My body like lead.

Tomorrow on my mind. The knock on the door.

Suddenly, I thought of the other six people who would also die tomorrow and the knocks on their families' doors.

The thought jolting through me like a bolt of lightning.

I wasn't the only the one who would lose someone they loved!

I had to keep trying. I couldn't just roll over and give up because Ben refused to cooperate.

I stood up from the floor, my mind racing, filled with purpose.

Who could I call? The transit system? No. I needed to tell the police. Once they knew about this, they could stop it and all seven people could be saved, including Ben!

Hope filled my heart as I ran downstairs and grabbed my phone. It didn't take long before I found the direct line into the Charlotte Police Department.

The phone rang twice before a woman with a thick southern accent answered.

"Charlotte Police Department," she stated.

"Umm, Hi…I need to report something…" I stuttered, feeling suddenly uncomfortable.

"Yes, ma'am, go ahead," she responded.

"There's going to be an accident tomorrow. The train…I mean, a transfer truck is going to stall out and then the train…well… it's going to hit the truck and derail…." My own voice unrecognizable as I tried to explain it to her.

The phone was silent.

"Hello?" I offered. *Had she hung up?*

"What did you say?" I could hear the wariness in her voice.

I repeated it to her, once again.

"Ma'am, the police department doesn't take kindly to prank calls," she huffed.

"Oh no…no! It's not a prank. I swear, it's going to happen," I said, my voice shrill and desperate.

It was quiet on the line again. I thought I heard mumbling, but I couldn't be sure.

Then she said, "Just one minute, please."

I was elated that she was putting me through to somebody.

Somebody who could help me.

There was a short succession of rings and a man answered.

"This is Detective Anderson. How can I help you?"

Shock ricocheted through my body, and I almost dropped the phone.

Detective Anderson? It couldn't be!

My entire body began to shake.

Why him of all people in that entire station?

But I had to talk to him even if I didn't want to. I had no choice. He was my only option now.

I steadied my voice as I spoke. "My name is Claire DuPont. I am calling to tell you that there's going to be an accident tomorrow. On the three o'clock train from downtown. A transfer truck is going to stall out on the tracks, and the train is going to hit it. One of the passenger cars will derail and seven people are going to die. Can you please help me?" I couldn't hide the desperation in my voice any longer.

"How do you know about this, ma'am?" he answered.

"I dreamt it…" I replied, already knowing that it sounded insane… but it was the truth. There was no other explanation.

"Ms. DuPont. We can't go out on a wild goose chase every time somebody has a bad dream. You understand?" His southern drawl sophisticated and clear.

My heart began to sink, but I was not deterred.

"You have to listen to me! Don't you understand!? People are going to die! You have to help me!" I shouted, my voice choked on tears.

There was silence followed by a long exhale. "Alright. Where did the truck stall out?" he asked.

"Where did the truck stall out?" I said aloud.

The realization came on fast that I couldn't answer him! The location, gone from my mind.

He was finally listening to me and I couldn't answer his question!

As much as I tried to remember where the truck had stalled out, I couldn't. Hazy memories from the dream rolled around in my mind as I tried to bring them into focus.

I struggled for several seconds before he spoke up.

"Look, how about this. If you remember any more details, why don't you give us a call back?" His voice more patronizing than comforting.

I had lost him.

"I'm telling you, it's going to happen…" Hopelessness resounding in my voice. Consuming me.

"What's your address, Ms. DuPont?" he asked.

"It's Mrs. DuPont…" I answered.

After we hung up, I got my purse and left the house as quickly as possible. I was afraid he was sending someone to pick me up to take me straight to the mental hospital. And I couldn't blame him.

I had no destination in mind and the boys didn't get out of school for another two hours, so I drove around aimlessly until finally coming to a stop in front of Saint Michael's Cathedral Church.

I don't know why I stopped there, of all places. But I couldn't help myself. It was as if some unseen force was guiding me here.

I parked the car and walked up the grassy hill toward the chapel.

The church was not elaborate. It was a simple square brick building with a tall steeple.

I walked up a set of stone steps and stopped in front of the double arched doors, wind catching my hair. The doors were glistening black against the intermittent sunlight and smelled of fresh paint. So fresh, I was afraid to touch them. The door to the right was slightly ajar, so I pushed on the antique-style curved door handle as it silently swung open.

I quickly looked around and saw no one nearby, so I stepped inside. A rush of silence and cool air surrounded me as my eyes adjusted to the dim lighting. The scent of wood polish and mustiness filled my nose.

I stepped in farther, gazing in surprising reverence at the sanctuary.

I looked up at the large majestic stained-glass windows standing in contrast to the dimness of the church. So similar to the ones we had seen in New Bern. The memory of them tumbling low and painful in my belly.

I walked across hardwood floor onto the carpeted aisle running down center of the room through rows of pews with elaborately designed hand-carved edges. My fingertips grazing the tops of them as I walked toward the front of the room. Being drawn toward a sculpture on the wall over the pulpit. A giant golden cross with a carving of Jesus hanging on it. It glimmered as spotlights from the ceiling shone down on it.

My feet padded lightly along the walkway as I stepped through rays of blue, red, and yellow as the sun filtered through the colors of the stained-glass windows.

When I got all the way to the front, I closed my eyes. It felt strange to be here.

I turned to leave and found myself stopping and taking a seat on a pew near the back. I sat with my hands folded in my lap and wondered how many others had sat in this very spot.

With their own grief.

Their own hopes and dreams.

Disappointed.

Lost.

What force had brought me here with the image of Jesus on the cross glaringly in front of me?

Words suddenly spilled out of my mouth.

"I don't know if you're really there or if you even can hear me. And if you can hear me, I don't even know if you would care. But I'm asking for your help. I'm so lost, and I don't know what else to do. I don't know if you're a cruel god or not. I would hope not. But this whole situation with the dream has been a nightmare. A literal nightmare, which I cannot wake up from. I want it to stop. I want this to be over. And I want my husband to be safe! Would you help me? Or at least send me a sign that everything is going to be okay? Can you do something? Anything! Please help me..." My voice echoed in the room as tears streamed down my face.

Suddenly, I felt a hand on my shoulder and I looked up. It was a man wearing a black shirt, pants, and belt, with a white collar around his neck.

The priest had a distinct gentleness about him.

His solid white hair was brushed and parted neatly to the side. His face soft but worn seemingly beyond his years.

"I'm so sorry...I was just leaving," I stuttered, standing up.

"I'm glad you came," he spoke softly.

I sat back down as he took a seat next to me.

We sat together in the silence for several moments.

His presence strangely comforting.

I finally broke the silence between us.

"What do I call you?" I asked.

"Some call me Father John, but if you're more comfortable, you can just call me John," he said, his voice soothing.

Was this a trick of the trade or was it just the natural sound of his voice?

"John, I'm Claire," I said, feeling out of place.

"Nice to meet you, Claire. Though, I am sorry it's under these difficult circumstances. Is there anything you'd like me to pray about?" He looked straight ahead as he spoke. I wondered if he was looking at the Jesus figure.

At first, I didn't answer. I didn't know how to respond. No one had offered to pray for me before. I hadn't grown up in church. It was not something that we did.

"Can I ask you a question?" I offered instead.

"Yes, absolutely," he answered.

"If God exists, why does he allow bad things to happen?" I asked.

He nodded. "Yes, that is quite a question. One I hear often, I'm afraid. I can't tell you that I know the answer. A lot of what happens in this world doesn't make sense, even to me. I lost my wife when we were very young. She died in a hit and run accident. I was never the same after that. She was the love of my life, and when she died, part of me died with her. I didn't know who I was or for what reason I had to live. I was standing on the edge of a bridge about to jump, and I heard the voice of God. He called to me in a way that only I could understand. I climbed back over the guardrail and decided to dedicate what life I had left to Him. But that doesn't mean that I didn't question Him. I questioned how He could allow such a beautiful and dearly loved woman to be taken from this world. Taken from me."

He paused for a moment before he continued, as I swallowed back my tears.

"The truth is, we don't understand. I don't think we are meant to understand. We are meant to trust and to lean on Him. We can't see things clearly from this human perspective, but one day we will. Until that time, all we can do is put one foot in front of the other and trust that something bigger than us is guiding all of our lives. The Bible says, 'We know that in all things, God works for the good of those who love him, who have been called according to his purpose.' If you notice, the verse doesn't say God causes evil and suffering, just that he promises to cause good to come out of it. It doesn't say we will see the good immediately or even in this lifetime, but that we are to trust that God has caused good to emerge from bad circumstances.

"In the end, I had to accept that this Earth is not our true home. There's more for us than we can see with our physical eyes, and I'm holding onto that."

When he finished speaking, he looked down at his hands folded in his lap.

He seemed so strong to have gone through such a tragedy.

"But how can I trust in a God that I am not even sure that I believe in?" I asked.

He laughed a little and said, "Just because you don't believe in Him, doesn't mean that He doesn't believe in you." He turned and patted me on the arm before getting up and walking out of the back of the church.

The big doors clicked shut and I sat in the pew, looking up at the figure on the cross. I still wasn't sure if I believed in God or not, but I knew that the things that John said made sense in some strange way.

Time rushed past as I sat pondering the profoundness of it all, and when I looked at my watch, it was time to pick up the boys.

When Ben got home from work, I had his favorite dinner waiting for him. Baked lasagna.

I walked from the stove and placed the casserole dish on a hot pad in the middle of table as the day slipped away across the darkening horizon.

"You feeling any better?" he asked.

He already knew the answer to that question. All it took was one look at me, with my red, swollen eyes.

I didn't answer. I didn't feel like a fight. Not tonight. Not when June 2nd was almost over.

I sat down with dinner, picking at it until everyone else was finished.

Ben took the boys upstairs and got them ready for bed as I cleaned up the dinner dishes.

I could hear giggles wafting down the stairs, but soon it grew quiet. After a few minutes Ben hadn't returned, so I went up the stairs to check on them.

He was in the boys' room. All three of them in Grayson's bed, with Ben reading them a story.

The book was called *Did I Ever Tell You How Lucky You Are?* The boys loved books written by Dr. Seuss.

I stood just out of sight and watched Ben tell the story with his usual antics and great enthusiasm. The boys mesmerized as always by his dramatics. Their eyes aglow with adoration for their father.

My heart was filled with joy and despair, both at the same time.

But I didn't cry. I couldn't. There was nothing left. All of my tears had been spent. The last three months had taken its toll on me, and here in the final hours I had given up hope.

When he was finished reading, I hurried back downstairs so no one would know that I had intruded on their moment. He put Oliver in his own bed and tucked both of the boys in for the night.

I had finished loading the last dish when he came around the corner.

He walked past me and got out a bottle of wine, opened it and poured us both a glass.

As he handed me my glass, his fingers grazed across mine, sending shivers up my spine.

He walked across the kitchen and put on a CD.

Soon, Marvin Gaye's smooth voice flowed out of the speaker and filled the room as "Mercy, Mercy Me" played.

Ben and I looked at each other from across the room. Neither of us saying a word.

He moved in closer and took my glass, setting it on the counter, never taking his eyes off of mine.

He took me by the hand and led me into the foyer, pulling me close to him as we began to sway together to the music.

I laid my head on his shoulder, taking it all in.

Feeling every ounce of our love captured in this moment.

In what I knew was our last dance.

The song faded into the background as he kissed my forehead, my nose, my cheek, running his hand up my back slowly, deliberately.

His warm tongue grazed my lips, and I kissed him ardently in return.

I threw my arms around his neck as he picked me up and carried me up the stairs to the bed, gently removing all of my clothes.

He took off his clothes and climbed in the bed next to me, trailing kisses down my neck and his tongue over my collar bone.

I was quivering from his touch as he caressed my breasts with his mouth.

He brought his mouth to mine and I began to kiss him gently at first, but then with more intensity. I grabbed at him desperately as if we hadn't touched in a very long time.

My body filled with an aching desire to feel him inside of me. I put my hands on his hips, pulling him closer.

I groaned as he entered me, deeply. I ran my hands up and into his hair, grasping, tugging, caught between desire and agony. I met each of his thrusts with equal push until we came together in rapture.

Lying together in the darkness, I wrestled with the thought of speaking up and telling Ben the things that I needed to say to him, but the words wouldn't come.

Before long I could hear his breathing slow and rhythmic. He was asleep.

The dream lurked in the shadows, taunting me, waiting to spring on me and take away everything that I loved.

Oh, how I longed to be free from this oppression. To be able to wake up in the morning and not be afraid.

But I knew tomorrow would bring reconciliation to the dream and me. One way or another.

The day had arrived.

The day I have been dreading for months.

Tomorrow was June 3rd.

I lay in the whispers of the night, listening to the hum of the fan and Ben's quiet breathing, fighting to stay awake.

Maybe, I could talk to him in the morning before he left…

I could try once more to convince him to stay home. To not take the train.

But sleep snuck in and overtook me.

CHAPTER 23

JUNE 3RD

I jolted awake the next morning, reaching frantically for Ben, and he was gone.

Icy blood pumped through my veins.

All that was left of him was a note that he left on his pillow for me, that read:

Had to get to work early to prep for this meeting.

See you tonight, beautiful.

I love you. Ben

I grasped the note and clenched it to my chest, screaming his name out into the empty room. Nothing but the sound of my own voice echoed back to me.

I sat in the kitchen watching the clock. My heart beating in perfect harmony with each tick. I sat silently listening to the sound of the refrigerator hum and the occasional dropping of ice. It had been hours since I had dropped the boys off at school. Earlier, I used the house phone to call Ben, to beg him again to not take the train home, but his response was more impatient than ever. I had called just as his client walked in the door.

I spent every minute after we hung up hoping against hope that something would change fate. That somehow things would end up differently.

I even tried to call Detective Anderson again, but he didn't answer his line.

I struggled, racking my brain for some scheme to stop this from happening. To stop the train. To stop Ben.

The warning Jonathan gave me about the Butterfly Effect nagged at my brain. I just didn't see how saving Ben could be a bad thing.

Yes, it would change the world.

The world for us.

I began to pace. Going outside, then back inside. Over and over again. Hoping. Wishing.

Before I realized it, it was one o'clock.

There were only two hours left.

As I looked at the clock, a feeling came over me that nearly bowled me over.

A rush.

A surge.

An overpowering determination that I knew no force on Heaven or Earth could stop.

"Damn, the consequences!" I called out.

I will do whatever it takes to stop this from happening!

I didn't care if I had to drive to his work and physically stop him from taking the train.

I wasn't just going to sit there and let him die!

Not now.

Not ever.

I didn't care about the damned Butterfly Effect anymore; I was going to save my husband!

I ran and grabbed my shoes then picked up the keys off of the foyer table, stopping only for a moment to remember last night's dance.

Joyous that it was not our last, after all.

I slammed the front door closed, not even stopping to lock it. I jumped in the car and turned the keys in the ignition, and to my horror the car didn't start. I was only met with a loud clicking sound. I made several attempts and got the same results each time. Eventually, even the clicking stopped, and there was only silence when I turned the key.

I slammed my fists on the steering wheel and noticed the headlights had been left on.

My battery was dead.

Dread coursed through me, but I wasn't deterred.

I got out of the car and ran back into the house.

I would have to go to plan B. I still had plenty of time to get an Uber to come get me.

The app to call them was on my cell phone, which had been missing since last night when I had let the boys play a game on it. I searched in all the normal places, but I couldn't find it anywhere. Frustration set in as I searched the couch cushions and under their beds to no avail.

I ran into the kitchen to check the countertop and looked up at the clock; it was 1:45 already. I gave up on finding my cell phone. I was running out of time. I dug in the junk drawer and found an old phone book. Within a few minutes, I found a cab company to call. Using the house phone, I dialed The Speedy Yellow Cab Company. They promised to arrive within thirty minutes. Cutting it too close for comfort, but I had no other choice.

I could still make it in time.

While waiting, I called my mom and asked her to pick up the boys for me. She happily agreed, saying that she would take them to the library and ice cream afterwards.

I paced the floor, looking out the window every few minutes for the cab. The world around me moved in slow motion as my anxiety grew.

At two thirty, I was in full blown panic. I had only 30 minutes left and I needed to leave now if I was going to make it to him before he boarded the train.

I called the cab company again, asking where my cab was, my voice shrieking. She informed me that there was no reservation for my address, but they could get a car to me within thirty minutes.

"Thirty minutes from now will be too late!" I screamed.

I hung up and ran out of my front door, desperately looking around for another way. I tried to start the car again and it returned with nothing in response.

I was overcome with the feeling that something was trying to prevent me from getting to Ben.

Was the universe working against me, because Ben was supposed to die today!?

I refused to accept that notion.

"I won't let you win!" I screamed up at the sky.

No sooner than the words had come out of my mouth, I saw Mrs. Parks backing out of her driveway. I was overjoyed at the sight of her, realizing that she could take me to Ben!

I ran toward her car and tripped over the edge of the driveway, face-planting in the dirt, cutting my forehead. I scrambled back up and made it to the street just as she was pulling away. I called out to her, but my mouth was dry and the words caught in my throat, only a raspy whisper coming out. I chased her car as it drove down the street. Waving frantically, calling out her name, but she didn't hear me. I kept running, choking on sobs, as the car got farther and farther away. I ran past eight houses before I gave up.

I turned to walk back with my head hung in defeat, touching my face as blood ran down my cheek.

When I got back to the house, I looked at the clock and saw that it was quarter to three. The realization dawned dark; there was no way I could get there in time. Not now.

My only hope was to call him and beg him again to not get on the train.

Suddenly it dawned on me. There was no way he would be taking the three o'clock train! I didn't know why I hadn't thought of it before! Foolishness washed over me as I remembered that he told me that he had a meeting at 2:00 with the new client to go over all the financials. I hadn't put two and two together until now. He would never be finished in time to catch the 3 o'clock train. He would still be in his meeting.

All this stress had been for nothing!

Joy washed over me like a tidal wave. I was so giddy with relief that I had to sit down.

I quickly realized that this was just like when I believed, wholeheartedly, that I had seen Ed's ghost next door, and it was his brother, all along.

I had let the dream warp my sense of reality again.

Ben was really fine.

He was safe.

But maybe I should still call? Just to be sure?

It was a few minutes before 3:00 and I hated to interrupt his important meeting, but I had to be reassured.

After all I had been through, a little reassurance wasn't too much to ask.

Was it?

I called Ben's cell phone and it went straight to voicemail. Most likely turned off because of the meeting. He didn't like to be disturbed when he was with a client.

I hung up and called his office line. The receptionist in the lobby put me straight through to his desk.

It rang several times with no answer. I didn't panic. I knew he was in his meeting.

I hung up and called the receptionist back, this time asking to be put through to his co-worker, David Taylor.

He answered on the first ring.

"Hey, David. I'm sorry to bother you, but could you tell me if Ben is still in that meeting?" I asked, my voice at a slightly higher pitch than normal.

David began laughing. "No, he actually walked out of the meeting with the client. He seemed pretty intent on getting home. He told me you had been worried about him taking the train home today, so he was going to catch the earlier train instead. I was surprised he left the meeting early like that, especially after he had worked so hard to get this client."

Darkness crept in slowly around me, then all at once.

"When did he leave?" I asked, my voice barely audible.

"Oh, about fifteen minutes ago. I think he was trying to catch the three o'clock train."

I dropped the receiver to the floor and it broke into pieces.

A scream rose from my gut, rattling the windows and walls.

I stumbled out into the backyard still screaming, quieting the birds.

"This can't be happening!" I cried out. Sobbing into the grass as the wind blew across my back, ruffling my shirt.

Fate had made up its mind and showed me no grace.

Despite every effort that I had made, I had failed at preventing what was to come.

Suddenly, the truth dawned upon me. Coming into sharp focus.

Suffocating me. Dragging me past the depths of despair.

Shattering my heart.

It was all my fault.

I had caused all of this.

I had been so absorbed in my own questions and fears that I never stopped to consider that I myself could be causing it to happen. I had inadvertently betrayed my own self.

I had set everything into motion.

If it wasn't for me, he would have cut back those tree branches. Ben warned me that they were dangerous, and I didn't listen. If I had, the branches wouldn't have been there to fall in the storm. His car wouldn't have been damaged, and he would've never had to take the train in the first place.

And NOW he took the three o'clock train because of me.

Because I was worried about him.

He left early, trying to come home to me.

Why didn't I just let it be? Why did I have to push and push?

I cried out at my own foolishness.

At God.

At fate.

And at the cruel trickery of the universe.

My voice grew hoarse and I stopped screaming. The birds began to sing again as I stood up on wobblily legs and went back into the house. I walked into the kitchen and looked at the clock. It was 3:45.

I numbly walked over to the television and turned it on. And sure enough, the local news was broadcasting a special report.

There had been a train accident.

A transfer truck had stalled out on the tracks, and the train had hit it and derailed one of its passenger cars. As the news camera panned the scene, I saw Detective Anderson in the background. I fell down in front of the tv, crying out Ben's name.

I moved forward in a place where nothing seemed real. I looked with unseeing eyes and listened with unhearing ears.

The roaring sound in my head made it difficult to think.

I walked over to the dish filled sink and began washing and drying them, one by one.

Even though I was expecting it, the knock on the door caused me to drop the mug I had been drying. It smashed on the floor, shattering pieces all around me.

I looked up at the clock and it was exactly 5:20.

I knew who was here.

I stood still for several seconds, paralyzed by dread.

I walked through the shards of broken pieces of ceramic as my blood pumped through me in giant swells.

I stopped in the kitchen doorway, desperate to halt time. I didn't want to live this moment. I knew what to expect, and I couldn't bear the thought of going through it.

Yet, I moved forward, seemingly against my will.

My breath came faster as something dark coiled around my chest.

My body feeling alien to me as I crossed the foyer. I stopped, remembering the touch of Ben last night right here in this spot, and a sob rose up in my throat.

Another more insistent knock came, followed by the doorbell ringing.

I stopped in front of the door, resting my head on the frame, my eyes filling with tears.

I reached for the doorknob with a trembling hand and twisted. As the door swung open, the sun's glare flashed into my eyes, blinding me. My vision went in and out of focus as I tried to see the face of the man standing in front of me.

"Mrs. DuPont?" he asked.

"Yes," I answered, my voice barely over a whisper.

"My name is Detective Anderson, and I'm with the Charlotte Police Department. I believe we spoke on the phone yesterday?" His voice, surreal.

"Yes, we did..." I stuttered, shielding my eyes from the sun as I tried to see his face.

We stood together quietly for a moment. The space between us filled with a knowing. I wondered if he could feel it too.

"May I step inside?" he asked.

My body grew suddenly weak.

I didn't want him to come inside.

Not again.

"You can say what you need to say to me right here." I crossed my arms defiantly.

"Mrs. DuPont, the reason I am here is because there was a train accident today…"

He was still talking, but his voice went completely out of focus. His mouth was moving, but I couldn't hear him. I stepped out of the doorway and onto the porch, walking past him and stopping at the top of the steps.

My eyes fixed on the street.

A yellow cab had stopped right in front of our house.

The cab that I had ordered, arriving too late.

Suddenly, the backseat door swung open. Someone was getting out. I strained to look as they stepped out of the cab and paid the driver, the sunlight still blinding me.

I put my hand up to shield my eyes but it didn't help. I walked down the rest of steps, stopping at the bottom.

I could tell by the shape it was a man, and he was walking up the driveway, coming straight toward me.

My heart began to race.

It couldn't be! Could it?

I stepped another step down, and when he passed under the shade of the oak tree, I caught a glimpse of his face.

For just a moment, time stood completely still as my mind whirred with the impossibility of what I was seeing.

Coming straight toward me, just like magic, was Ben.

I met him on the walkway, collapsing in his arms and sobbing.

"You're okay!" I cried out. "Oh my God, you're okay!" I touched his face, still trying to absorb the fact that he was really here.

"Of course, I am. I told you I would be." Ben laughed, hugging me tightly.

He put his arm around me and we walked up the steps and onto the porch where Detective Anderson was still waiting.

"Who's this?" Ben asked.

"I'm Detective Anderson, and I'm here to talk to your wife about her prior knowledge of the train accident that occurred today at three twenty," he said, sounding frustrated.

Ben's face turned an ashy white as he looked at me, then quickly looked back at the detective. "Train accident?" he stammered.

"Yes, your wife called and reported the train accident yesterday, and I would like to know how she knew about it."

Ben shook his head in disbelief and turned to face me.

"I was coming home early to appease you because I felt bad about how upset you had been…and I actually missed the train," he stuttered, his face still pale. "And I would've been on it, if it wasn't for this bicyclist. His tire popped as he crossed the courtyard right in front of me. He fell over the front handlebars of his bike and broke his arm. I stayed with him until the paramedics came. Because I stayed with him, I missed the train. So, I called a cab to bring me home…" He shook his head, clearly still trying to process what had just happened.

A sob rose up in my throat.

He would've been on the train…

But somehow, by some miracle…he wasn't.

I looked up at the sky and gave a silent thank you to God. Someone had heard my prayer, after all.

Soon after, I explained to Detective Anderson about the dream again. He had a few more questions, but for the most part left just as baffled as he had arrived.

After he was gone, we went inside.

Ben stopped me in the foyer and pulled me close to him.

"I'm sorry I didn't believe you, Claire…" Ben's voice cracked.

"All that matters to me is that you're okay. God, I am just so thankful that you are okay." I hugged him tighter as tears ran down my cheeks.

Just at that moment, both of the boys came rushing in the front door, followed by my mom.

Oliver came up to me and tugged on my shirt. "Momma, you okay?"

I kneeled down next to him and Grayson, wrapping my arms around both of them.

"I am now," I said.

I looked back at Ben and he was smiling.

He walked over and knelt down next to me, putting his arms tightly around all three of us.

And I finally released the breath I had been holding for the last three months.

EPILOGUE

─ᴑᕤᴑ─

The church bells rang as I lifted my hand to my eyes, shielding them from the bright sunlight. Wisps of hair blew into my face as the fresh spring air swirled around me. Ben stood close to me in his tuxedo. Handsome as he'd ever been.

I couldn't believe it had been year since I had that awful dream. The memory of it long past.

I stood at the bottom of the church steps in a lavender gown and smiled as the bride and groom appeared.

Jonathan and Sheila came down the steps together, eyes bright with joy, caught up in love and the promise of happily ever after. The crowd showered them with birdseed as they ran to their getaway car. I smiled and waved as they passed by. Jonathan winking in my direction.

They waved out the window with the crowd cheering as the car pulled away, trailing tins cans and streamers.

We watched until they were long out of sight.

Ben turned and kissed me, long and deep, as the crowd began to disperse. Warmth spread all the way through me, down to my toes. He never ceased to have that effect on me.

I felt a tap on my shoulder and turned around. Mandi stood behind me, smiling and holding baby Sarah, now just five months old. A beautiful strawberry-blonde haired girl with brown eyes and yellow flecks. Chubby fingers reaching out to Ben.

A few seconds later, Oliver and Grayson came running up with my mom and dad in tow. A look of exhaustion on my parents' faces, but their eyes full of happiness.

The leaves rustled in the trees overhead as the wind rushed through them, making Bradford pear blossoms float down all around us.

Ben and I looked at each other with a knowing smile.

I closed my eyes and let the sun warm my face. My heart overflowing with the love for life.

And I was thankful. So very thankful.

Thankful for the good days and thankful for the bad days.

I knew I didn't always make the right choices, but I always lived from my heart. Each day that the sun rose, I gave my all. Focusing on every moment in the present tense. Not living in the past—or the fear of tomorrow.

I came to realize that my life, even with all of its twists and turns, in the end was truly a gift. And that even the terror of that dream had been a gift to me. It gave me the gift of insight and a chance to learn how to really live life the way it is meant to be lived.

It also helped me to learn and to grow into a better human being. I learned to let go of expectations and to just embrace life, with all of its beauty and imperfections.

None of us on this Earth are promised a tomorrow. All we can do is learn to live and love in the place right where we are at. To appreciate the ones we love while they are here with us. And to live our lives to the fullest that we can.

Because in the end, all we really have in this life to hold onto…are the moments between.

Dear Readers,

It is my great hope that you thoroughly enjoyed my novel. Would you do me a great service and leave me a review?

This helps me tremendously with getting the word out about my books!

Also, please be sure to sign up for my newsletter to be informed of future releases and also follow me on Facebook and Instagram too! I would love to see you there!!

Until next time!

Love,

Natalie Banks xoxo

Other titles by Natalie Banks:

The Water Is Wide
The Canary's Song
The Dark Room

That Year by the Lake coming Spring 2020

CONNECT WITH NATALIE:

WWW.NATALIEBANKS.NET

INSTAGRAM: @officialnataliebanks

FACEBOOK: @nataliebanksnovels

NATALIEBANKSNOVELS@GMAIL.COM

NATALIE BANKS

N atalie Banks is an award-winning international author and a previous recipient of The North Carolina Governor's Writing Award. She weaves characters with relatable humanity and stories that touch the heart and soul. She has quickly become a favorite among readers. When not writing, she spends time on the beach in North Carolina with her husband and children.

For more information or to schedule an interview please contact Natalie at:

NATALIEBANKSNOVELS@GMAIL.COM

CPSIA information can be obtained
at www.ICGtesting.com
Printed in the USA
LVHW031827130220
646864LV00005B/884